The Windsor Love Pact

Can fake-dating turn into love?

Windsor Riverside Romances
Book 1

Lizzie Chantree

PUBLISHING

Formatted with Vellum

Chapter One

Maya gasped in shock as a man barrelled into her, knocking the lukewarm coffee she'd been sipping straight over her white vintage lace t-shirt. Time froze for a second before she realised that he was holding her arms to steady her and apologising profusely. 'I'm so sorry!' he said, his tone breathless as he pushed the black baseball cap he was wearing further back to reveal more of his face and then glanced behind him. Maya felt another punch of surprise as she recognised the piercing blue of his eyes first and then the fact that they were filled with panic. She looked over his shoulder and noted a crowd forming on the other side of the pretty little flower-adorned bridge they were standing on and frowned, before understanding dawned.

Recalling the feeling of having no privacy, she quickly wondered how she could limit the damage to this escalating situation. 'Please let me pay for your dry cleaning and coffee,' he said hurriedly, as he tried to draw her away from the crowd, who looked as if they were deciding how much they could push their luck by approaching their idol. Maya's own eyes sparkled as she had literally just been thinking that her days were pretty quiet, after her own touches with fame. Now she was standing on the bridge next to her rental house with devilishly handsome bad boy, Noah Benedict! It was like a scene from one of his movies.

'It's fine,' she said lightly. 'It looks like you're in a bit of a predicament,' she nodded towards the crowd who were just now beginning to walk towards them as Maya and Noah rapidly turned back towards her house and the docks along that side of the river.

'I was feeling a bit stir crazy and thought no one would notice me if I had a quick early morning stroll,' he shrugged and then grinned self-depreciatingly, which made a few butterflies take flight in her stomach.

'We all start pretty early here if we're working on the boats and the cafés on that side of the water bring in droves of early morning dog walkers. I live here...' she pointed towards the first town house, then flushed as that might seem a tad stalkerish and forward. 'I meant to hide in!' she hurried on and he chuckled, but then looked over her shoulder again and grimaced. 'But they already know you're here and if that's your boat,' she nodded towards the shiny black powerboat that she'd seen docked outside his mansion situated further up the river when she helped on the river cruises, 'then that's your best bet. Jump in and I'll walk back across the bridge and hold them off. I probably know most of them.'

He heaved a huge sigh of relief and quickly took her hand to thank her. 'Your clothes and coffee. What can I do to compensate you?' he asked again as they reached his boat and he threw the cap in, leaving his dark blonde hair all mussed-up and sexy.

'It's nothing. It will take me two seconds to change

clothes and I work across the water, so I won't even be late for work.' She smiled warmly at him, to show him she was sincere and he breathed a sigh of relief.

'Thank you,' he said as he jumped into his boat and set off. 'I don't even know your name,' he called back, but she'd already turned and was walking rapidly towards the bridge and he had to quickly start the engine and move the boat back into the centre of the river.

After persuading the group on the bridge that there was nothing to see now, Maya caught her breath and stepped aboard *Bertha*, the timeworn steamboat that was docked on the river Thames, and waved to Joe, her grandad's best friend and one of her favourite people on Earth. What a morning! Joe ran the only steamboat on this stretch of the river, with its black and gold railings and cream and black lifebuoy rings that were tied at intervals with bright orange rope. The forest-green awning that covered the seating area had seen better days and the paddle wheel needed a lick of paint, but the boat was still majestic despite being weathered from the water and passing of time. *Bertha*'s faded grandeur caught the interest of tourists walking around the dock area, and she often featured in people's holiday snaps. Joe's business was largely based on ferrying tourists up and down the estuary and regaling them with local history, even if Maya was pretty sure he embellished his stories here and there for his own entertainment when she wasn't around to chide him. She wouldn't be surprised if he added in a visiting humpback whale or a dragon living in the nearby castle at some point.

She ran her hands along the wooden handrail and enjoyed the feeling of her feet being back on board the solid timbers of *Bertha*'s deck. She'd missed this... both being on the water and part of a bustling community. The river path was still a feathery assault course of swans and geese, hopeful that a passing child might drop a morsel of food and she breathed in the honey-sweet scent of the golden Marsh marigolds and tall grasses that were swaying in the slight breeze across the water, reminding her of home. Sometimes she couldn't believe how much her life had changed, but it felt good to be surrounded by so many memories of her childhood.

Maya grinned and waved to Roman, the guy who helped Joe with the river cruises. Roman had his long dread-locks held back with a headband as usual and he sent her a winning smile as he helped a customer step over the threshold of the deck, holding her walking stick, handbag and half-empty bottle of vodka! Maya's mouth dropped open and then she giggled as Roman handed the items back to the woman once she was safely on board.

'Roman,' she called out, 'do you need some help?' The woman was certainly unsteady on her feet, but Maya suspected it was more likely from the drink than the need for her walking stick, as she was currently waving it at a huge seagull, who was regarding her with keen interest.

Roman shook his head, which made the ends of his hair fly around his shoulders. 'I think I can manage.' He winked, already reaching out to assist the next passenger on board. Maya made a note to sit near to the wobbly customer, just in case she fell overboard. There was a wooden-panelled bar in the centre of the boat with art deco effect mirroring along the back wall, that would have been opulent and glamorous in its heyday, but they only really served lukewarm rosé wine now so it was unusual for them to have to worry about customers overindulging, as they spent most of their time gazing at the lush river views, or into the verdant gardens of the exclusive houses that lined the waterfront. Maya eyed the woman who was laughing uproariously at something her friend said, then saw that they were celebrating something by the way the second woman brought out a slightly squashed cake and some candles that she quickly discarded after a glance at *Bertha*'s wooden bench seating. She pulled a couple of plastic forks from her turquoise bag and they both tucked in with relish and more giggles. One of the ladies caught Maya's hand as she passed and she turned to them with a polite smile.

'Are we likely to see Noah Benedict on this cruise?' asked one, as she took both their plates and slipped them back into her bag, crumbs and all, which made Maya wince. The other lady sat forward eagerly and Maya bit her lip in mirth. Most of their customers mainly wanted a glimpse of Noah, the charismatic movie star who lived along the river in a beautiful glass and metal house that must have incredible views of the river. Before he'd crashed into her that morning, Maya had actually glimpsed Noah herself on the grounds of his estate a few times and she could understand everyone's excitement. Being so close to him for a few moments had been a whole different experience. Magnetism shone from him, even in his harassed state. He had the usual Hollywood film star classic good looks; blonde tousled hair and piercing blue eyes with a requisite droolworthy body that must take hours of punishment in the gym. The hunted look on his face had surprised her though. She'd assumed he courted publicity, as he was always featured in the press.

'I can't promise anything,' she said, much to the ladies' obvious disappointment, 'but there have been more sightings of him from *Bertha* than any other cruise on the river,' she added quickly, not mentioning that some of the villagers had seen him up close and in person that very morning. These feisty ladies might lynch her!

Despite her broken-heart, Maya had started to feel that she was – slowly – starting to heal. It was good to be back again, back among people who'd known her as a child. Living beside the ebb and flow of the river after the glitz and glamour of the life and relationship that she'd had to leave behind, had brought her a quiet joy. Her old routine involved a fast-paced work life, creating intricate jewellery for influencers, celebs and attending non-stop parties. Now she spent her time by or on the water, on Joe's boat or on the bank sketching wildlife, while she tried to come to terms with the loss of her jewellery design business *and* fiancé.

Walking in on him in bed with Portia, one of their models, had brought her glittering career and what she'd thought was a good life with her fiancé crashing down around her.

Maya thought back to her first sight of Blake. He was tall, dark and handsome, and surrounded by a group of eager women. He had been sitting astride a chair in their art class, where they were studying jewellery design, and his eyes met hers as she'd walked in. She'd felt a frisson of heat go down her spine and her cheeks flush. He'd sat next to her when their lecturer arrived and her heart was already metaphorically in his hands. They'd been so young. Together, their ideas were magic, though. Maya's designs were unusual and customers adored her work. Blake quickly realised his genius lay in marketing, so he left the design work to Maya. An up-and-coming reality star had been photographed wearing one of their Luna Moth neck-laces with delicately arched wings and sweeping tail in a nightclub in Soho, and suddenly everyone wanted to know their brand. Influencers were talking about them and their phones buzzed from morning to night with requests from stylists asking to borrow jewellery for events. They had been a dream team for a while with high-profile parties, celebrity endorsements and a swanky new flat.

Their list of clients had grown and although she'd been shy and hadn't relished the spotlight, Blake had courted it.

'Our success is down to my marketing skills,' he'd repeated like a mantra.

'Of course,' she'd always appeased, as she'd sketched some new jewellery ideas, keeping her eyes down and firmly on her work.

'Pieces landing in the right person's hands takes weeks of networking,' he'd crowed, making excuses for why he was always out late at night, but people came back time and time again for her beautiful designs. Most of their customers thought Blake was the designer because he was the public face of the company – and he didn't disabuse them of that notion. To them she was the boho partner in her glamorous one-off pieces that her grandmother had designed and her love of vintage. Maya glanced down at her current attire of an A-line skirt that sat a few inches above her knees and looked like it had been scattered with flowers as the print was of regal purple dahlias, the contrasting pink and white petals of cosmos and flowering sage on a white woven background. Above that she had a cute little white short-sleeved shirt she'd tied at her waist and a pretty little nasturtium flower brooch, with its wide petals and splashes of colour at its centre. She'd taken a second look at her coffee stained outfit of a lace top and jeans earlier, and decided to make a bit more of an effort, as you never knew who you might bump into in this town it seemed, she smiled to herself. Not that she was ever likely to stumble across Noah Benedict again and she was definitely not attracted to sexy rogues any more. She'd learned that lesson the hard way and her heart carried the scars.

Blake clearly preferred sleek blondes like Portia. Portia had been wearing an incredibly expensive 18-carat diamond necklace Maya had designed and nothing else. Maya had looked at them both and felt like the air had been sucked out of her lungs. Portia had gasped and grabbed the bloody diamond necklace – as if Maya was about to rip it from her throat – and then darted to the bathroom to lock herself in. Maya hadn't smashed anything, nor screamed accusations at Blake. She'd just let the bottom fall out of her world while Blake scrabbled around to find his jeans and trademark white tee. Then she'd turned on her heel and run, tears streaming down her face, heart smashed into a million tiny pieces.

She'd swept up the few personal items from her desk, leaving everything else behind. Unfortunately that included a folder of her designs for their forthcoming, much-antici-pated collection.

For a long time after the breakup Maya had hidden herself away at her grandparents' house where she'd grown up with her siblings and dissolved into all-too-frequent tears at the world and the injustice of loving a man who didn't value her.

Maya had barely left the house, her family tip-toeing around her and whispering in corners in hushed tones. She'd hardly been able to eat because she felt that the affair must have been her fault; she wasn't attentive enough, talented enough, sexy enough, clever enough. Maya had never been short on admiring looks from men, but Blake had chipped away at the way she dressed and behaved until she'd been reduced to being grateful that he loved her. She wouldn't put herself through the pain of a broken heart again.

Slowly, with the help of her family and her best friend Leah, she'd begun to heal. Being close to the water, riverside plants and the wildlife they attracted, like the ever-darting dragonflies and busy bees, had helped and she'd started designing again. Smaller jewellery at first and then bolder and more intricate pieces that were inspired by the shapes and forms of the flowers she discovered growing by the river.

Maya rested her elbows on the rail as she watched the world pass by and a couple of fish darted along in the frothy white ripples that *Bertha* created in the water. As the boat steamed along, Maya wished her troubles would wash away with the breeze and she could truly start again.

Leah had popped round the night before and tentatively suggested that she consider dating again. The friends had met a couple of years previously, but to Maya, it felt like they'd known each other their whole lives and she didn't know how she'd survived without a confidante and cheerleader like Leah before that.

'No thanks,' Maya had replied as she reached into the fridge for a second chilled bottle of sauvignon blanc.

'But...' Leah had begun, but Maya had given her one of those stares that told her to shut up and drink her wine.

This conversation seemed a recurrent theme with her friends and family these days. Her grandparents constantly tried to match-make her with the grandsons of friends or neighbours. Dodging the topic was becoming an art form. No way, she wasn't ready.

It had taken everything she had to pick herself up again and she'd spent the last two years building up a new jewellery brand that was hers and hers alone – No.1 Ethereal Lane. She'd worked from her workroom in her house by the river, sketching new ideas while helping Joe and on *Bertha*, and now her brand was being noticed. A particular piece, an exquisite cluster of white-gold bell-shaped comfrey flowers with shimmering emerald-winged stalks and curved silver leaves, had just gone viral, the collection selling out immediately. Post after post appeared on social media about the collection and the press were now on the trail of the mysterious designer behind the brand, because no one seemed to know who that was. Had it been Blake's marketing wizardry that had propelled them to the level of success their business had reached last time, or was it her designs that customers fell in love with and were clamouring to buy?

Joe beckoned her over with a wave and Maya slid her sketching pencils and sketch pad back into her canvas tote bag, leaving it tucked under the bench by her feet so no one could trip over it. 'How are the birthday girls getting along?' he asked, inclining his head to the women who were currently leaning over the guard rails to look at the fluffy-downed cygnets that were paddling at the side of the river.

Maya bit her lip in mirth. 'They've been nattering about how to get the attention of our gorgeous captain to persuade him to go off course,' she teased. Joe laughed. Customers often flirted with Joe as he was so handsome. He looked like a dashing pirate and certain female clientele seemed to think he came with the boat and was there for the picking! Joe would shake his head and roll his eyes with good humour.

Maya moved over to nudge hips with Roman as he stood at the guard rail by the port side of the boat and he grinned and nudged her back. They enjoyed flirty banter with each other, but although Roman was gorgeous, he still occasionally dated his extremely fiery and vocal ex-girl-friend from the next town and getting thrown into the middle of an argument was the last thing Maya needed. Roman's angular cheekbones and cheeky smile often got schoolgirl giggles from their female customers and he enjoyed every moment, she knew. 'It's quiet again today,' Maya noted, glancing around at the almost clear decks.

Roman winced and shrugged. 'I know. The worry lines on Joe's face can't get any deeper!' he tried to joke as they both glanced at Joe, who was standing by the huge black paddle wheel. Maya put her arm around Roman's shoulders and gave him a squeeze of comfort. 'Olive needs her hip op and Joe can't afford to stay at home and help her. We don't have enough passengers as it is.'

'I agree. Olive's been hobbling around their bungalow for months.' Maya sighed and tears sprung to her eyes. 'He's so stubborn.' Joe's wife, Olive, needed him at home, but the business required him to be on board. Maya helped as much as she could, serving drinks from Joe's collection of mismatched glassware and checking tickets. It wasn't enough. 'We must come up with a plan to help,' she added and Roman hugged her back before moving away. 'Let me know if you think of anything.'

She watched Roman walk towards Joe and noticed that his shoulders were sagging in defeat. If *Bertha* was dry docked, she might not make it back into the water – and both Joe and Roman would lose their livelihood.

The boat drew up near Noah's waterfront pad and Maya leaned over the guard rail and breathed in the fresh river air, closing her eyes for a quiet moment of contemplation as the breeze touched her face. Noah's sleek black power boat was moored by the wide raised wooden jetty to the front of his property, so he'd made it back alive! She thought of those piercing blue eyes and the way they'd briefly settled on her dark brown ones and then shook the image away.

Working on the deck of a boat might be unusual for some, but it suited her. After all, she could work pretty much anywhere that inspired her. Maya sat cross-legged on the bow and considered Joe's options, which were limited. As she watched the riverbank glide past, she sighed when she saw a young couple strolling along with a frolicking dog, smiling as they held each other's hands. That had been her once. She took her phone out of her bag, glancing despondently at the screen. She was sure that her ex, Blake, would have loads of inspired ideas about how to help Joe. He'd texted her constantly when they split up, but there had been over a year of silence now. She swiped open an old text and flinched, waiting for the pain they usually brought. She needed to permanently delete them and move on, but she'd kept one or two and she didn't really know why. It was as if she couldn't quite let go of the last strands of their relationship, which was ridiculous because she'd definitely moved on. Maya almost snarled at the phone and the woman sitting next to her frowned and turned her way.

'Are you okay, dear?' she asked, patting Maya's hand.

'Sorry!' Maya shivered, wishing she'd brought a jumper as the wind was picking up as they neared the halfway point of the cruise and her hair kept flying in her face. 'Old message from my ex,' she explained, grimacing and not wanting to explain further. The face of the woman next to her hardened and she urged her to take a fork and a mouthful of the remaining squashed cake, which Maya gratefully accepted.

'Delete it,' she advised sagely. 'This will help,' the woman insisted, patting her hand in solidarity. The cake was deliciously chocolaty, which immediately restored Maya's good spirits and filled the air with the indulgent scent of earthy cocoa and sweet vanilla. She shook her head at the offer of a tipple of vodka, but was sorely tempted. She shoved the phone firmly back into her bag and knew she wouldn't receive another text. Other than that one time... Blake had always been predictable. She had nothing to offer him now and he always had his eye on the prize.

Maya sat back to let the sun that peeked through the clouds for a minute or two warm her face, then pulled her sketchpad back out of her bag. She began sketching the common reeds that were swaying in the wind and the oval leaves and beautifully scented, spiky-looking flowers of the water mint on the river bank as they sailed slowly by.

She was building something new after feeling like she'd been without an anchor for the past two years. Her heart was finally healing and being back home with the inspiration of the river and all its surrounding natural beauty was inspiring her creativity. Her new-found success would annoy the hell out of Blake. Suddenly – unexpectedly – she was taking over the world of high-end jewellery design again, this time with no one knowing her name. People were beginning to know her brand, No. 1 Ethereal Lane, but the designer behind the intricately cut designs was unknown and she intended to keep it that way.

Chapter Two

Maya waved goodbye to Joe, blew a kiss to Roman and nodded to the Bowen brothers, Alex and Luca, the somewhat ruthless operators that ran the other cruise boats that had the license to run along that stretch of the Thames by Windsor Promenade. Both men were beautiful to look at with dark good looks and honed, athletic bodies that they'd earned through sheer hard graft on their boats. They worked and played hard and fast. They had no choice but to accept Joe's old steamer, but Maya knew they would rather scoop it up, modernise and re-brand it and run the entire stretch of river on their own. She also knew that they enjoyed flirting outrageously with her to wind both Joe and Roman up.

They hated sharing the dock with Joe and *Bertha*, as both sets of boats ran up and down the river to deliver guests to a popular racecourse and a beautiful castle that stood proudly amongst the trees. The entire area was picturesque, with a bustling town leading up to the dock and several riverside restaurants.

Unfortunately for Joe, most tourists preferred the plush

air-conditioned bars of a Bowen boat and the glossy interiors with velvet padded seats and fancy cocktails. You got the best tour guide ever on Joe's steamboat, but you also had to sit your bum on seats that may or may not leave splinters. The drink choices were lukewarm beer or lukewarm wine, as the fridge was often on the blink.

Maya wandered up to the little coffee shop called Riverside that was situated at one end of the dock and stepped inside. 'Hi, Penny. My usual please?' Maya's stomach rumbled at the scent of freshly baked bread and the strawberry jam from the slices of Victoria sponge cake that were displayed in the glass counter top.

'Sure thing!' said Penny as she set out three takeaway cups for Maya's order. They'd become friends after Maya moved into her house across the bridge from the café and frequented the place a bit more. The café was aimed at tourists, with artworks of the plants found by the river on the walls and a vast window to the front and side to maximise views of the water. Most customers sat there as it was a prime spot to wait for their turn to get on one of the Bowen boats; they could see how big the queues were getting and jump up to join them at a moment's notice.

Maya grinned at Penny as she handed her a lemon muffin – her weakness, along with anything else made with sugar. Maya always picked up a muffin on her way home when she'd been helping on the boat and Penny would save her one from the morning rush, or have to put up with ten minutes of huffing and sighing while Maya chose something that wasn't her favourite. She ate everything except for bananas, which covered her skin with scratchy hives every time she had the misfortune to eat one by mistake. Who the hell added dried bananas to cereal, for goodness sake? Her mouth watered at the tangy scent of the lemon muffin and she bit into the silky centre and sighed in bliss, jiggling her hips to the 80s music that Penny often had playing in the background.

'Thanks, Penny.' She grinned, admiring the way Penny had woven ribbons into her long blonde plaits that day and how pretty she looked in her fitted jeans and branded collared t-shirt with the cafe's scrolling lettering and a coffee cup.

Penny brushed a stray hair out of her blue eyes and smiled back.

'Busy today?' asked Penny, making Maya cringe a little. She ran her mind back over the day's steamer cruise and knew that all the locals, minus the Bowen brothers, wanted Joe's business to do well. Alex and Luca were arrogant enough to want to run the whole dock outside, but they were newcomers compared to Joe, who had lived by this stretch of the river his whole life. All the town had been his passengers at one point or another. Olive and Joe were right at the heart of the local community. *Bertha* had been one of the first on this stretch of river, offering short cruises. Out-of-towners might prefer the flashy new cruise boats, but people who lived in or around the town would still use Joe's steamboat to offer support. Still, Maya didn't know how much longer *Bertha* would cruise if she didn't get some kind of renovation soon, but she was determined to help. She'd also heard that Olive had loved and left Alex and Luca's grandfather at one point – a long time ago, but she wondered if that was why the boys' father had chosen this particular dock in which base their business. It was only rumour, and she had found no truth in the tale so far, but Olive was a beautiful woman, so you never knew!

'Umm...' said Maya, pulling a face, scooping up some used sugar sachets into the nearby bin.

'Your grandmother was in earlier,' called Penny over her shoulder as she served a young mum with a pushchair and offered to carry her drink to the table for her, which was greeted with an appreciative sigh of thanks from the woman, clearly desperate for caffeine.

'What did she want?' asked Maya, never knowing what her grandmother was up to at any time.

Maya and her siblings, Romy and Arthur, were raised by her grandparents in a rambling house that sat on a bend in the river Thames. Maya's parents were doctors for an overseas charity. Their mum was from Windsor, but her dad had grown up in a pretty little Mexican fishing village. The vividly painted houses there and handmade fishing nets swaying in the afternoon breeze had inspired many of Maya's earlier designs and she was hoping to go back and visit sometime soon.

'She ordered two dozen cupcakes for an afternoon tea she's holding next week, but she asked for rainbow icing and edible glitter.' Penny clamped her lips together with mirth, and Maya couldn't help but chuckle.

It certainly wasn't a conventional childhood and her grandmother flew in the face of every convention that she could – Maya was sure just for fun – but it worked for them. Ettie was certainly more than the tiniest bit eccentric.

Her granddad bred exotic plants from huge Victorian glasshouses in his garden that made you feel you'd entered Kew Gardens when you stepped inside. The humidity from the controlled climate settings hit you as soon as you opened the door and then the scent of the bountiful flowering vines made you stop and draw in a breath of Heaven. It was a paradise of brightly coloured flowers or the gentle tones of the King Protea from South Africa. The flowering evergreen shrub had red and cream blooms and leaves that appeared to swirl and dance around the crown of petals.

Women were always calling at her grandmother's house trying to reach her brother, Arthur, but Ettie never let them in. That would mean she'd have to stop whatever she was doing and give them a cup of tea and sympathies that they hadn't heard from Arthur, or Art, as they all called him. He artfully avoided commitment. But then Maya supposed they all did now. Maya's sister, Romy, was a law unto herself and very vocal, especially about relationships since her own recent woes. Her answer had been to buy a ramshackle old boat and store it by a pretty little cottage opposite *Bertha's* dock, then turn it into a coffee stop for dog walkers, much to Alex and Luca's disapproval as that was now the view from the start of their cruises. Maya thought this was hilarious because it was their own grandmother, Clara, who rented the berth at the end of her garden to Romy in the first place, although she didn't think Romy was aware of the connection and Maya certainly didn't want to cause her any more stress.

Romy poked her head round the café door. 'Hi,' she said, stepping in and nodding a greeting at Penny, who handed her a chilled bottle of orange juice and her usual order of a cheese toastie in a paper bag. She was wearing mud-plastered jeans and a fitted once-white t-shirt that seemed to be covered in straw. Romy's long dark-blonde hair was piled up on the top of her head and she immediately started munching on her sandwich, eyeing her sister over the top of the bag. She had a question in her eyes and Maya felt like angry little soldier ants were marching up her back. She knew full well what Romy was going to say. There was a big family party coming up, and she'd promised them she'd bring a date.

'About the party...' began Romy. 'I know Gran wants us all to bring a plus one, but we have to actually go on a date to see if we like someone,' her sister said pertinently, arching an eyebrow at Maya.

'I've heard about this party!' said Penny, joining the conversation and making Maya groan out loud. 'Romy told me that you haven't found a date yet.'

Maya sighed, the weight of obligation landing firmly on her shoulders. She'd sensed that they were all ganging up on her and she'd had enough. 'For goodness sake! I've already got a boyfriend!' she snapped, then immediately wished she could take the words back.

'What?' said Romy, aghast. 'When did this happen?'

Maya could hardly say ten seconds ago, so she looked around wildly for inspiration and the only thing she could see was a magazine on a table with Noah Benedict's face on the front cover. 'We met recently, but he travels a lot for work,' she hedged not mentioning the first time she'd seen Noah in real life was that morning.

'So... this boyfriend?' demanded Romy. 'Who is he and why didn't I know about it?' Romy added, but Maya detected traces of hurt in her voice, which made Maya feel even more guilty about her lie.

'I didn't tell anyone because it's fairly new and I didn't want you all to ruin it for me,' snapped Maya. Then she cursed under her breath as it was unlike her to be rude to Romy, even though she was the one being pushy. Maya didn't understand why she needed to bring a partner to the party. She'd gotten used to being alone. Romy was bringing an old school friend she dated occasionally and Arthur would have a gorgeous starlet on his arm. 'Sorry, I didn't mean to blame you. I just wasn't ready to announce it yet.'

Romy nudged her shoulder to show there were no hard

feelings and finished the last bite of her food. 'What's he like and when can I meet him?' Maya's insides tightened because she'd created her new boyfriend out of thin air and now really wished she hadn't.

'You'll meet him at the party,' Maya said breezily, trying not to faint at the lies stacking up. 'He's tall, handsome and you'll love him!'

'Fab, but I expect to meet him before then. It's months away!' said Romy with an expectant smile as she paid for her order at the till and then waved goodbye to Penny. 'I can't wait!' she said as she turned and headed back home as Maya's stomach sunk like a lead balloon. Penny was serving a couple of late customers now.

'You know that art class you mentioned last time you were in?' asked Penny, as she put a slice of chocolate cake in an empty box and handed it to her customer, who looked like they couldn't wait to run home and scoff the lot.

'Yes,' said Maya, smiling as the chocolate cake man paid. 'The one that's on Joe's boat? There are about ten people each week now. I didn't know it would be so popular when I suggested Bertha as a venue to Mason, who runs the class. And it gives Joe a little of extra income when people buy drinks. It's not as if the boat is busy.'

'I'm not surprised at all if Mason's work is anything like yours. Your paintings are beautiful.' Penny looked at the café walls and Maya followed her gaze. Penny sometimes hung Maya's paintings of delicate plants from along the riverbed that she sketched while she was sailing on *Bertha* with Joe on the café walls, and they always sold pretty quickly, even though they weren't cheap. The paintings made the basis of her jewellery designs, which were crafted from precious metals and stones.

'Could Gio join Mason's class?' Penelope's cousin, Gio,

had followed her over from Greece, but was struggling to settle in. 'Gio is so quiet; I thought a class might help his self-confidence.' Penny sighed, twirling her braids around her fingers, which she always did when she was worried about something. 'He wants to be an actor, but I think he's just too shy.'

'I'm sure he can join in,' said Maya, thinking that twelve was probably the most students Mason could handle.

Maya picked up the other two coffees she'd ordered while she'd been chatting. 'I'm late.'

Penny whipped the paper cups away and gave them a blast with the milk whisk to warm them up, and Maya smiled gratefully. 'At least Leah has that gorgeous boyfriend of hers to keep her warm at night if the coffee is cold by the time you get there,' joked Penny. 'I don't think I'd leave my bed if I had a man who looked like that,' she added and Maya smiled before picking up the cups and going to meet her friends.

Chapter Three

Leah glanced up when the bell above the door to her flower shop chimed and grinned when she saw Maya and the coffee. Maya adored walking in here because the sage Leah liked to use in her arrangements added an earthy aroma with a herbaceous note that reminded her of her grandad's potting sheds. Leah finished tying a peony bouquet with pale-pink petals and plump buds surrounded by tiny white fluffy gypsophila and soft green eucalyptus leaves and picked up scissors to curl and secure the gold ribbon.

Maya loved that her best friend's shop was just along the river from where Joe's boat was moored and across the bridge that connected this side of town to her own riverside townhouse. The flower shop wasn't huge, but the double-fronted Victorian windows gave Leah room to show off her floristry skills to everyone on the river and people came from miles around to buy her latest arrangements and admire her displays. The shop was a floral paradise with a deep Parisian-blue paint on the woodwork and window frames. Discreet lighting directed the eye around the room and Leah's own range of floral scented candles stood proudly by the front door. It worked well because river cruise customers often popped in. Unfortunately, it didn't translate to many sales for Joe's old steamboat, but Maya had placed leaflets advertising *Bertha* by the till.

'Good day?' asked Maya and Leah nodded and gripped a piece of ribbon between her teeth to hold it in place whilst she finished the bouquet in her hands, gratefully accepting the coffee afterwards, taking off the lid to sip it.

'Bliss.' It was cool in the shop's interior to keep the flowers fresh, so a warm coffee from Penny's café was always welcome – Leah often wore fingerless gloves, even in summer. 'It's been hectic as usual,' she answered. 'Matt's in the back if you need him?'

Maya grinned, as she always needed Matt — just differently to how Leah needed him. He'd made himself indispensable. He was a huge part of her life, as was Leah.

Maya always thought that Leah looked like a Flower Fairy, her red hair often loosely tied up with a ribbon from the shop to keep it off her face. She was petite and when they visited a bar outside of town, security or bar staff always asked for ID.

'I'm ready for a break,' sighed Leah, taking a packet of chocolate biscuits from a drawer and waving them at Maya.

'Have you been on the boat?' asked Leah as she led the way to the fairly large back room that they used as an office. The space was white and modern and had backlit images of models wearing Maya's jewellery in slim metal frames on the walls. They were walking into the heart of Matt's fledgling modelling agency and Maya still felt a thrill of excitement every time she walked inside, and she knew Matt was enjoying his new role as her model agent as much as she was. Maya was so thankful that her brother, Arthur, had set her sparkling new website up because she wouldn't have known where to start. It was high tech, but had been of minimal expense to her because of her brother's know-how. An overnight success: two years of slog and experience running a business before.

Maya hugged Matt and then sat down in the chair next to him, Leah did the same. There was another screen; to alert Leah if a customer came in. Maya gave Matt his coffee and he sipped it gratefully and filched two biscuits before Leah could eat them all.

Matt was Maya's very own James Bond. He was one reason that the company had reached the stage it was at now. Being the first No. 1 Ethereal Lane model held kudos and the publicity from the furore that had surrounded their first campaign had catapulted him to fame and helped him raise the money to start his own agency from the space behind the flower shop. His own modelling career had kept him busy and travelling for years, but now he wanted a new challenge and he'd hated leaving Leah because their relationship was getting pretty serious and he'd even tentatively mentioned to Maya about designing a very special ring at some point. How she'd managed not to let that slip to Leah she didn't know, but the thought of Leah's face when he did eventually ask her would be worth the subterfuge.

'You two are sickening,' Maya joked as Leah picked up some digitals of a recent photo shoot and handed them to Matt with a flourish and an air kiss.

'You need to find your own Prince Charming,' teased Leah and Maya pushed her chair back and bumped into the desk, almost knocking her half-full coffee cup over as that reminded her she'd just told her sister she had a boyfriend! She knew Romy would mention it to Leah if she saw her, as she'd expect her to know, so Maya needed to come up with a plan for the family party and quick. She patted her flushed cheeks and picked up her coffee, then paused mid-sip.

Maya saw a look pass between her friends.

'What's up?' she demanded, glancing between them as they clearly wanted to tell her something and Leah should probably be back in the shop by now.

'There's a lot in the press about Blake at the moment,' said Matt, who always sounded affronted to have to mention that name.

'He's just launched his most popular collection yet,' said Leah with a slight snarl in her voice, even though she'd never met Blake. As Maya and Leah had grown close, Maya had decided she needed to trust. This time, she'd chosen well. Leah was the best person she knew outside of her own family. Maya was a solitary soul by nature, but Leah had scaled the walls she'd built around herself through sheer persistence. She'd popped up whenever Maya was sitting watching the river meander. They'd discovered mutual creativity; Maya had helped Leah set up her floristry business. She was a gifted florist who didn't have a business head. After a previous business failure, Leah had been in debt. Maya had immediately seen her potential and, one day, they'd walked along the river and peered into the windows of the run-down shopfront that was partially covered by ivy.

Maya had seen the potential of the property, but Leah had been reluctant. She was scared to fail again. But after agreeing the lease and weekends spent scrubbing and painting the woodwork, the shop shone. Two years later, Leah's debts were paid off and her gorgeous shop was a destination in itself. Matt being able to work there too worked well for the couple as it saved paying for extra office space. Maya felt that in her own way she'd had a hand in her friend's happiness by finding Matt, even though Leah had chased him a bit at first – but that was another story.

'Blake has run out of the hummingbird designs now, so I won't have to see them out and about any more,' said Maya, straightening up a stack of paperwork on the desk in front of her and tutting at the stray used teabag that sat on the edge of a plate by an old mug of tea. Maya swiped the teabag into the bin by her feet and put the cup on the plate, before realising that her friends were watching her with half smiles because she was a little obsessive about cleanliness.

'He's certainly milked them for all they were worth,' said Matt, shaking his head.

'He's a businessman,' said Maya sadly. 'It didn't occur to me he'd use the designs in so many ways, adapting them to bracelets, earrings, belts and everything else he could think of. He's smart. He was always smart,' she added quietly.

'Not always,' said Leah with another eye roll of contempt. 'These are your designs, not his. He's just taken the credit for them.' Leah's hair bobbed up and down as she spoke, and Matt put a calming hand on her arm. She stopped ranting and smiled in apology.

Maya felt warmth fill her veins at her friend's loyalty. Blake hadn't actually been that awful of a designer, but he'd realised where his skills lay early on. He could manage talent – hers, anyway. They'd been a winning combination until he'd broken her trust. All the love and passion had drained from her designs for a while and that had almost been as devastating to her as losing her relationship, which should have told her something. She'd been too upset to take a deeper look at how she felt and was full of self-pity.

Then she'd started living by the river again, met Leah and drawn every day. No. 1 Ethereal Lane had evolved from a different place. She made exquisite jewellery of the grasses and flowers that thrived around the river bank and intricate designs incorporating precious stones that she set into her designs, which seemed to drive her customers wild.

'Leah is right, though. He's a thieving git,' said Matt after a pause.

'I signed the company over to him to get out of our partnership. The finances were tricky at that point; we'd both invested heavily.'

'You lost your investment, though!' Leah raged.

'But I also walked away from the risk of any debt chasing me later. I just wanted out.'

'He made a fortune from your designs,' seethed Leah, clearly attempting to tone her voice down for Maya's benefit, but she could almost see the steam coming out of her ears.

'He's within his rights to exploit the designs,' said Maya, eyeing the almost empty pack of chocolate biscuits that Leah was waving around. Her stomach grumbled, but from too much sugar, than hunger. She really must get back to swimming at the local pool to stretch her muscles out again. She was a strong swimmer and loved the solidarity of head and arms pushing through the water without having to talk to anyone else.

'He manipulated you, for sure,' ground out Matt, snapping her back to reality. She zoned out of Blake-bashing, even though she'd been the instigator often enough. She didn't really care what he did now, unless it directly affected her business, which she didn't think 'his' latest designs would. He could pretend as much as he liked. He'd pretended to be in love with her for long enough, why stop the pretence now?

'I don't really care... I've moved on...' she hedged,

wondering if this was the right moment to spill her new boyfriend news. Leah raised an eyebrow at this and Matt stayed silent for a moment, which spoke volumes, as both of her friends often voiced their thoughts out loud and they equally spoke over each other when feeling cross. They thought it was about time she began dating properly again and had tried to set her up with friends often enough, which Maya found exhausting and sad. Now she'd thrown a fake boyfriend into the mix to Romy, she'd have to pretend to Leah and Matt as well, and she hated lying. The problem was that it was too late now because she'd already blurted it out to her sister, who was like a dog with a bone when she happened upon interesting titbits of information about her siblings. Maya was *very* selective post Blake, and it got her into no end of trouble now.

Leah had fallen madly in love with Matt the first time she'd seen him, and she hadn't understood why Maya wasn't already in love with his dashing good looks. To her (and many of the female population), Matt was the perfect male. He was tall, dark and handsome, as well as being astute and kind. Maya would never cross the work/life divide again and although she loved Matt dearly, and he had an extra special place in her heart for being her first ever No. 1 Ethereal Lane model, there was no spark. She was grateful for that now, as Leah had come into Maya's house and fanned her flushed face when she'd first met Matt and had to grab a cool glass of water to ease her parched throat. She hadn't stopped talking about him for days and she'd stalked his social media to find out if he was interested in anyone else, even though Maya had told her he wasn't.

These days Leah and Matt were inseparable, even working out of the same space, which would drive Maya nuts. Maya had never fully worked Blake out when they were together, so there was no reason for her to do that now.

'That model he shagged probably thinks he's a genius,' scoffed Leah and Maya flinched. Leah refused to call Portia by her name, even though she and Blake were still together two years later. Both had benefited hugely by their association, and Blake often paraded his prized girlfriend out to the press, something he hadn't done with his fiancé. Portia never cracked a smile to the photographers and had been dubbed the 'ice queen' as she was always draped in diamonds. Maya squeezed her eyes shut and refused to picture Portia draped in her diamonds. It had taken her ages to use the stone again, but now she did with bravado. Her most successful design to date had a stunning diamond draped in a delicate flowering eelgrass, as if it had just been unearthed and pulled from the river. The well-known interior designer Maya had created it for was powerful, talented and an advocate for sisterhood, so it had found its rightful home. Plus, she felt like it was her own private way of sticking two fingers up at Portia when it was worn and photographed by the press.

'Why don't you tell everyone the truth about your new work?' quizzed Matt. It was a question he'd asked repeatedly, but her answer was always the same.

'I'm not ready.' She knew that response still wouldn't satisfy Matt or Leah, but it was all she could give them because it was the truth. Maya was happy producing her best work from the steamboat or studio on the top floor of her rented house, often sitting on the little balcony at night and letting the breeze from the river wash over her as she listened to late-night radio.

'You might get asked to loads of exclusive parties and meet lots of delectable men if you tell everyone how amazing you are and how popular your brand is getting,' winked Leah as she pulled the ribbon out of her hair and tied it tighter, preparing to go back to work.

'I don't have time for parties.' Maya could feel her heart-beat ramp up as she knew what was coming next.

'You've got that family party coming up soon, so it could bag you a date for that,' said Leah.

Maya knew she needed to get out more, but her space and time was sacred, especially now that she was making more expensive pieces with delicate gems like sapphire and ruby which took her breath away with their beauty. Her days were spent on the river with Joe, sketching and, once in a while, she'd join one of Mason's art classes. People came and went as their circumstances changed, but the ethos of the class remained: everyone was welcome. Now the looming family party was on her mind. She had thought that she might bring Mason, as they had a lot in common and she had a feeling he liked her by the way his eyes always sought her out, but neither of them had overstepped the friendship mark... yet.

'I've got no interest in being famous...' she said finally, 'but I am over my ex.' That wasn't exactly the honest answer. She knew she'd been using Blake as a barrier for not jumping back into the real world and living again. 'Plus, I've just started dating someone else,' she added and then ran for cover as Leah chased after her, demanding to know more. Luckily Maya was faster, and a customer had just walked into the flower shop, so Leah had no choice but to slap on a smile after sending Maya a ferocious glare that told her she would be made to give up more information later. Maya leaned back against the side wall of the shop and caught her breath while her mind whizzed over all the other things she could have said. Why had she told two people she was dating someone new? They might assume he was special for Maya to have told them, but it was their own fault for hassling her to find someone for the dratted family party. Her family went all out for these kinds of events, so it would be flamboyant, dramatic and completely bonkers. If she dragged someone along it might scare the life out of them! Maya stomped home muttering to herself at her own stupidity, whilst wondering how to sign up for several hundred dating apps in one go.

Chapter Four

Robbie strolled into Noah's vast kitchen and grabbed a beer from the huge industrial fridge. 'I heard you almost got mobbed in the village,' he teased, throwing a beer towards Noah as he was sitting rather glumly at the end of the central granite breakfast bar and reading the papers. Noah looked up just in time and caught the beer with one hand. All of the training for his action roles came in handy when his best friend was around, as you needed quick reflexes for his constant jokes and tricks. For Robbie, comedy was inherent. He couldn't help himself from teasing and annoying his closest friends, Noah grumbled to himself as he sipped the beer and enjoyed the cool liquid hit his parched throat. He'd been in a bad mood since he'd tried to take a simple walk along the river. It had one perk, he supposed, even if he had made an absolute jerk of himself and knocked coffee all over her white top. It had to be white! He groaned and leaned his head on his hand.

'Your housekeeper told me one of your groundsmen had to haul you up from your boat, quick smart!'

'I drove the boat up the river and jumped out to stretch my legs. I forgot that people find the regular stuff that I do interesting.'

'I don't understand it either,' Robbie said with a straight face. 'It's not as if you're pretty or anything,' he winked. 'You're in half of the movies they watch these days. They're fascinated about everything from the shoes you wear to what snacks you eat...' Robbie eyed the huge bowl of crisps that Noah was lazily snacking from, even though he knew he'd have to do an extra hour in the gym to work them off. Robbie filched a few and happily munched away as he wandered around.

'They think I'm the action hero though. I'm just a guy who wanted a walk by the river.'

'Your life sucks,' joked Robbie, gazing around the huge open-plan kitchen, state-of-the-art wine fridges and enormous windows with views across the rolling lawn, down to the water's edge. Noah grinned suddenly and his sense of humour reasserted itself. It was unlike him to feel maudlin, but something about that morning had unsettled him. He didn't know if it was bumping into the beautiful woman by the bridge, or the fact that he'd clearly ruined the start to her working day.

'You're an idiot,' Robbie told him helpfully.

'Thanks,' Noah replied sarcastically as Robbie rounded the huge island unit in the centre of the kitchen and poked Noah in the ribs, making him jump and almost knock his tooth out on the beer bottle. His agent would love that! It exhausted him sometimes at how demanding his agency could be. He sighed and sipped his beer, still giving Robbie death stares over the top of the bottle, which Rob seemed to find hilarious.

Robbie grinned widely and sipped his own beer. 'Have you decided what to do about your awful dating life?'

Noah shrugged. 'I'm not sure that I can handle another relationship after what happened with Tabitha. It's all a bit raw and there's another story about what a lothario I am in a gossip column again today.'

Robbie snarled and Noah finally smiled. 'Maybe I need to meet someone from a different world to mine? Someone who isn't interested in fame at all.' He pictured the dark haired woman on the bridge and how she hadn't asked questions of him, she'd just helped him get away, without even telling him her name. He wondered if he could risk going back and trying to find her, but squashed that thought immediately. It could only bring more chaos.

Robbie opened the fridge to search for food. 'If you prepare me a sliced beef sandwich and add some of that amazing chutney your housekeeper makes, then we can come up with a Tabitha battle plan.' Robbie batted his eyelashes at his friend and Noah sighed. Robbie never stopped eating! He must work it of in nervous energy when he was on stage because he was slim and fairly athletic for a lazy guy who loved nothing more than slobbing around on Noah's couch.

He stood up and shoved Robbie out of the way of the fridge to actually start making them some lunch. Robbie piled several jars into Noah's arms until he complained and began unloading them onto the island unit.

'You can't eat all of this,' said Noah, eyeing the tower of food.

'I can try!' replied Robbie happily. 'We need sustenance and also to make sure that our plans for your revamped sex life are Tabitha proof.

Chapter Five

Lying to your loved ones was never a good idea, Maya had learned – the hard way. After a few exhausting weeks of pretending to go out on dates with an extremely busy fictional boyfriend, Maya's fingers ached from the intricate work on her latest designs. She'd put off a meeting with her family and friends so far by explaining they both had impossibly heavy work-loads and actually didn't see each other that much. The part about how hectic her own life was becoming was true, even without her non-existent other half.

The sun was just rising over the river and creating a hazy dappled effect on the ripples in the water so she squinted as she repositioned the metal shields she used to draw the warmth of the flame away from the precious gems she was setting so that they didn't overheat while she soldered a tiny bezel cup. She'd been working for most of the night and had finally dozed off after adding the final gem to her design. She never worked on two pieces at once, but she had a very important client that could not be put off. The first was a bespoke piece for a famous client, whom

Maya already loved, even though the client did not know who she was. Her personality shone when they had chatted online and Maya really wanted to get the piece right. Their conversation had been light, fun, and vivacious. Sahara was a much-loved daytime television hostess. Maya was numb with shock that her clients would pay so much money for a piece of her work. She no longer undersold her gift for design and she was reaping the benefit.

She jumped as her phone rang and she picked it up after seeing who was calling. 'Hi, Mason,' she said, her mood instantly lifting at the sound of his voice. 'Haven't bumped into you for a while. Work has been hectic.' She glanced around her immaculate workroom and realised that the turmoil was inside, not around her. She'd been worrying about the family party again and the secrets that were mounting up.

'We've missed you,' he teased, his Irish lilt making her skin tingle. Mason wasn't her usual type; tall, self-assured and handsome. He was definitely good-looking, but in a quiet way. He wasn't flashy or pushy, but he was often smiling. Could he be boyfriend material? she wondered. 'I'm holding a class today, but we only have a few people booked in. Want to join?'

'I do!' she said happily, a burst of fresh energy filling her veins at the thought of seeing Mason and her other friends. 'I want to start a couple more paintings for Penelope's café, so I need to do some preliminary drawings.'

'Maybe seeing me – and the others – will inspire you?' he teased, and she flushed and realised he was right. She was very much looking forward to seeing him now. Perhaps she *could* find herself an actual date for the party. She'd been thinking of staging a tearful break-up with her current faux beaux because he never had time to meet her family, but that might bring even more problems with her family wanting to hunt him down and give him a piece of their minds. Subtle, they were not!

'It's a date,' she answered Mason without thinking, and then pulled the phone away from her face and stared at it in shock. Had she just called a casual meet-up a date? How embarrassing! 'Umm. I'll see you there, Mason,' she added, finishing the call and not waiting to hear his response because her cheeks were burning and she needed to stick her head in a bucket of cold water for being such a moron. Mason was just being friendly and now she sounded desperate, which she actually was – for a date. She really was going to have to make up a scenario where she broke up with her imaginary boyfriend soon if she didn't find a replacement. Her friends and family knew Mason well, so they'd realise it wasn't him. She sighed.

The delicate necklace she'd placed on her beautifully curved wooden jeweller's desk took her breath away and every twinge in her joints was worth it. Her work tools were within easy reach, but tidily stacked in different sized racks.

Maya looked out towards the double doors and balcony on the top floor of her home and enjoyed the glorious view of the river and the swans drifting by as they watched people outside Penny's café, in the hope they might throw in a morsel of food. With no time to linger, or for a coffee, she hurried herself along.

Maya carefully lifted the necklace and placed it in the safe. It was hidden behind a watery landscape painting from a fancy gallery and Maya had been frightened to move it at first lest she damage it. Now she deftly slid it across the discreet rails it sat on, opened the safe and checked that her platinum and diamond No. 1 Ethereal Lane tag was secure on the clasp of the necklace. Someone already flooded the market with cheap copies of her branded tag and people wore them on simple chains or added them to other necklaces or bracelets. Authentic originals were easy to distinguish as the quality shone with the intricacy of her designs. That there was only one of each numbered piece made fakes very easy to spot.

Closing the safe and then locking her office door, she hurried back downstairs. Maya's client had a big charity gala and auction to attend and was raising money for a pretty little local museum that had fallen into disrepair, so the intricate necklace had to be ready on time. Maya hated to leave a client waiting, and the extra work had been back-breaking.

Maya grabbed an apple from her fruit bowl and a bottle of water from the fridge, then glanced down at herself and checked she'd remembered to get dressed because she was so tired. She was wearing an old pair of Levi's and a textured sage-green cotton shirt with a wide laced collar she loved.

She stopped to take in the vista of the quintessentially English old town as she stepped out of her front door and walked towards the river – it truly was a picturesque sight. The honey-hued cobbled main road ran from the dock, past the riverside café and up the hill towards the stone castle and bustling centre of town. Pretty little shops lined the high street with red-tiled roofs and deep sash windows. It was picture perfect. Ideal for a painting session! She shoved her sunglasses on top of her head, because the sun had finally showed itself. Picking up her pace, she half walked, half ran, to jump onto Joe's boat before *Bertha* left for her first cruise of the day.

Joe shook his head; she was usually early for everything. She hated the stress of worrying about being late. She'd rather get there early to relax with a coffee and watch the world stroll by. He grinned and pulled her in for a hug and a kiss. 'I will pay you for today,' he said. 'You never take a wage, and that fancy house you're renting must cost you a fortune. You need a wage,' he added, mock sternly. Maya grinned as he said this pretty much every time she stepped aboard. She kissed his leathery cheek and admired his neon-green shorts and red top as Joe refused to conform to uniforms.

'Your t-shirts don't need to be viewed from space,' she said cheekily. He rolled his eyes theatrically. Joe's one concession to conformity was the giant word CAPTAIN across his back on his T-shirts.

'I like to let my customers know who I am,' he chided playfully. 'By the way... your grandparents told me you have a date for the party! Who is the lucky chap?' Maya's insides squirmed as the subterfuge was getting too hot to handle. She glanced over to see Mason setting up his art class, and he waved. Joe glanced his way and raised a busy white eyebrow in question as she still hadn't answered him. She waved back to Mason, who was looking handsome in washed-out jeans and a pale-blue t-shirt that day and used that moment to steer the conversation away.

'I'm sure I'll have time to introduce you at some point,' she assured breezily, then added, 'Penny sold four of my paintings, so you really don't need to worry about me.' Joe's eyes lit up and he pulled her in again for a congratulatory hug. She saw they had about twenty guests that day and about eight for the art class. Hordes of people were queuing for the Bowen Brother's boats. The eldest brother, Alex, looked her way and blew her a kiss. She mock fainted, laughed and caught it. Maya would secretly love to steal all of Alex's customers. Hordes of young women waited to get on their boats and Alex and Luca lapped up all the attention as if they were rock stars! They flirted with Maya relentlessly, but she'd had her fill of playboys, however much she'd toyed with the idea of finding one to mess about with recently. It wasn't her style... not that she didn't enjoy looking at handsome men, though! It made her day brighter, and they seemed to enjoy the flirting, too.

Roman winked at her as she walked past and they slapped hands in a high-five. 'Ready?' he asked. Maya nodded and settled herself on the bow, after checking that the handful of guests didn't need anything and saying hello to Mason and his art class.

'You cut it fine,' Mason noted with a grin as he settled his group. He already had a splodge of ochre paint on the back of his hand and his jeans pocket was full of paintbrushes.

'I know.' She smiled up at him and took his hand to brush the yellow paint off with the pad of her thumb. 'I was working late and then fell asleep at my desk.'

'Maybe we should meet up for a coffee after the cruise ends and get you a sandwich?' he suggested, his hand still in hers. She let her hand drop and wished she had that fizzy feeling of excitement that she felt should come with an offer of a coffee date from a very attractive man. The way she'd felt when Noah had stopped to check she was okay after knocking into her, even though their 'meeting' had been fleeting and embarrassing. Was it bad that she was looking forward to the coffee more than the company with Mason? She was determined to try harder and upped the wattage of her smile, which he seemed to appreciate as he held onto the guard rail for support.

'Sounds good!' she said, making sure she sounded keener than she felt. She'd been friends with Mason since he'd come over to her one day while she was sketching and told her he was thinking of starting a local art group. She really liked him, but wasn't sure if it was anything more just yet. The problem was that she'd already told her family and friends that she had a boyfriend, so she'd better start dating for real, or be doomed to failure and more family meddling in her love life. Mason would solve all of those problems, but he might create more if she wasn't as invested as he was, and she wasn't sure her family would believe it was him, anyway. There would be no reason for them not to have met before now, because Mason wasn't exactly busy and he held his art classes on Bertha! 'They sell double-shot coffee at Riverside and Penny might even sneak in a drizzle of caramel if we're good.' Mason's face lit up.

'It's a date,' he said over his shoulder as he turned back to his class and she kind of wished she'd kept her mouth shut earlier. If she bumped into her family or friends now, they would think she was two-timing a guy who didn't exist! Every simple coffee with a male friend was seen as a potential life partner to them, which was ridiculous. She'd only been single for two years and wasn't exactly desperate... She sighed as she realised that's exactly what she was, now that she'd blurted out she had a boyfriend.

Sitting cross-legged on the bow, she pulled her small drawing pad and pencils out of her canvas tote bag. She loved sitting on the edge of the boat and drawing, but currently her nerves were shot to pieces. Joe liked to have her on board, but he and Roman could easily manage this amount of guests on their own if she suddenly decided to jump ship and scamper back to dry land. She'd been back to the local pool lately to try to ease the tension in her body, but she wondered if she might give river swimming a go again soon, because that was where she could float about and still be immersed in nature. The sterile environment of a black-and-white tiled pool hadn't made her want to rush back. There were ten superb wild swimming spots that Maya knew of along the Thames and Hurley Lock was her favourite with its shallow beach, tall grasses, mild current and pretty tearooms.

As the boat moved away from the dock, Joe started his tour speech and she heard guests murmur to each other about famous film star Noah Benedict and his mansion being situated further up the river. Maya could understand the excitement as she'd had often sat up late with Leah and watched one of his films, drooling all over themselves. Matt joined them occasionally, but he preferred the action movies and when Leah and Maya had commented that they liked a different kind of action and fallen over laughing childishly, Matt sighed and got them all a glass of wine.

He had a movie coming up later in the year that was being filmed in one of the big London studios, with Dame Rosalie Alton – who was a megastar – so the whole town was fizzing with excitement. Noah lived here now, and he had been adopted as one of their own, so the locals had become quite defensive when he was branded a wife-stealer by the press. It had turned out later that Noah was meeting his date to talk about a charity gala and her husband – his good friend – was actually at the restaurant too! It seemed to Maya that that particular newspaper had it in for him, as that was the third viper-like article she'd read from them.

The occasional glimpse of Noah walking across his lawn and sitting on the grass reading a book often sold Joe's tours, as people didn't have to fight for space by the railings to get a good look at their idol. Maya had seen him a few times recently, but he rarely had company, and she wondered if the photos of him in the press with various companions were true. She knew from her own experiences that stories could be way off the mark, or too close for comfort, so she had an open mind and was curious – but just because he was local, not for any other reason... She kept thinking about his disarming smile, but she was still resolutely off men who looked as good as he did. He was bound to have an entourage the size of his ego.

The boat steamed down the river and Maya opened her pad and drew. Even though the river network was sometimes damaged by the environment or people, it still provided a magnificent home for a variety of plants and animals in the ancient wetland landscape. Being part of one of the longest rivers in England meant it was an area of outstanding beauty, in Maya's opinion, with wide paved pathways running along the riverbanks, which were surrounded by grasslands and soft-petalled river flowers in hues of cream and pink. Swans dipped their graceful necks into the water and ducks and Canadian Geese flocked around brightly coloured boats or bobbed on the ripples of the river as the boat steamed by. Today she was looking for the flowering grasses that grew in this area, so she immersed herself in her sketching until Joe mentioned over the Tannoy that they were passing superstar Noah Benedict's house.

The chatter from the guests picked up volume, and a few rushed over to Maya's side of the boat. One woman screamed and fanned her face with her hand as her friend held her arm for support. Another woman frantically waved at the house as they saw Noah walking towards his outbuilding with a determined stride. He had a towel slung over his shoulder and he was wearing denim shorts and a casual white T-shirt, looking breathtaking. Maya's heart almost stopped as their eyes met and she could have sworn that he smiled at her. He was probably smiling and basking in the attention of the fans who were manically trying to catch his eye, but he'd reached the door to the modern natural wood and tinted-glass-windowed building and slipped inside. Maya's heart was racing, and her skin was incredibly hot suddenly, but she guessed that was why he was a film star. His charisma shone, close up or at this distance. Be still her beating heart! If only he wasn't such a miserable git, according to one of the co-stars of his new film —Tabitha. He'd seemed pretty friendly when he'd accidentally poured coffee all over Maya's chest. Tabitha was scathing about him, so he'd clearly done her wrong at some point to have so much venom directed at him.

Maya wondered how it would feel if a man this dangerous looking and sexy as hell ever turned his attention her way, but she couldn't in her wildest imaginings see how that would ever happen. He was an impressive actor and could make an audience nearly hyperventilate and pass out in excitement from the way the woman next to her had just screamed. She had almost given Maya a heart attack and was wobbling and holding her friend's arm for dear life. 'He smiled at me!' she bellowed, her face flushed, as Maya jumped up and grabbed a bottle of water from the bar and rushed her way to calm her down. The woman took the drink gratefully as Maya guided her and her wobbly legs safely to a seat. The customer opened the bottle and gulped the cooling liquid down. 'I'm not sure I'll ever recover,' she gasped, clearly trying to catch her breath. 'Did you see, Agnes?' she asked her companion, who was rummaging in her bag to pull out a floppy sun hat and perch it on her friend's bouncy grey curls.

'I did, Melony!' her friend replied, touching Roman's arm as he walked past to get his attention and ordering two enormous glasses of rosé wine. 'We need to celebrate!' she stated, enjoying their rapt audience, as all the other passengers had moved to this side of the boat to see what the commotion was about. 'Let's hope our luck stays with us when we get to the racetrack. There might be a horse named after Noah,' she cackled gaily and Maya couldn't help but laugh. Both ladies were short, loud and curvaceous, with long, flowing colourful dresses. They had flirted outrageously with Joe as the boat had departed and he'd blushed and smiled. Maya knew he was worried about his wife, Olive, at the moment, as she needed a hip replacement and then a holiday. Joe couldn't afford to keep the boat out of the water for the two weeks for her to recuperate, or staff it while he was gone.

Ten minutes further up the river, the guests disembarked at the racecourse and new guests climbed aboard for the journey home. There are only five of them and Maya served drinks and then settled them on the top deck as Joe turned the boat around. While it was quiet, Maya took her chance to grab a moment with Joe. She knew he would be concentrating on the river and also understood that Olive's operation was the following week. 'Joe,' she said, making him look up for a moment. 'Olive is going to need you at home for the next two weeks at least.'

'I know,' he said, not taking his eyes from the river. 'I can't be in two places at once though,' he sighed, rubbing his white beard, his bushy eyebrows as wild as ever.

'You know that Gran and Pops will help,' said Maya, 'but could I ask you to trust me?' She tried to keep a straight face and not look shifty because Joe was supersensitive to anything to do with his precious boat, *Bertha*. 'I've had a plan for a while and I want to look after the boat for two weeks for you. You won't need to check up on us and I'm sending you to Cornwall so that Olive can recuperate properly. Before you can protest,' she held up a hand to stop him from speaking. 'You need a rest, Joe. We can handle it here and I promise I won't let you down.'

'But...'

Roman strolled behind Joe and agreed with Maya after catching the end of the conversation. 'We can do it, Joe,' added Roman with a smile, putting a hand on Maya's shoulder and giving it a squeeze of support. 'Olive needs you and it's about time that you let me sail Bertha. I've been working here weekends from when I was a teenager and since I've been full time, you know I can run the boat with Maya. You've taught us both well.'

'I can't afford a holiday,' harrumphed Joe, his eyebrows almost in his hairline. Joe still had a thick mop of hair that he swept back with gel, so he looked like a dashing Father Christmas.

'I won a competition, and it's two weeks in a beautiful cottage by the sea,' Maya lied, crossing her fingers behind her back and hoping Joe would forgive her for fibbing. It was the only way she could think of to help her friends. 'I can't go because I've got a painting commission of the riverbed and it's one of Penny's customers. The holiday is a set date, so we will waste it.'

'Surely you could paint there, or you must know someone who needs a holiday at the cottage?' said Joe. 'Ettie and Owen would love it!' Maya smiled at the mention of her batty grandparents, but they were in on the plan too. In fact, it had been their idea! Her whole family had chipped in to rent the cottage for Joe and Olive.

'Grandad is doing a talk at the local horticultural society that week and you know how obsessed he is about his plants.' His garden was overflowing with beauty, and growing up there had been an adventure and a pleasure. She was pretty sure her love of nature came from him. They'd spent hours and hours lying on their tummies, examining the tiniest flowers over the years. Her favourites were Sweet Alyssum, that had miniature blooms that smelt of honey and pink or purple Egyptian Star Clusters the bees loved.

'Oh,' said Joe, understanding dawning. He knew that his best friend was obsessed with plants, so that definitely counted them out. 'What about Leah and Matt, or Penelope?' he asked.

'Leah's overrun with orders and they have a holiday booked at the end of the summer. Penny hasn't finished training her new manager yet, so it doesn't work for her either.' Joe stopped and thought about it for a moment and Maya saw his shoulders sag in defeat and knew at that moment that she had won... for now. She could see how exhausted Joe was and his usual raucous, sunny nature was gradually being worn away.

'Okay,' he surprised her by saying. She had expected to have to pin him down and force him to go. He smiled gratefully at her as if he'd finally acknowledged that he needed to accept help, and pulled her into his arms for a hug. She sank in gratefully and realised that he'd lost weight, as the hug didn't have his usual all-encompassing warmth and happiness. She hated lying to him and she hoped that what she had planned for his boat and his business, were worth it.

Chapter Six

The next week had been a whirl of activity for Maya and her family, which culminated with Joe and Olive being safely packed off to Cornwall for two weeks of rest and recuperation after her operation. Maya's coffee date with Mason hadn't been as relaxing as she'd hoped because she'd worried about Romy walking in and joining them at any moment. Then she'd have barraged Maya with questions about it later because she was clearly affronted not to have met him yet. Maya and Romy might be different, but their childhood had created deep bonds and they looked out for each other and meddled a little too. This boyfriend issue needed to be squashed soon, or she'd have to admit she'd lied to keep the peace. The party was not far away now and Maya was sweating about it, as preparations were in full swing and her grandmother never ceased to mention how excited she was about the gathering when they were together. Maya was pretty sure she was trying to trip her up as she still hadn't let them meet her boyfriend and Leah was champing at the bit to have a couples' dinner with Maya's high-flying and often-travelling boyfriend.

Standing with her hands on her hips and surveying the boatyard that she'd had *Bertha* transferred to, she caught sight of Alex and Luca and beckoned them over with a wave.

'You know you're not to touch Joe's pitch through pain of death?' she arched an eyebrow at them and they both pretended to quiver in fear. Alex held his hands up in surrender, and Luca's grin widened.

'You think you'll get this old girl back on the water?' he asked in amusement, as they both turned to look at *Bertha*, who was looking rather shabby and as if to make a point, one of the lifebuoys dropped loose and clunked to the floor, which made Maya jump. Luckily, the outer paintwork just needed touching up, but the inside was another story all together and the floorboards needed sanding and varnishing.

'Of course we will,' assured Maya, not sure exactly how confident she was about that fact, but she'd had to take drastic action to help Joe. 'I know you're both worried about the competition, but I'm sure the ladies will still flock to your boats to see our biggest local attraction...' Both men preened a little and then she laughed and nudged hips with Alex. 'I meant Noah Benedict,' she added playfully and Alex roared with laughter and swept her dramatically over his arm for a quick kiss on the lips which stunned her to silence, but which she also quite enjoyed. She put her hands to her lips and he winked at her and then he and his brother turned and left. She'd always had flirty banter with the Bowen brothers, but neither of them had ever kissed her before!

Maya turned and saw Mason waiting for her next to

Bertha, and his face was just as stunned as hers was. Blast! She plastered on a smile and as she walked towards Joe's boat, she felt a lump in her throat and dread in her stomach. Alex and Luca had agreed that Joe's boat needed updating, and they respected him enough not to be threatened by a little of competition. They probably thought Maya could do much with the old girl. But *Bertha* still had fight left in her yet. She greeted Mason with a friendly kiss on the cheek and then tried to act as if she hadn't just been kissed by Alex, but Mason was still frowning.

Maya didn't know if she had made the right decision about anything in her life, but there was no going back now. She waved to Mason's art group as they all clambered on board and started looking around with interest as they listened carefully to Maya's plans. Two of the artists, Bobby and Phil, were about Mason's age and in their early thirties. Both were unemployed right now and the art classes were a lifeline for them both. Phil spoke softly and was tall and skinny with a mop of brown hair, whilst extrovert Bobby had a loud belly laugh that made his stomach wobble when he joked around. He was larger than life and he gave the best cuddles. Another regular was flame-haired Margot, whose personality matched her hair. She'd just lost her home, husband and job, but she still arrived at the classes with a smile and determination to find happiness again, according to Mason. They'd been sending mildly flirty texts quite a lot now, and it hadn't progressed from a close friend-ship even after the coffee, but Maya got the impression he'd like there to be more. She didn't know why she was stalling, but she wanted to feel fireworks and not just a slight fizz of attraction.

'Hi, Maya,' Phil said shyly, as she gave everyone a welcoming hug.

'Thanks for helping, Phil. I appreciate it,' she responded and had the wind knocked out of her as Bobby swung her into his arms for his hug. 'You too, Bobby!' she gasped when he'd put her back on her feet and she'd caught her breath.

'I can't wait to get stuck in!' he said, eyes shining with excitement, but then Bobby found joy in most things, which was one of his most endearing qualities. He had no permanent home, but he tackled each day with vigour and Maya knew he'd be back on his feet soon. She quickly hugged the rest of the artists and thanked them profusely for being there.

The engine of the boat was sound, but the interior and exterior were washed out and tired. Maya, Matt, Leah, and Penny had spent the previous night scrubbing *Bertha* until every speck of grime was erased. Even her brother and sister had turned up for a few hours to help and had both gone home with grease on their faces. Penny had gotten little work done after that, as she'd spent the time mooning after Arthur, who, to his credit, got stuck in with the cleaning. Maya's back already ached, but she was determined to get this right. She was taking a tremendous risk taking the boat off of the water for two weeks for a refit. She risked Joe and Olive never speaking to her again if they didn't like what she'd done, but her gut was telling her to press on as she would never have this opportunity again.

The green banquette seating she'd had custom-made would arrive to be fitted in a week, so they had until then to bring the boat back to life. Penny's cousin Gio came and stood next to her. He grinned shyly at her. He was a giant of a man, with broad shoulders and a gorgeous smile. His thick dark hair and Mediterranean good looks make people stop and stare, but he shied away from engaging in conversation with the others in the group and Maya was determined to help him find confidence somehow. Penny had confided that his gentle nature meant he'd been taken advantage of by overbearing men, his last ex included, who had milked his bank account dry and then left him broken-hearted.

They'd found that they had much in common when he'd joined Mason's art class at Penny's insistence. His art was delicate and beautiful for a man with such enormous hands. 'Okay, everyone,' said Maya, corralling the group into the bar area. 'I've drawn out a plan of exactly what I want for Bertha.' She took out a detailed drawing and spread it over the main bar. Everyone crowded around and Elliot, the youngest of the group, who was a very talented autistic artist, pushed his glasses further up his nose and pressed his face closer to take in her vision. He'd visited *Bertha* one day with his mum and become fascinated when he'd watched Maya pull her sketchpad and pencils out of her bag and begin to draw. They'd come and sat next to her and spent the journey chatting about Elliot's love of art. He'd joined Mason's group a week later, and he was probably one of the most outspoken of the group.

'How's Mum?' Maya asked, ruffling his hair and receiving a wide grin in return.

'She's at a job interview!' said Elliot with pride.

Maya clapped her hands in excitement, her eyes shining. 'Oh, Elliot! That's brilliant news.' Everyone crowded around him to hear more, and he glanced at them all with pride. 'What's the job?'

'It's about talking to customers at the bank in the high street. Mum says lots of them are closing down, but this one is getting bigger! Mum's brilliant with people and loves a chat,' he said innocently and Maya suppressed a giggle because his mum certainly was a chatterbox in the loveliest way and would suit a customer service role perfectly. This role sounded ideal for her, and she'd be near Elliot's school. Double win! Elliott was an absolute joy to be around and he helped Mason run the classes by organising the setting up of the easels and distributing the paints each week.

'Your plans are great, Maya!' he said happily as he took his time to check them out properly and her heart warmed. Elliot could be a harsh critic if he felt a tone or angle needed to change, but his insight was more often than not on point, and she grinned and high-fived him and a few others who all murmured their approval. She felt the grip of fear loosening and finally drew in a full breath of air, enjoying the easing of the dizziness she'd felt all morning.

Maya had marked out in great detail what she wanted them all to do and knew they would be pushing it to finish the project in two weeks. Most of them had refused when she'd insisted on paying them for their time, but she'd been immovable. Joe often let the art class members travel on the boat for free when it sailed from town and up towards the next village, which was by the racecourse. It was about a twenty-minute trip up, but *Bertha* also sailed in the opposite direction past the historic castle that nestled amongst the trees, before turning by the dock by The Fisherman's Arms pub and returning home. The Fisherman's Arms served the best steak and ale pies and mash for miles around, so that route was popular too. The artists wanted to repay Joe's generosity for those journeys.

In Maya's usual organised style, the bar had small piles of paint pots and brushes. 'There's food and drink behind the bar for anyone who hasn't had time to have breakfast,' she called out after them, but she could see the excitement of creativity had already taken hold.

Maya sighed and the feeling that a lump of lead had been sitting in her stomach for the past few weeks had finally dislodged. Maybe they could do this and it might actually work. 'I love your style,' Gio said softly, glancing down at her paint-splattered denim dungarees and scruffy off-white t-shirt. Maya grinned and squinted at his shorts because they were so grimy you literally couldn't tell which colour they had started off with. He held his hands up playfully, which was the first time Maya had seen him relax a little. 'I know. Awful, aren't they? I wear them when I'm working backstage on the sets and the grease won't come out however hard I try.'

'Well, they're perfect for this job!' she said cheerfully, linking arms with his. 'Come on. You and I have got to do a patch-up job on the outside and start sanding the floorboards on the deck.' She hoped she had enough energy for boyfriend hunting later!

Chapter Seven

'I can't believe it,' said Mason. *Bertha* was magnificent, and practically every surface now reflected the sunlight that shone through the windows around the bar. She was transformed and for a moment it stunned them to silence, even though they'd all been part of the refit.

'I added some finishing touches,' admitted Maya as she ran her hand along the new black granite bar that was an off-cut that a kitchen shop situated at the top of the hill in town had donated. The local community had gotten behind the makeover and they'd turned up with coffee and sandwiches for the workers. Maya hadn't let them on board, but a few had craned their necks to get a glimpse. She worried that someone might let slip and tell Joe, but the community was pretty tight-knit and she knew they all loved Joe and Olive and were excited about this surprise.

'It really is mind-boggling and I bet Alex and Luca have been trying to see what you've done,' said Leah as she and Matt handed out glasses of fizz or orange juice, and Penny distributed cupcakes that filled the air with toffee and the spicy cinnamon that was dusted on top, which made Maya's mouth water. Someone switched the radio on and the smooth jazz playing seemed to fit with *Bertha*'s new look. The interior had plush velvet seats in green and matching cut-glass vintage glasses were lined along glass shelves at the back of the mirrored bar. As the sun filtered through the windows, ripples of colour reflected on the completely refurbished bar.

'They have popped by a couple of times,' Maya admitted, then felt her cheeks go warm at the mention of Alex's name, but she'd also seen him around town with three different women and she wasn't about to become number four this week.

The interior walls of the bar nearest the seating were painted a deep green and smart black and gold inlaid panelling had been added to match the theme of the boat. The grandiose interior had windows everywhere but still felt sumptuous and welcoming – now the inside was just as beautiful as the view of the river would be. It was like stepping back in time to an art deco masterpiece with chandeliers, lush greenery and sophisticated, rich colour schemes. 'To Maya!' they all chanted as they raised their glasses. She blushed and brushed the compliments away.

'To teamwork!' she exclaimed, raising her glass back to them all as they burst into chatter and the team arrived to get the boat back to the riverside. 'Joe's returning in the morning and I've heard from Gran and Pops that Olive is healing well,' Maya sighed in relief.

'I've sent Joe a few images of the river that I took weeks before and told him everything was fine,' added Roman, who was walking around and opening cupboards behind the bar to find out where everything was stored. 'He's not asked about *Bertha* or discussed ticket sale numbers, so maybe he's finally realised that he needed a rest.' He shrugged, brushing his long hair from his shoulders and grinning at Maya.

Bertha looked film star glamorous, and stepping aboard now was an experience. Over the years, quite a few famous people, including local actress and national sweetheart, Dame Rosalie, had cruised along the river on *Bertha* in her heyday and signed their names above the bar. Maya had highlighted this with lots of tiny gold stars in between the names and left the room for lots more. She hoped that when people saw who had been there before them, they might spread the word, or come in and pose for a social media post in front of it.

As they all jumped off the boat and prepared to welcome Joe back to the other love of his life, Maya felt sick. Leah leaned in and gave her a warm hug. 'It will be okay', she reassured. 'How could anyone not love this?' Maya looked around the inside of the boat that was almost unrecognisable and prayed that Leah was right.

Chapter Eight

'Urgh.' Maya tried to open her eyes, but the sunlight streaming through her curtains wasn't helping with her hangover. She'd drunk too many glasses of rosé the night before to ease her nerves and then passed out watching a rerun of one of Noah's films. It was almost sacrilege to miss any of it, but she must've been bone-tired, as she'd finally fallen asleep on the couch. Maya glanced at her watch and groaned, dragging her legs off the couch and trudging to the shower where she got a fright, as she hadn't given it time to warm up. After lathering her hair with strawberry-scented shampoo, she washed the suds away and then wrapped her body in a big fluffy white bath towel and dried her hair. She didn't have time to straighten out the waves today, knowing Joe would be eager to get on the water and be back with *Bertha* as soon as he could.

Roman had offered to pick Joe up that morning, but Joe had insisted that he wanted to walk. Maya pulled on red shorts and a top with the new logo on it. It was the image of the castle peeking through the trees and she'd bought stock for staff of all shapes and sizes. Maya knew how important branding was. The image was colourful and vibrant and had *Bertha* written in scrolled lettering underneath. Joe's own t-shirts had CAPTAIN written across the left side of the breast.

As she crossed over the bridge and reached the promenade opposite her house where the boats collected the passengers, she stopped and shuffled back a step or two, as quite a crowd had formed. She took a deep breath and gripped her bag to her chest. She noticed Margot from the art class as her vibrant hair was tied back with a green scarf and Phil and Bobby were standing next to her, both wearing the branded t-shirts that day, which made her heart melt a little. Leah, Matt, and Penny were all standing proudly beside *Bertha*, and Maya raised a shaky hand in greeting.

Leah grabbed her hand as she approached and squeezed it in solidarity. 'What if he hates it?' Maya asked her friend.

'He'll love it! It's stunning, Maya. I can't believe you pulled this off in two weeks and word of what you've done has spread like wildfire!'

Maya turned and almost walked into Alex and Luca Bowen, so Alex caught her arm and straightened her up. 'You must stop falling for me, Maya,' he winked, and she rolled her eyes and squared her shoulders.

'You must stop kissing me, Alex,' she said pertinently and Leah's jaw dropped. 'I've got a boyfriend,' she added with a flourish and then wished she hadn't because she saw a flash of challenge in his eyes.

'I stand corrected,' he said with a bow, and she wished he wasn't so handsome. 'Well done with *Bertha*. She'll definitely bring more tourists to the area.'

'Can we come on board and have a look now?' asked

Luca. 'You've been avoiding us all week, but now I think that's more about Alex.' He laughed and slapped his brother on the back who grinned good-naturedly and took the hit.

Leah was almost bouncing off the floor with questions about Alex kissing her and excitement about Joe's imminent arrival, so Maya touched her arm to calm her down. 'I'll tell you later.'

Maya headed towards *Bertha* before Leah could ask more, but Alex gave her a hug of congratulations, which shook her further, his arm slipping around her waist afterwards as he guided her closer to *Bertha* and the crowds. She kind of quite enjoyed it, but now she'd told him she had a boyfriend as well! Their friendly rivalry was legendary and even though Alex and Luca did flirt with her, she didn't think they meant it. They'd probably fall off the dock in shock if she actually ramped up her response. She'd never betray Joe and cross that line, though. Maya knew they wanted Joe's boat, however cute they both were. After finally turning and hugging Alex back, the level of noise grew to a din. He kissed her on the cheek, brushing her hair out of her eyes with his fingers, and then he winked at her cheekily, making her grin. 'Your boyfriend's one lucky guy,' he whispered into her ear, which made the hairs on her neck stand up and then he moved away and into the crowd. Joe had just arrived, and Maya blinked and rushed forward to greet him. His eyes were out on stalks and his mouth dropped open in shock, so she didn't have time to think about Alex and his antics.

'Um, Joe,' she said, grabbing his arm, but he stood mutely and looked at his boat – his shining star of a boat. 'There's been a few changes.' She turned to the boat just as flashbulbs went off behind her. She'd forgotten how much everyone here loved Joe and what a big part of the community he was. The photographer was lining up Joe and Mason's art group for a photo and they looked around the crowd for her, but she ducked behind Alex, who frowned and then shrugged. In the end they called for her, so she groaned and joined in, but hid behind the hulk that was Gio at the last moment, because she hated being photographed. He looked down at her and probably assumed she was feeling shy like he was, so he slung an arm around her and she enjoyed the warmth of it for a moment, before kissing his cheek, which made him blush. She blinked as a few more photos were snapped and she had nowhere to escape to, so she grit her teeth and put up with it.

She scrambled up the rear ladder onto the boat and stepped aboard when everyone else boarded from the front. Leah saw her and led the photographer on a tour in the other direction so that Maya could have some time alone with Joe to find out what he really thought.

Blake had been featured in the press again lately and he had turned up at her grandparent's home a few times since their breakup and gotten a sharp retort from her grandmother. Maya grinned, as she wouldn't have been surprised if she'd 'accidentally' tripped him up with her walking stick. She didn't need the stick, but kept it by the door if she needed to act like a frail old woman to get rid of people, rather than the sprightly pensioner that she actually was, who still occasionally went rollerblading. Maya hoped with all her might to turn out like her grandmother when she was older.

Maya turned to face Joe, who was looking around in wonder. 'How did you do all of this?' he asked her.

'Everyone helped,' she smiled shyly. 'Do you like it? I'm sorry for lying to you, but you'd have never left her in my hands if I'd have told you what I was going to do.' She held her breath and waited for Joe to answer.

Joe wandered around the bar and trailed his hand along the surfaces, picking things up and putting them back down again. 'I want to bring Olive to see it! Bertha is reborn! It's unbelievable, Maya,' he said excitedly, making her smile in relief. Joe spotted the pile of t-shirts and swapped his own eye-scorching orange one for his Captain shirt, proudly turning so that she could see the bright logo of a castle peeping through the trees on the back. The tension she'd been holding for the past few weeks finally left her body and she shook her arms out to get the blood flowing again. Joe squeezed her into the tightest hug and the breath was knocked out of her again.

'It's magnificent!' he exclaimed, eyes shining with tears and joy. 'It's stunning, Maya. How can I thank you?' Tears spilled out of his eyes and he hugged her again. 'I thought *Bertha* was as washed up as I was. Now I've had a holiday, Olive's hip is healing – she's had a good rest – and I have come back to a whole new business. I can't believe it!' Maya finally grinned and Leah slipped into the room and took a few snaps on her phone for Maya and then leaned in to join the hug. Gio and a few of the art group saw them as they walked past and they piled around Joe, congratulating him.

'Right, you lot. You are officially my first customers,' said Joe in a booming voice. 'Let's get this party started. The drinks are on me!' he chuckled. 'Let's see how Bertha takes to the water with her shiny new makeover.' He looked around in wonder. 'I can't believe you all did this transformation in two weeks,' he said, mirroring Leah's earlier sentiment. 'Thank you, Maya,' he said, eyes misting over for a moment. He took her hand and kissed it, making her blush. 'You are an absolute gem.'

Mason walked in and handed her a glass of chilled white wine, which she took gratefully. 'Care to join me for a walk on the deck?' His face seemed sombre, so her mood immediately shifted from euphoria to uneasiness as they stepped outside. 'I just heard you tell Alex that you had a boyfriend,' he said.

Chapter Nine

'Y ou're becoming a bit of a celebrity. Don't let it go to your head!' teased Maya as she boarded *Bertha* and gazed around at the hordes of customers and queues of tourists still waiting to have their tickets checked by Roman. She'd heard the buzz of conversation as she'd passed and the excitement level to get on board and meet the captain was palpable. The steamer was usually fully booked now and Maya had helped Joe to hire two new staff. Maya kind of craved the simple times when she could sit on the boat and draw, but Joe was much happier now and Olive had visited and exclaimed how much she loved *Bertha*'s new look. Maya's chat with Mason hadn't gone that well the week before and he was avoiding her now, but there was no way she could explain that she was resolutely single when she'd spun such a yarn to everyone else. She'd had to pretend that it was very recent and not that serious, but Mason's texts had dwindled to nothing, which stung a little but was her own fault.

Maya stepped into the bar, and ordered their signature strawberry lemonade, which had kind of happened by accident when Roman had been gazing dreamily at a woman who kept asking him about the makeover. He accidentally put strawberry puree in the lemonade, and it created a *Bertha* classic. Lots of people enjoyed it with a hint of gin, but tonight Maya wanted a clear head. She had quite a demanding client this week, expectations were high.

She blew Roman a kiss and headed out to the main deck. Joe waved and then continued with his spiel about the local landmarks. The sun was dipping and because it was early summer, lots of houses along the river were having barbecues and parties. Maya could see lights strung across the garden of Noah's house and people milling around the grounds, drinking fancy-looking cocktails and laughing. A few women were wearing long, floaty summer dresses in hues of orange and green that were the height of glamour right now and as the boat approached, there were guests on the private jetty, which had steps down to the boats that were tied up at the water's edge. As they drew closer to the boats, Joe's customers started murmuring in excitement at being so near to Noah's house and the fact that they had just spotted a famous comedian, Robbie Latton, who she knew from the gossip columns was Noah's best friend.

One woman on the jetty of Noah's house cackled and pushed the chest of the man next to her in jest. He stepped back and lost his footing, which sent him tumbling into the water. Maya kept her eyes on him and, as he fell, his head struck the edge of a sleek black powerboat moored below. She didn't think twice. She called 'man overboard!' to Joe and dove straight into the water, right where the man fell. It was quite a leap from the height of *Bertha's* deck, but Maya had leapt off of *Bertha* thousands of times before when they'd been quiet. Maya heard the woman's hysterical screams as she plunged into the icy water and reached to secure her arms around the man, who was by now a dead weight. She felt her lungs strain and pushed up to the surface with all her might, gasping for air as she surfaced and feeling relieved to hear the splash of someone else diving in to help. Joe had thrown a buoy into the water and the other person grabbed it and then them. Between them, they dragged the inert man back to the jetty as arms reached down to lift the three of them back onto dry land.

Maya's teeth started chattering as river water streamed from her hair and clothes and she attempted to catch her breath and push herself to stand up on wobbly legs, but they gave out and she leaned on her arms and sat next to the unconscious man instead. He was still out cold. She knew from protocol that Joe would have already called an ambulance. She held out a hand to stop the man, who was dripping with water next to her, when he called for someone nearby to contact emergency services. 'Joe will have called them already,' she whispered, seeing the lines of fear on his face and nodding towards the boat in the river.

She didn't have time to really register that the person who dived in after her was Noah before she checked the inert man's vital signs and started resuscitation. All the boat crew had safety training regularly, and she was sending up a prayer of thanks whilst trying to remember what to do and blocking out the sobbing woman who was still hysterical. Noah asked someone to take her into the house and the other guests crowded round, trying to help the inert form. Maya was too busy concentrating on the man who had hit his head to notice too much else, but he had a huge red lump on his forehead and a slight cut to his cheek that was now bleeding. She tried to calm her own breathing and suddenly the man who hit his head came round and started coughing and spluttering, gasping for air. Maya put her hand on his heart to calm him and told him quietly that he was okay and that an ambulance was on its way. 'You fell into the water and hit your head, but you're going to be fine,' she added, keeping her tone soothing and praying that what she said was true. She gently dabbed at the cut on his face with her t-shirt, but it was superficial and had already stopped bleeding.

He groaned in pain and the ambulance crew pushed through the throng and took over, checking their patient and asking Maya several questions which she answered as best she could, shivering at the realisation of what had just happened. The second crew member also checked her over after they had the guy who had fallen into the water on a stretcher and wrapped in a blanket. They gave Noah a quick check too, although he assured them he was fine and had gotten there at the last minute. Smartly dressed house staff arrived and towels were placed around their shoulders as the crew lifted the very dozy man into the air and carried him to the ambulance.

Maya stood up shakily and walked to the end of the jetty to where Joe and a crowd of onlookers were standing on *Bertha*, who had been anchored in the same spot. Maya waved to show that everything was fine – at least she hoped it was, and Joe nodded and turned to tell his customers to get ready to resume their journey. She knew he'd have been worried sick and would have kept *Bertha* there to stop any other boat from going overhead while she was in the water. She also knew he'd be watching for her signal to leave, but that he'd be back for her when the clients were safely at their destination, now that he knew she was safe.

Noah spoke to the paramedics, as they were about to leave, then turned to face Maya. She didn't feel anxious or shy, so she presumed she was still in shock. They just stood looking at each other for a moment, before he blinked and then walked over and put his arm around her. 'You're an absolute hero and you're shivering!' he said. Maya was so cold now that her teeth started chattering again.

'Come on,' said Noah, taking her hand and not really giving her a chance to run and hide. 'There are fresh clothes and hot showers in my guesthouse. We need to wash the river water off of our skin. Thank you for saving Robbie,' he added gravely.

'You'd have gotten to him in time,' she said croakily when she finally found her voice. 'I'm Maya,' she added shyly.

'I'm Noah,' he said unnecessarily. 'I didn't know the exact spot he'd fallen in as the sun had dropped. Plus, the boats were in the way and Tabitha was screaming, so I couldn't think.' He waved his arm in the general direction of the hysterical woman, who was still sobbing into a rather good-looking young man's arms. 'You saved him and we are forever in your debt,' added Noah sombrely. 'Plus I owe you for dry cleaning... twice now... and a coffee,' he quipped and her head snapped up that he'd recognised her. 'You saved me that day on the bridge too.'

Maya laughed at how serious he looked, even though his wet hair was bedraggled and his face and his clothes were plastered to his body, giving her a glimpse of firm chest. 'Anyone would've done the same. I'm always alert when I'm working on the boat, maybe not so much on my way to work...' she bantered. 'I was just in the right place at the right time,' she said self-deprecatingly.

Noah led her through the crowds, who made room for them as they got closer. 'Get everyone a fresh drink,' he said to one guy as they passed and he nodded and ushered everyone back up the garden and towards the house.

Maya could hear music playing as they walked towards the modern building in the garden that she'd always wondered about. Noah's guesthouse! She was going to see inside it! She couldn't wait to tell Matt and Leah. Matt would faint because he was such a Noah fan. Leah would want to know about the interior furnishings and plants, after asking what Noah looked like drenched in water from the river, of course! She chuckled to herself and admired Noah's broad shoulders as he led the way to the building and opened the door for her to step through.

'Thank you.' She looked around in awe at the interior of what seemed to be a huge annex. It had a gym area and a stunning glistening pool that looked out on plate-glass windows that had views out to the river. There were over-sized concrete urns with lush green plants that contrasted to the industrial feel. The main area before you got to the pool had comfortable seating and a fully stocked bar with tall bar stools in front of it. The furnishings were plush and in deep rich tones of plum, dark blue, green and inky black, reflecting the tones of the river.

Some wooden stairs led to a second level, which was behind an enormous sheet of glass where she could see a vast bed and more windows out to the water. The view from the bed must be incredible to have views over the pool to one side and elevated views of the river from the other. Most of his actual house was made of weathered metal, wood and glass, but she could live here and die happily. That whoever stayed there with Noah was so lucky – but just because of the view! She bit her shivering lip to stop herself from shaking and half-wished she could just jump into the pool, as it looked warm and inviting. Who'd have thought that she'd meet the ultimate player? She was so glad he wasn't her type, or she'd be blushing and stumbling over her words right now.

The air in the guesthouse was cool as he led her upstairs to the bedroom. It was such a weird sensation to be so close to the man she'd seen on the big screen and on her own television. She'd drooled then, but she hadn't been serious and she watched his taut derriere ascend the stairs in front of her eyes, blinking a few times to make sure she wasn't dreaming and had actually knocked her own head somehow. Noah beckoned her inside his guest suite and pointed to where she could find clothes and a shower. One of her own artworks hung above the plush headboard of the bed and she stopped walking in shock. He must have bought it from Penny's café, but Penny hadn't mentioned it and she was pretty sure that everyone locally would ram themselves into the café if they thought he'd been there.

Even soaking wet and exhausted, he still oozed glamour and sex appeal. Her heart was racing after all the drama of the accident and it was just her luck to be looking like a swamp monster the both times she met a film star. She plucked a stray piece of river weed out of her hair and sighed. It always ended up like a wavy mess when it got wet, and it wasn't her best look. Less sexy siren and more horror film extra.

Noah saw her looking at the painting of Wood-sorrel with its distinctive trefoil heart-shaped leaves and white flowers that hung from tiny green stems and he smiled her way. He had magnetism on the screen, but in person, it radiated from him. Maya gulped and tried to shove the first burst of lust she'd had for a while away in confusion.

'Do you like the art?' asked Noah as he grabbed a fresh fluffy towel from a drawer for each of them and handed one to her. It smelt like heaven with its soft, citrusy fragrance and she draped it around her shoulders to mask the stench of river water. 'There are some spare clothes in the wardrobes. I keep them here for when I'm working late and come for a swim, then I fall asleep after I've dried off.' Maya pictured him pulling himself out of the water half-naked and then shook that thought away. The next image was of Noah, all sleepy and delicious, waking up tousled and in the vast bed they were standing beside and she frowned. She really must have hit her head on something when she dived into the water because she was behaving like a teenager with her first crush! He'd asked her a question, and she'd rudely ignored him.

'I... um. The paintings look nice,' she mumbled, trying not to look into the big blue eyes that were looking worried as he gazed at her.

'I should get you into the shower and warmed up. Are you sure you didn't hurt yourself when you heroically dived in?' he asked with concern, not seeming like the dark and dangerous sex-god who was splashed all over the papers for a moment. 'If you leave your clothes out here, I'll get them washed and dried quickly up at the house. There is a dressing gown on the back of the bathroom door.'

'I'm fine, really,' she protested, finally finding her voice. 'I think I might have been in a bit of shock, as it all happened so fast, but I'm warming up now. A shower would be great. I'm sorry if I wasn't listening earlier.' Noah laughed and led her nearer to the bathroom that had a huge bath in front of another river view and a double shower. Maya's eyes went wide in shock. 'Anyone can see you take a shower?' she asked.

Noah chuckled and tapped the wall with his fingers. 'It's a one-way glass. You can see out, but no one can see in.'

Maya frowned. 'Are you sure?' she ran her hand over the glass, before stepping back and flushing. 'Sorry!'

Noah threw back his head and laughed again. 'I think it might have been headline news if a local resident was having showers and flashing to the river cruises!' Maya spluttered and finally the knot of tension in her stomach eased and she sighed.

'Sorry,' she giggled. 'You like this artist's style?' she said after a moment, glancing over her shoulder at the Wood-sorrel.

'I asked my assistant to find me pieces from local artists that reflected the river and he said this lady was popular. He tried to find her contact details and reach out to her directly about a further commission, but the café owner gave him a short sharp shrift about respecting privacy.' He grinned with a mischievous twinkle in his eyes and Maya gasped. She might have met Noah again sooner if Penny hadn't been so vigilant, but in the end, it would probably have just been a phone call with his stylist and Penny knew she didn't take on private commissions for her art. She was too busy with her jewellery line. Might have been fun to know about though. She smiled shyly.

The painting certainly reflected the river, as Maya had drawn the original lines of the flower against the edge of the swirling river, on her sketchpad while sitting on *Bertha*. Tonal blues and greens of Noah's furnishings echoed the paintings beautifully, and she felt pride swell in her chest. The guesthouse seemed to complement the surrounding river. Calming colours welcomed them, but the room had an eclectic edge, with art and sculptures dotted around.

'Please make yourself feel comfortable. I'll have a shower by the pool so that I don't look so much like a drowned rat and scare my guests,' he joked, and she laughed.

'I hope your friend is ok,' she said quickly, wishing she'd thought to say that before. He should have been her first thought, but her mind had been groggy. His eyes clouded over and he frowned.

'They said they'd let us know. His brother was here and they only let one person go with him, so he's been giving us all text updates. My phone is waterproof, but I don't think they expected it to be dunked in a river,' he joked. He pulled his phone out of his rather wet jeans pocket and luckily it had a clear rubber case around it. He scanned his latest texts and his shoulders sagged with relief. 'Apparently Robbie is already regaling the ambulance crew with his awful jokes, so it looks like he might be ok,' he grinned and turned to smile at her. She drew in a sharp breath.

'I was so worried about getting him breathing again that I didn't really register who had been knocked out,' she said, a tremor in her voice as she reached out to put a hand on the wall to steady herself. She'd just given mouth to mouth with one of the nation's favourite comedians - Robbie Latton! 'Bad jokes?' she raised one eyebrow in question and snuggled further into her towel.

Noah grinned cheekily and shrugged. 'Okay. Maybe the knock to the head has improved them.' He winked, and she grinned back at him, eyes full of mischief in mirth. Robbie sold out packed stadiums and people clamoured to hear his sets.

'Thank goodness he's okay. He was out cold.'

'Get into the shower. You look freezing,' encouraged Noah, moving back towards the door and motioning that bigger bath towels were in the cabinet next to the shower before leaving her standing alone and not quite knowing what to do with herself. She was glad that her own phone was tucked into her sketch bag that was still on the boat and safe with Joe. She quickly stripped off, leaving her clothes outside the door as instructed and stepped under the water-fall shower, that was instantly warm. Fancy! She wondered if she could get one of those at her own house as she lathered her hair to wash away the river weed and breathed in the manly scent of the shower gel, which was spicy and immediately perked her senses up.

She didn't hang about after that and towelled herself dry and wandered into the bedroom, noting that someone had pulled huge curtains across the guesthouse and pool side, so the bedroom felt snug and private, even though it was huge. Turning and catching sight of the river almost took her breath away. Realising now that this was also one way glass, the hazy early evening light was dappled across the water and the fairy lights from the garden that were moving in the gentle breeze sent darts of light across the surface. Wishing she had her sketchpad to capture that moment, Maya glanced at the view briefly, but needed to get a move on or appear rude. She'd have liked to have sunk against the shower wall and tried to work out how she was going to get out of there with so many glamorous people milling about.

Maya opened one of the modern wardrobes and ran her hands over the rows of clothes hanging in an orderly fashion and smiled. Perhaps she wasn't the only neat freak in the world? She selected a white t-shirt and pulled it on. After using her fingers to comb her hair into some semblance of a style, and grabbing the hairband she'd left at the side of the fancy double granite sink to pull it into a slick, high pony-tail, she put her still disgustingly damp underwear back on, before rushing back down stairs.

Noah looked like he'd just stepped out of the shower, as he was all tousled and sexy. He was wearing a discreetly branded blue shirt with the sleeves rolled up and some washed out jeans that made him look like he'd just taken part in a fashion shoot. She smiled tentatively and smoothed her hands down the t-shirt, tugging at the hem. He grinned at her and reached out for her to take his hand. She blushed and complied. 'You must need to get back to your guests?'

'I need a minute to breathe before we go back out into the throng. Is that okay?' he asked, shifting uncomfortably in his seat. 'My ex-girlfriend, Tabitha, is out there and she definitely wasn't invited.'

'Sure,' she replied, worrying that he had actually hurt himself in the river. 'Why is Tabitha here if she wasn't invited? I wasn't exactly on the guest list either,' she joked, but was curious now. 'I understand if you don't want to tell me. We have literally just met... for more than five minutes anyway,' she countered.

Noah looked at her for a moment as if deciding something, then offered her a cup of steaming tea that he poured from a china teapot. Next to it was a bowl full of sugar lumps and a plate of crumbly looking shortbread. 'Apparently, I'm a reprobate and not to be trusted – especially if you believe the stories that Tabitha feeds the press,' he sighed, and rubbed his temples. 'Sorry. That was uncalled for. She's making me second-guess everything I say and do. Rob falling into the river will probably be my fault by the end of the night.'

'The Tabitha that's outside?'

'Yes. Our producer has told us to "get along" hence I couldn't ask her to leave once she'd shown up with a mutual friend. Weirdly, Tabitha wants us to date again and feels the way to do that is to tarnish my reputation in the press, so no one else will want to date me. I just can't understand her logic.'

'Wow!' Maya's eyes were out on stalks. Noah slumped in his seat and rubbed his eyes, before propping himself on the bar.

Maya blinked as the scent of his spicy aftershave drove her senses wild and quickly drank the heavenly sweet tea he'd made for her. She sighed and put her teacup down on the fancy saucer, eyeing up the biscuits, but deciding now was not the time to stuff her face, especially when Noah seemed to want to open up. 'It's put me off dating for life!' Noah groaned and pushed the plate of sugary shortbread her way, as she was clearly hungry. She grinned and nibbled the end of one piece before putting it on the edge of her saucer. 'It gets worse,' he joked. 'my family hates the fact that I'm over 30 and not in a committed relationship, but Tabitha has made me wary of everyone's motives. You helping me on the bridge, even though I'd just thrown coffee over you, intrigued me though.'

Maya flushed and ignored the last comment, as what could she say to that? 'It's a genuine dilemma when you should be having the time of your life,' Maya sympathised, patting his hand and then frowning and putting her hands primly in her lap. A shiver went up Maya's spine at how similar both their exes sounded. 'I can relate to that. I'm 29 and my family and friends are always trying to set me up. It's a nightmare!' she sighed dejectedly. 'Maybe you need a new relationship to let Tabitha know you aren't available?' she added thoughtfully. Noah sat up straighter suddenly and looked directly at her, his features bright and alert.

'You're right! That's it! We both need to be in a relationship by the sound of it. Let's have one and then they'll all back off!'

'What! Wow... that's not what I meant...'

'If we pretend to date, they'll leave us alone. It's genius!' Noah was looking at her with those piercing blue eyes that were even harder to dodge in person. Maya wanted to lick her lips, but she sipped her cooling drink instead. Noticing her clothes sitting on a nearby cabinet, she slid off of her seat, backing away. Frowning at Noah's daft idea, she remembered his guests outside. She could sit with him and listen to his nutty plans all night, but Joe would be worried. It felt like she'd been with Noah for hours, but it had probably been about half an hour, so Joe would have had time to drop off his customers by now. 'I should get back to the boat,' she said apologetically, as this evening of make-believe had almost been fun. 'Turn your back so that I can slip my shorts and top back on.' She raised an eyebrow at his amused glance and he looked away while she changed, quicker than she ever had in her life. She folded the dressing gown and t-shirt in a neat pile and turned back to him. 'You can turn around now,' she instructed, and he fixed those blue eyes on her, which made her heart beat faster and the hairs on the back of her arm stand up. He had a good sense of humour and she was sorry that he'd been so ill treated by his ex, just as she had. The fake date idea could be hilarious to shut everyone up, especially Matt and Leah who were relentless in their matchmaking, but dating a man as famous as him could only bring bigger problems for her with her business growing at such a pace. Thank goodness he was just joking!

'I can take you home in my boat. I remembered that you said you live by the river, or have a driver to take you back to your place?' he offered, sad to see her go, which was weird when he had a house full of guests. She didn't know what to think of the fact he'd recalled where she lived.

'It's okay. Joe will come back for me, but thanks.'

'Joe?' he asked, his eyes still on her. 'Is that your actual boyfriend?' Maya snorted and tried to hide it behind another sip of her drink.

'Joe is 75 and his beautiful wife, Olive, has just had a hip replacement,' she laughed. 'Joe owns the boat I jumped off of.'

'Is that the boat you were walking to when we first met? I've seen you drawing from the bow.' Maya's face went bright red. He had seen her! She didn't imagine their shared glances. She frowned again. What did that mean? Probably nothing more than that. He was curious about the goings on, on the river, nothing more. 'Um... I help Joe out from time to time. I'm an artist.'

'Amazing! Can I ask what you paint?'

'River scenes mostly. Like the ones that you have hanging in your bedroom,' she grinned suddenly and couldn't contain her laughter.

Noah turned to glance up to where Maya had opened the curtains again and looked at the artworks. 'You painted that? I've been trying to get my hands on another one for the house, but they're always sold the minute they hit the walls of the café that sells them, apparently. I keep meaning to wander up there or take my boat to see if it's busy.'

'Umm. After the coffee-bridge disaster? I think it might cause a bit of commotion if you did!' said Maya. 'Is that your shiny black boat by your dock?'

He grinned, seemingly in no rush to leave. 'Yes. It's flashy, but it sang to me in the boatyard.' Maya smiled because she'd felt the same way about the sleek, cream powerboat that came with her house. She imagined gliding up and down the river in it as it was far less congested than the roads around town, but she was fearful of scratching it.

'I can understand that because I've got a mooring underneath my house. My landlords store their boat there.'

'You enjoy living by the river?'

'Yes. My place is pretty much opposite *Bertha's* dock.'

'*Bertha?*'

'Joe's boat.'

'The huge steamboat? I have seen nothing else like it on this stretch of water. I didn't get a moment to register anything when Robbie hit his head, other than Tabitha's screaming that Rob had fallen into the river,' he shook his head at the memory. 'I'd love to see what it's like inside, but as you mentioned earlier and we both recently experienced, it's usually a bit of a furore if I don't plan things ahead of time.'

'That must be tough,' she said and his head whipped up to see if she was mocking him. Then his shoulders relaxed, and a glint of mischief came into his eyes that sent her pulse racing. This man was lethal! She was so thankful right now that he wasn't her type. She let out a breath of relief.

He answered self-depreciatingly, 'It can be, but I'm not complaining. It certainly has more upsides than downs.' Maya thought about that for a moment because for her it had only caused stress and pain to be even remotely in the public eye. She was soon forgotten though, and the brand evolved around Blake, but there had been press interest in them both even then.

'I have contacts,' she smiled cheekily. 'I can probably get you smuggled on board for an out of hours visit to tour *Bertha*, as long as you promise to sign the wall of fame by the bar.' The corners of Noah's eyes crinkled, and a smile tugged at his lips.

'I'd love that. It's a date!' Maya nearly had a heart attack! She hadn't meant it like that. He looked down, and they realised that he'd taken her hand. 'Come on. We should get you back to your friends if you won't let me take you home. Can I see where you paint?' he asked suddenly, stepping away slightly.

Maya was already missing the contact from his warm hand. She hadn't expected him to actually want the tour of *Bertha*, or to see her again. 'You want to see inside my house? That was my line last time and you couldn't run away fast enough,' she said incredulously, an eyebrow arching with humour.

Noah burst out laughing. 'Sorry. I assumed you had a studio. I wasn't inviting myself to your place, although I wouldn't say no to that either. I was in a bit of a hurry last time,' he added cheekily with a grin, his eyes twinkling, his smile suddenly wolfish. Her stomach filled with butterflies in flight and she almost looked around for somewhere to hide from his magnetism. She was only human, after all.

'Can I get your phone number... to keep you up to date on how Robbie is?' he asked innocently, batting his eyelashes at her and making her laugh. She wondered how many women's numbers he already had stored in his phone and frowned, then shook off the sudden tension in her shoulders. It might be fun to chat to him and it wasn't as if he wanted to date her. He just wanted to see her etchings - literally!

She took his phone as he held it out to her and tapped her number in, saving it under the name SwampGirl. He took the phone with a smile and slipped it into his jeans pocket, then led her back outside where a cool breeze and music floated all around them, bursting their bubble of intimacy and making her shiver. Just before they stepped away from the relative safety of the guesthouse door, he turned and faced her again.

'Sorry that we ruined your evening and your boat ride.'

Maya looked into his beautiful blue eyes. 'It's kind of been fun... except for the your-best-friend-nearly-dying-part,' she joked. As they walked into the garden, all eyes were on them and she smiled shyly at a few people and tugged at the hem of her shorts. 'You must get back to your guests, Tabitha included,' she nudged hips with him playfully. 'You can do this. Try acting. Pretend to be someone who doesn't care if she's here.' she bit her lip and tried not to laugh.

He paused mid-stride and then grinned with mirth. 'Good idea. I'll text you about Robbie and our plan,' he said, putting a protective arm around her as everyone gazed their way but didn't approach them.

'Oh... okay,' she faltered suddenly, her bravado slipping. What plan? Surely that had all been a joke?

'It's an excuse to speak to you again and for us to organise that private tour of your floating piece of history,' he whispered into her ear, making the hairs on her skin stand on end and a frisson of heat zip around her body. Her eyes went wide with shock and she flushed and began fussing with the end of her ponytail. She noticed Joe standing at the edge of the jetty in his *Bertha*-branded T-shirt and bright red shorts. He stood out from the other guests. But as far as she was concerned, it was for all the right reasons. Noah shook Joe's hand and thanked him for stopping for Robbie and they spent a few minutes chatting, before she urged Joe to take her home.

'Thanks again for today, Maya,' said Noah, a little dejectedly. 'You too, Joe.'

Noah waved them off with a wistful look, as if he'd like to jump on board and sail away with them, then he turned and walked back towards his guests.

Chapter Ten

'I s Gio joining Mason's art class on *Bertha* today?' Maya asked Penny as she handed her a steaming cup of coffee at the café.

'Yes,' replied Penny, as she glanced up from placing a huge, crumbly slab of Victoria sponge cake that smelt of vanilla and strawberries, on a plate. 'He's actually looking forward to it and I've told him I'm proud of him for stepping out of his comfort zone. Since he helped you with *Bertha*'s new paint job, he's been painting everything in sight.' She handed the cake to one of her regulars and rang the sale up at the till before turning back to Maya, who was leaning against the wall by the end of the counter. This was her favourite spot for a chat as she could look out towards her own house and also see the goings on along the river.

'He seems to love the fact that the lessons are outside,' commented Maya.

'*Bertha*'s bright new awning is the perfect place to paint,' agreed Penny. 'Plus, I've noticed that he chats to a few of my customers now. He'd have never done that before.'

'I think it's because he's comfortable on *Bertha*, so he talks to the other artists. Plus, Margot has taken him under her wing.' Maya's face lit up at the memory. 'She's been bringing him into conversations with others and he's gradually becoming more comfortable in his own skin.'

'She's a ball of energy!' laughed Penny. 'A total whirlwind.'

'I know!' laughed Maya, but being around Margot and the gentle friendship he's found with Bobby and Phil have been great, too. 'I think Bobby might have a teeny crush on Gio, but he thinks Gio is way out of his league. Gio would probably think the same about Bobby because he's so friendly and everyone loves him.'

'I think it's a bit too soon after Gio's breakup for matchmaking,' agonised Penny as she tapped an order into the till. 'I love Bobby though!'

Maya nodded and tilted her head while she listened to Penny. But she had her own plans for Gio and hoped it was something he'd want too. They'd become good friends over the past few weeks, but his star quality was hidden beneath a wall of insecurity.

'Have you got any more paintings for me to display?' asked Penny as she made a coffee for her next customer and looked over to make sure her staff were cleaning tables as guests left. Penny was a stickler for hygiene and it was one reason Maya came in so often. That and the fact that she got all the latest town gossip from Penny and it was about a hundred foot from her own front door. They both looked up at the empty wall spaces where her paintings usually hung, and it looked bland without them.

'How about putting up some of the work from Mason's art group?' Maya suggested, thinking back to the blank café walls. She'd been so busy lately that she hadn't had time to paint.

Penny didn't look convinced. 'I have a few small artworks you can hang, but you've seen Joe's boat.' Penny tilted her head to one side, and Maya could see her mind whirring. The boat was hugely popular, and she'd hung some art from the group in the bar, as they painted views from the river which complimented the decor. Every income stream helped, and this was a way for them to make their own money. Penny served her next customer, and they both looked up at the framed newspaper article of *Bertha's* transformation that Penny had proudly placed behind the till. Customers often enquired about it when *Bertha* wasn't in dock and Penny always sent them to the little white ticket office by the promenade to find out more. When *Bertha* was idle, she created quite a stir now and had crowds waiting to board her every single day. Maya stayed silent and patiently sipped her coffee while Penny decided what to do. Checking the big clock on the wall because she was due to paint alongside the art class soon, Maya needed to hurry now, but this was important. She didn't know why she hadn't thought of it sooner.

'Please, Penny,' she urged. 'It could really help Gio's confidence to see his work showcased here. I'll still send over my artworks when I can and I will ask Mason to curate the pieces from the art class first.' She finished her coffee and placed the cup in the bin at the end of the counter. 'I know what you like and what we can sell them for.'

Penny grinned suddenly, and handed her a lemon muffin, which made Maya smile from ear to ear.

'When did you become such a businesswoman?' she asked. 'You usually just pop in whenever and hand me a box of your paintings.' She smiled as she turned to her next customer.

Maya laughed good-natured, too. The sales of her artworks had helped pay for her jewellery supplies, now she was on top of every single transaction.

'I'll think about it,' promised Penny, as Maya bid her goodbye and set off to jump on *Bertha* and join the art class.

'Hi, Mason,' she said as she walked up to the area they had chosen for the class that day. *Bertha* was gradually becoming busier and Maya wondered if the class might have to relocate to the pretty little village hall that was on the other side of the river, if more customers kept booking steamboat cruises.

'Hi, Maya,' responded Mason with a smile, but it didn't quite reach his eyes and she hated that she might have hurt him. She didn't really have time to join the class today, but she needed to make sure that Mason was okay.

'I haven't heard much from you lately,' she said as she unpacked her drawing pad and pencils from her tote bag and sat next to him on the side of the boat in front of the shiny new gold guard rails. A few swans floated up towards the side of the boat and a couple of teenagers snapped selfies with the watery backdrop before the birds realised there wasn't any food on offer and swam off.

Mason flushed and busied himself with setting up his portable easel. 'I guessed you'd be busy with your boyfriend and I didn't want to intrude,' he said, not looking up, his hair covering his eyes. Maya flinched and then Noah's face came to mind for some reason.

'That's fair enough,' she said quietly, chewing on her lip and not sure how to mend this situation without more lies. 'As I mentioned, it's quite new and nothing serious right now, but I can see where you're coming from. I'd like us to still be friends?' she asked hopefully, and he finally looked up and stopped what he was doing.

'I'd like that,' was all he said before he checked he had all the paint he needed by running his hands along the tubes in front of him. He cleared his throat and stepped out from behind the easel. 'I just need to check on Elliot,' he added, excusing himself and moving around her.

Gio was already sitting further along the bench, his face turned up towards the sun, his eyes closed, enjoying the warm air. Maya wished she had the camera to capture that moment, then remembered her phone and took a few snaps. She didn't paint portraits, but if she did, she'd start with Gio. His bone structure was chiselled, and he'd obviously been outdoors a lot lately, as his skin was turning an even darker shade of brown. He looked serene, which she knew he rarely felt inside. He was full of self-doubt and loathing because he felt he should have stood up to the ex that bled him dry. Maya scowled when she thought about that man and the damage he'd done to the gentle soul that was Gio. He had thick black hair and firm muscles and his t-shirt looked clean but well worn. She thought he might be one of the most handsome men she'd ever seen and that was after she'd been alone in a shower room with Noah Benedict, so that was saying something! She pictured Noah's piercing blue eyes crinkling up with humour and sighed because he'd crept into her thoughts rather a lot lately.

Leah hadn't let her off the hook about meeting her new boyfriend and the excuse that their schedules hadn't worked out yet was wearing thin. She had thought about how Noah's fake date idea could help her too, but as it had been a joke, it didn't play on her mind too much.

'Hi, Gio.' She waved a pencil at him and he waved a paintbrush back with a smile. His dark eyes shone from under his too-long fringe. If she hadn't had her hands full of watercolour pencils, she'd have needed to fan her face. She could imagine Gio gracing the front pages of glossy magazines and shook her head to clear it from anything other than the business in hand. The next No. 1 Ethereal Lane model choice could wait. Not everyone who could model wanted to and not everyone who wanted to could model. It was a skill, and she wasn't yet sure if it was something such a shy guy, however beautiful, could handle. Gio kept his head down as the other group members arrived, but then brushed his fringe out of his eyes and offered a few of them a tentative smile as Margo breezed in and blew them all kisses with a flourish and a twirl, her long red skirt flowing around her legs and her white fitted top rolled up at the arms, ready to get to work. Elliot walked over, giving Gio and Maya a huge, genuine grin and they high-fived. Maybe there was hope for Gio yet?

Chapter Eleven

Noah felt like he was skulking around in a murder-mystery movie. He had a baseball cap pulled down over his eyes and he was dressed in black as he usually was when he was out in public. The sun was shining and the dry heat made him wish he'd worn something cooler. A lush lattice full of climbing plants concealed the front door. Alongside that was a thick hedge that ran up to the riverbank. In front of Maya's house there was a dock for a boat, which could come and go on the river.

He'd been concerned about how to send Maya flowers to say thank you for saving his best friend's life, but a courier seemed impersonal. Delivering them himself meant he had an excuse to see her again, but he'd dithered about being spotted by the press or the villagers. They seemed to have a sixth sense about wherever he went, which was becoming more and more oppressive.

After pressing the doorbell, he noted some sort of fancy security panel by the door, which he guessed was telling Maya who her guest was. He frowned and then remembered to smile, as she might be watching him. She'd given him her exact address over a text after they'd exchanged phone numbers at his party. He'd been thinking about her a lot and really wanted to see her again in person. The door buzzed open and Maya stood before him in cute denim shorts and a cutoff T-shirt, which gave him a glimpse of her toned waist, making the blood fizz in his veins.

Noah gulped and turned the voltage up on his smile. She was looking at him with her head tilted to one side as if assessing him and he felt like a 12-year-old schoolboy. He thrust the bouquet into her hands that he'd ordered from the florist across the water. His assistant had picked them up that morning and Noah was impressed with the quality of the flowers and design. Supporting local businesses whenever he could was important to him, but he couldn't imagine a nicer arrangement from a big name florist.

'Can I come in?' he asked, and she grinned and stepped back, taking the flowers and inhaling the delicate scent of the honeysuckle and sweet peas. She didn't seem unhappy to see him, so he sighed in relief and followed her inside, looking around with interest. The walls were white and the interior was modern with simple, with elegant light fittings, but it was the art that caught his eye. The walls were lined with four hauntingly beautiful riverside landscapes like the one that he now owned.

She led him into her vast all-white kitchen with parquet wooden floors and floor to ceiling double doors overlooking the river. It flooded the room with light and had a seating area at one end and a cream marble island unit that separated the kitchen from the lounge. It was elegant and full of bespoke art pieces that were strategically placed around the room from what he could see.

There was already a humongous bunch of red roses in a square vase in the centre of the island unit. Next to it, his own colourful bouquet – that he had been thrilled with moments before, suddenly looked paltry. He sighed theatrically. 'I need to up my game,' he inclined his head towards the other bouquet. He hadn't wanted to overwhelm her with his gift, but now he wished he'd gone all in! Maya laughed and offered him a glass of wine after grabbing two glasses from a built in glass cabinet that shone as the light hit it from the windows at the front and side of the house.

She waited for him to settle on one of her bar stools and then grinned a secret smile that did something to his stomach. 'Robbie sent those,' she laughed. 'Thanking me for jumping into the river after him.' Noah's mouth dropped open until he snapped it back shut. Bloody Robbie - although to be fair, she had saved his life.

She opened a huge double fronted modern fridge, and her eyes sparkled with mirth. It was full of branded produce and immaculately ordered. 'He sent me all of this in a hamper, too! I literally won't have to shop for weeks.' Noah rolled his eyes, but noted some labels and congratulated his good friend on his immaculate taste.

'Thank you for your flowers,' she said, her cheeks going rosy suddenly, as she poured the crisp white wine into two sparkling glasses. 'We might as well enjoy the wine Robbie sent too,' she joked, showing him the fancy bottle and brand and he couldn't help but smile.

'Thank you for what you did,' he said simply. 'Every second counted, and you didn't hesitate.'

'It was a bit like watching something in slow motion,' she said as she handed him a glass of wine.

Noah accepted the glass and smiled into her eyes, but she blushed again and turned to take a few snacks out of the fridge. 'We need to sort out that date on *Bertha* and talk about how our *plan* is going to progress.' He grinned, his own eyes full of mischief.

'Plan?' she squeaked, putting her glass back down before she'd taken a sip.

'The idea you had at my party. It was genius!'

Maya frowned, and she held a hand to her heart as if she was afraid for it. 'You can't be serious? I was clearly joking and I'm pretty sure it was your idea.'

'Tabitha has ramped up her plotting, and there are fresh stories about me most days. I'd never be at home - or be able to hold down a job, if I was gallivanting all over the place, breaking hearts, like she says I am. I really need your help,' he pleaded, and she sagged against the counter.

'There must be someone else you can ask, surely?'

'I have a close circle of friends and they'd tell each other,' he grimaced. 'You said you needed my help too?'

'I just said we were both single and were getting grief from our families about our stagnant love lives.'

'Ouch!' he laughed.

She grinned and fiddled with her hair, making him wish he could sink his hands into it and ruffle her composure. This was a woman he'd dreamt about ravishing, and his eyes kept getting drawn to her lush lips, which were more than a bit distracting. 'We'd just been dragged out of the Thames and were more than likely in shock,' she added, not giving an inch.

'But it could work...' he urged, taking her hand and then realising what he was doing and dropping it gently again. 'We could solve a problem for each other, don't you think?'

'I've stupidly told my family and friends I've got a boyfriend to keep them off my back...' she pulled a face as she admitted this and he almost punched the air in excitement. This was getting better and better. 'I hate lying to them and it's not something I'd usually do, but I blurted it out.'

'I can help you with that!' he said earnestly, trying not to sound too keen and scare her off.

'I love the flowers. They look like my friend Leah's work,' she changed the subject rapidly, picking up the pretty handwritten card and showing him the branding on the back. 'Yep. Great choice!' She moved to the window and opened it to let some air flow through the room as it was getting hot in there and the sun was beaming through the double doors to the water.

Noah felt warmth spread through his body at her praise, and realisation dawned that this could actually work. He hadn't known Maya for long, but he definitely wanted to impress her, which worried him slightly, but he brushed that thought away. He was beguiled by her dark hair and eyes and very kissable lips - but she'd given him no inclination about her thoughts on him, other than just being friendly, so he was in unchartered territory. It was hard to sustain relationships longer than the length of a film in his industry because they were all portraying someone else, and emotions got mixed up and accelerated at times. Relationships could be pretty transient and seemed to whiz past at warp speed compared to 'civilians' and then, when the movie ended, the fizz of excitement drifted away. Sustaining emotional connections when you lived in different parts of the world became almost impossible.

He lived in a world of decadence, travel and possibilities, but the flip side was isolation, fear of trusting anyone and loneliness. Noah was often too busy to date and not to be big-headed, women seemed to seek him out, which he presumed was because he was wealthy and famous. He'd certainly never had that level of success as an unknown, which made him wary of people's intentions. It was also the reason he didn't actually date much, not that you'd believe that if you read the papers. They made out as if he had a different woman every night! Popping to a woman's house in broad daylight was something he'd never normally do, but this was the only time free in his schedule and he'd acted on it. Plus, he was a man of action and this could actually help them both out of a troubling dilemma.

'I bought the bouquet from the shop across the water. I'd noticed the beautiful Victorian windows when I was sailing past on my boat one evening.'

'That's the one. It's just across the bridge from here.'

Noah grinned at last and let the last vestiges of tension about whether this was a good idea ease away. He wasn't usually nervous around women, but Maya unsettled and intrigued him in equal measure. He couldn't quite work her out. He had the urge to run his fingers across the frown lines on her forehead to ease them, and his breath hitched when she self-consciously rubbed the base of her neck, his eyes following the movement of her hand.

Noah watched the sun dipping over the river and had an idea. 'Can I make you dinner from all the goodies that Robbie sent so that we can chat more? Are you free tonight, or do you need to throw me out?'

Maya's eyebrows rose. 'I'd actually love that,' she laughed. 'I'm worse than useless at cooking. My grandmother finds my lack of culinary skills appalling, as she's an excellent cook.' Noah smiled and went to open the fridge and peer inside.

'I can definitely work with this.' Her eyes shone with what he hoped was excitement, and he felt a pull in his guts. He had a feeling that he was playing with fire, but he was enjoying himself more than he had in ages, so he was ignoring the warning signs that this woman could be dangerous to his heart and mind.

'My plan was to order a takeaway and watch a movie. I've only just finished work,' she said, standing on tiptoes and peering over his shoulder at the contents of her fridge. He felt her breath on his neck and he had to grit his teeth and remember to keep this friendly and not turn around and sweep her into his arms.

'We could watch the movie together?' he hedged, wanting to make this time together last for as long as he could and closing his eyes for a moment as her subtle floral perfume sent his senses into overdrive.

'Maybe...' Maya laughed and perched on one of her tall bar stools by the island unit, as he expertly began sorting out what he needed to cook them a meal. They chatted companionably as she pointed to where everything was and he thanked the heavens that he'd had to go to cookery school for a movie and had actually learnt to be fairly decent in the kitchen.

'If you cook me a delicious meal, I might even let you take another painting home,' she laughed, and he stopped in shock as her artworks were expensive.

'If we were dating, I could cook for you any time,' he slipped into conversation and she almost choked on her wine.

'You're too famous to date,' she sighed.

'How do you know if you've never tried it?' he stepped back and crossed his arms over his chest, which made his muscles bunch up, but she didn't even notice. He'd never had to work so hard to get a date before, especially a fake one. 'If you pretend to be my girlfriend, then Tabitha might leave me alone and you'd be helping a man in need,' he reasoned. 'You said the same about your family and friends.

Especially if you've already told them you have a boyfriend. My job takes me abroad a lot, so that could be why I haven't met your family yet. It could help us both.'

'You're serious about this whole fake relationship thing?' Her shoulders slumped, and she didn't seem as ecstatic as he'd hoped. 'Surely you could find any number of women who'd jump at the chance to be seen out with you?'

'I don't trust just anyone. You've already helped me twice and we could make it a hat-trick.' Her eyebrows shot up into her hairline at the compliment. 'We haven't known each other long, but I feel that we have a bond after what happened in the river and I'd love to help you out, too. It could be mutually beneficial. We could tell them what happened on the bridge and say I contacted you after that, as that part is true. It's actually quite romantic,' he pondered while she started at him incredulously.

'But I jumped in the river outside your house!'

'We can say we'd only managed to go on a couple of dates before that and saving Robbie was a coincidence.'

'My family will ask why I wasn't invited to the party.' She shook her head because she clearly felt this would never work, but he was determined to try.

'We could say I invited you, but you felt it too soon to meet everyone, because I was too busy to see you, so you were going to cool it off, then you ended up saving Robbie and we began spending more time together as my new film is based here.'

'I was going to dump Noah Benedict?' she scoffed, and he tried not to let his ego run away with him because she'd shown no inclination that she even fancied him.

'It has happened,' he chuckled, and she didn't seem convinced.

'I don't want to be splashed across all the papers,' she

said seriously and he frowned. Most of his dates courted publicity.

'It could help promote your art,' he answered, trying to work out what he was dealing with. Most people in his inner circle had to work hard to maintain their fame.

'Thanks, but I don't need help with that. I literally can't paint my canvases fast enough. Penny has agreed to substitute them with ones from an art class that my friend Mason run's on *Bertha*, to keep the café walls full, although if Joe's steamboat keeps growing in popularity, they might have to move venue.'

'Ahh. That makes sense.' Noah hung his head and tried to still the thoughts whizzing around his mind. This wasn't working out the way he'd hoped. He sliced some carrots and seasoned two lean steaks, drizzling some oil into a frying pan. 'Okay. Let's do it privately,' he hedged. 'We can just tell our close friends and family and present a united front when required.'

'Mine would want to meet you,' she shook her head at his innocence it seemed and he paused what he was doing and looked at her.

'They can't be that bad?'

She laughed at that. 'They aren't bad at all! They're amazing, but after my last serious boyfriend broke my heart, they'll grill you until you weep and then welcome you into the bosom of the family so you can't get out!' Noah actually liked the sound of that after the frostiness of his own relatives.

'I'm sorry to hear about your ex. You definitely need a handsome new man in your life to help you get over him,' he said, a sardonic smile flickering on his lips. He tried not to think about the spark of anger that lit when she'd mentioned her heart breaking and enjoyed the humour in her eyes now.

'Your family sound divine. It's better than mine who make you feel that the temperature drops when you walk into a room and nothing you do is good enough.'

'That sounds inviting,' she chuckled, but did briefly touch his arm in sympathy.

'Sorry. I always seem to over share with you.' He sighed and turned back to the saucepan as he threw the carrots into a pot of boiling water and pinched the sprigs off of some herbs that she had growing in a little pot by the fridge.

'I wondered what to use those for,' she joked. 'I chose them because they smell nice.' He grinned back, and she picked one of the rosemary sprigs and inhaled the minty scent rubbing the plant between her fingers and filling the air with the fragrance of camphor and eucalyptus. She came and put her arms around his shoulders and gave him a hug, which surprised him, but he gratefully sank into it. He liked the feel of being in her arms and had to restrain himself from pulling her in tighter and keeping her there. Or kissing his way up her delectable neck.

'Okay,' she grinned. 'You've convinced me. I'm a sucker for someone in need. Just keep me out of the press.' Noah's heart leapt and before he knew it, he'd laughed and swung her around before kissing her on the lips. When he put her back on her feet again, they were both wide-eyed and breathless, so Maya quickly refreshed their drinks and they didn't mention one more word about the kiss, even though the earth had shifted for him.

'I need a partner to attend a family party in a couple of months. I warn you, they are as batty as they come. You up for it?' she asked, looking up at him.

'It's a date!' he said happily, turning back to the steaks before she changed her mind.

They took their plates to the comfortable rattan table

and chair set that was on the ground floor balcony, as the sun had dipped below the horizon and the sky was now inky black and dotted with twinkling stars. Maya didn't turn the light on out there so people couldn't see in, in case Noah was spotted, but the river was pretty empty at this time of night and the pubs and bars the townsfolk frequented were further into town or along the river. Noah didn't know if his senses were heightened because he was sharing a meal with a beautiful woman, or that they seemed to talk about any topic with an ease he hadn't felt in years, but every morsel of the meal made him salivate for more. When Maya had taken the plates inside and started loading the dishwasher, he'd followed and they'd cleaned up together as if it was the most natural thing in the world.

Then she'd pulled out a tub of caramel ice cream with a smile and they'd sat watching a film with the tub between them and two spoons. He'd lifted his full spoon, but instead of eating it himself, he'd held it up for her, which had made her look at him in surprise, but she rose to the challenge and tasted it, her eyes closing in bliss as the caramel hit her tongue, which made his own mouth go dry. The mood shifted, and he'd desperately wanted to kiss her again, but she'd slipped from the sofa and called over her shoulder to ask if he wanted a coffee. The problem was that after spending an evening in Maya's company; he craved more. He knew she'd promised to be his fake girlfriend for a while, but when it came to the end of their charade, would he be able to let her go?

Chapter Twelve

Maya reread the newspaper on the table and her heartbeat fluttered. The hunt for the No.1 Ethereal Lane Designer was hitting a peak and she didn't know whether to be scared or excited at the prospect of more sales! The last piece she designed - white gold layers of entwined White Willow with its silvery slender leaves and heavy diamond clasp, had been worn to a gala and the customer, who had worn it, was on the front pages of practically every newspaper and magazine. This would mean even more enquiries for Maya, but her mind was distracted recently by a certain popular movie star who lived just up the river and his indecent proposal, she grinned. He was clearly already comfortable in their fake relationship as he'd kissed her in her kitchen and again before he left to seal the deal. It had almost blown her mind, and he'd grinned cheekily and said they needed practice if they were going to convince friends and family that they were a genuine couple. Her legs had almost buckled after the kiss and they'd been messaging in the few days since.

Maya was sure the meal meant nothing and Noah probably cooked for multiple women and kissed anyone he cared to, but she was enjoying flirting for the first time in ages, even if it was all make-believe. Her slumbering libido was waking up at full pelt and she was suddenly raging with hormones and thinking about sex every five minutes! She'd sent Romy a photo of Noah cooking dinner in her kitchen as they'd decided this was a way to prove they were dating and had got what felt like a million questions back. They'd spent an hour on the phone the previous night and Romy now understood why they hadn't met yet, which was a relief. She had agreed to let Arthur know, but otherwise to keep it to herself until Maya had a chance to speak to their grandparents, Leah and Matt.

Maya grabbed a fresh sketchpad and her bag and headed out to meet Joe. She'd been slack on updating her ideas for her designs lately as *Bertha* was way too busy most days and the vibe wasn't relaxing, but she was determined to draw a few flowers that day and hoped to see some Meadowsweet with its lace-like blooms and Geat Willowherb with its small pink, four-petalled flowers with paired, opposite leaves, cream centres and long seed capsules. Heaving her bag onto one shoulder as she walked, she picked up her pace and, after checking the time, jumping on board as they were throwing the ropes off of the side of the boat. Joe chuckled when he saw her red face. Roman grinned and took her bag for her. He gave her a signal of some sort with his eyes, but it came out like a lopsided blink.

'Are you okay, Roman?' she asked in concern, but he just nodded and spoke to the customer who was asking about the best place to sit to see Noah's house.

Maya frowned and then noticed that the boat was jam-packed with people and more were running up the pathway to get on board as they departed, then they stopped and slumped with disappointment as the boat moved away from its mooring. Turning to Joe and happy that business was booming, she came face-to-face with Robbie Latton. Maya gasped in shock, but her first instinct was to run her eyes over him to check that he was okay. He greeted her and then pulled her into his arms for a hug and planted a kiss on her lips.

The crowd of people around them whooped and cheered and took pictures of them on their phones. 'What are you doing here?' she asked breathlessly, looking around at their rapt audience.

'Noah told me you were here today, and I wanted to see you as soon as I could to say thank you.'

'You already sent me flowers,' she flushed bright red and then dipped her head as everyone was listening to them. Maya grabbed his hand and led Robbie through the throng to Joe's captain's cabin, which was more of a storeroom - much to the disappointment of the crowd. Already wondering how many of those posts would immediately be displayed on social media, she groaned, but at least it wasn't her and Noah splashed around just yet.

'I wanted to say thank you in person,' Robbie grinned, snapping her attention back to the chaos. She didn't know what to think other than he was gorgeous and still holding her hand. 'Let me take you to dinner?' he asked, brushing his hand through his thick red hair. He had slight stubble and a solid jawline. He was taller than her, but not by much, and he wore designer jeans and a very expensive-looking shirt, with sunglasses in his chest pocket. She tried to catch her breath, then remembered that he'd mentioned Noah.

'Does Noah know you're here?' she asked with interest. He raised an eyebrow in question, then let it go.

'Nope. He'd tell me to go to your house, but I think on my feet and I was nearby.' Robbie looked through the window at the crowd now situated outside the captain's quarters, who were trying to pretend not to be staring. 'Noah might have been right,' Robbie admitted, 'in hindsight. I can see how he came to knock coffee all over you now.'

Maya giggled and twirled her hair around her fingers. 'You are bonkers! I don't know how to get you off of this boat safely because you're so famous. You'll have to stay in here forever,' she indicated the small room.

Robbie beamed cheekily, and a sparkle came into his eyes. He did an evil, mwah ha ha ha sound and then laughed. 'My plan to get you alone worked,' he said rubbing his hands together theatrically. He grinned as she spluttered with laughter.

'You don't have to take me out to dinner,' she added, quite enjoying the attention now and ignoring the fact that someone might plaster her picture all over social media in the arms of this heartthrob.

'I know. I want to,' he said simply, his eyes ever watchful.

'Like a date, or as friends?'

'Friends,' he answered after a heartbeat. 'I heard from a trusted source that you have a boyfriend,' he winked, and she blanched.

'It's just something I said in jest that Noah took seriously.' She wasn't sure how much Robbie knew of what was going on, but he seemed pretty informed on what was supposed to be a secret, but then she herself had blabbed to her siblings to get some relief from their questions about her new boyfriend. She hadn't told them it was fake though, as what would be the point of that?

'Noah told me,' Robbie apologised, but didn't look in the slightest bit sorry. 'I hope that's okay, but when he explained he had a gorgeous new girlfriend, in my usual style, I didn't let the matter drop until he told me every single detail. I feel I'm part of the plan because you jumped in the river after me and set this whole love pact thing in motion.' he waggled his eyebrows at her.

'Love pact? It was a joke,' said Maya in exasperation, her hackles raising.

'I'm sorry if you feel ambushed,' soothed Robbie, taking her hand. 'Noah definitely needs you if you feel up to helping him?' he carried on without waiting for an answer as if it was a given. This guy was quite dramatic, waving his hands around in expression and she wasn't sure he was even listening to anything she said. 'Tabitha is a nightmare and Noah seems to think that you are the answer to all our prayers. You certainly are to mine. You saved me and I won't forget it,' he said earnestly and Maya's heart softened a little. 'I want to take you to dinner to make sure this works for you, too. It's not all about Noah, however much I love him.'

Maya flushed at the mention of Noah. She'd agreed to go to a garden party he was hosting soon, but she wasn't sure if that was his way of letting everyone know about them. She was still resolutely single in real life and how often did a girl get asked out by one of the nation's favourite comedians, even just as friends – a hot comedian to boot?

'What did he tell you about this pact?' she asked, hoping for honesty.

Robbie regarded her thoughtfully for a moment and then replied, 'That you were both agreed about dating to stop Tabitha from bothering Noah and to get your family off your back, but if I'm being completely honest, he didn't sound too ecstatic when I told him I was going to ask you to dinner.' She blushed again and wondered if she could find a window to open. 'He's my best mate and I want him to be happy. It's unlike him to want to do something like this, so...'

'He must be desperate?' she finished for him, making him falter and give her an apologetic stare. 'I'd like to go to dinner,' she decided suddenly, brushing her hair out of her face and looking up at him. 'What have I got to lose?' Robbie slung his arm around her shoulders and she noticed Roman was ushering their very reluctant guests back towards the exit, as they must have docked. 'We've just docked. Are you staying aboard for the journey back?'

'Nope. I've got a gig tonight and wanted to speak to you first. Can I call you?' he asked.

'Yes. I'd like that,' she replied, her stomach fizzing with nerves. She handed him her phone, and he added his number. 'Text me your number and we can set up a date,' he grinned and kissed her on the cheek. She laughed at his confidence, but she certainly wasn't complaining. Getting surprised at work by one of the world's hottest men while another popped round to watch a movie with her! Maybe Noah's proposal could be the bit of fun that her life was lacking and get her friends and family off of her back at the same time about her dormant love life! She couldn't wait to see the look on their faces when she actually brought home the very sexy movie star, Noah Benedict!

Chapter Thirteen

Maya grinned as a walking plant with tall leafy fronds and two arms holding a glazed terracotta plant pot, came into the kitchen. Her grandad's smiley face bobbed out from behind it as he carefully placed plant on the table, before her grandmother walked in and tutted, briskly shooing him out (with his plant) to take them back to his huge glasshouse. 'I thought they'd look nice in the conservatory?' her grandad winked at Maya as her grandmother forcibly tried to shove him back out into the garden with the tea tray she was carrying. As they stepped into the conservatory Maya was accosted by an ancient lemon tree that her grandmother used for her gin and tonics, and she almost tripped over several potted succulents that had spiky leaves and Maya already knew were painful to land on.

'It's already full, as you well know!' scolded her grandmother. 'It's becoming like a jungle in here and it's so hot I was thinking of putting on my bikini!' Maya grinned, as that was probably her grandad's goal, knowing him, but regardless the sun was beating down and the catmint and evergreen magnolias in the garden were beginning to flower and fill the air with their rich lemon-vanilla scent. Never ones to stick to convention, the huge Victorian house they lived in by the River Thames, with its rambling garden, had rooms full of curiosities. You never knew what to expect every time you arrived. Her grandmother was a law unto herself and did as she pleased and her grandad was just as incorrigible when it came to plants. It was a floral assault course just to get to the front door at times and she was sure this was pre-meditated to test the merit of any visitors. Woe betide anyone who damaged one of her grandad's plants!

Watching her gran take tea with several famous faces and some royals had filled Maya with awe as a child. She'd worked as a fashion designer to the stars, in her heyday. Maya, Arthur and Romy had often stretched out on their stomachs and propped their faces in their hands while they peered through the upstairs bannisters and listened to their gran greet a famous face at their door and welcome them into her dressing room for a fitting. The children hadn't been allowed to say hello very often, but they had always been curious enough to see if the client was anyone they recognised.

Moving in here at the tender age of thirteen had been an adventure, and it felt more like home than the small house she'd grown up in, in central London, with the endless stream of nannies. When her parents had been assigned abroad, everything had changed for Maya and her siblings. Her parents had always worked long hours, and it had been a relief to finally have the 'stability' of living with their grandparents. Arthur was one year younger than her and Romy three years younger. Being ten, twelve and thirteen might have seemed a delicate time to leave your children with your parents, but for Maya, Arthur and Romy, it had been a dream. They got to play in the vast garden at the back of the house and make forts under the branches of the rambling willow tree by the water. In contrast, their parents had always been uptight because they had demanding jobs and three small children. Both were surgeons, and although they loved their children, their work calling seemed to be stronger.

'He knows full well we can't fit more of his plants in the house,' grumbled her grandmother good-naturedly, placing the teapot on the little coffee table in the centre of the room, and moving a couple of plump cacti to make space. The steaming teapot was snuggled into a very fashionable tea cosy that her grandmother had made. She poured them both a cup of tea, and then got up to retrieve some homemade biscuits from the larder. They were various sizes and covered in different chocolate toppings, as her grandmother didn't do conformity, making them any size she felt like.

'Have you been making mischief this week?' she asked.

Her grandmother lifted her chin slightly and ignored her for a moment, then grinned and grabbed her hand.

'Well... I did bake a cake for my women's group, but it went down rather well. Just as well it was huge because they kept going back for more. Most unlike them, must have been those dried green leaves your grandad gave me to sprinkle into the mixture. He said they were medicinal, and they smelled funny.' Maya rolled her eyes and stifled a laugh. Her granddad was a world-renowned expert in exotic plants and he also had a passion for healing herbs.

Maya decided that the topic was best left alone. She turned her face up towards the sunbeams that were filtering through the glass windows and felt them warm her skin.

'How have you both been?' she asked, biting into the nutty, chocolaty biscuit.

Her grandmother's eyes ran over her and she tilted her head to one side, as Maya often did and regarded her granddaughter. 'How are you, more to the point?'

'I'm fine, Gran,' Maya wouldn't meet her eyes because she knew what was coming next.

'Have you found the man of your dreams yet?'

'You know I've been dating someone,' Maya scolded lightly.

'Well why haven't we met him yet?' her grandmother asked in a scandalised tone, eyeing her over the rim of her teacup, like a falcon about to pounce on a helpless mouse.

'He's busy. We both are,' Maya paused and remembered the plan Noah had devised for them to integrate into each other's lives. 'I thought that we weren't suited, but just lately he's home more and we've reconnected.' She recalled how a few of Noah's friends had looked her up and down because she looked like a drowned rat. But she had just saved someone's life, so she hoped they accepted her at some point.

Her gran was gazing at her thoughtfully, which always meant trouble. She hoped she hadn't voiced her last thoughts out loud. 'You know my brand has grown and I'm trying my best to keep up with it. It's all been a bit of a shock.'

'It wasn't to me,' her grandmother said haughtily. 'Your designs are simply beautiful, Maya.'

'You might be slightly biased, gran.' Maya smiled.

'I am not!' she refuted. 'Are you dating Robbie? He's rather handsome. I saw you both on social media and I can understand why he'd be rather busy most days, but is he making enough time for you?' She barraged the questions and then raised one eyebrow and nibbled on the edge of a biscuit. Her gran was addicted to social media and loved to have a gossip on various topics online.

'We aren't dating!' Maya puffed out her cheeks because her gran clearly wasn't listening. 'He asked me to go to dinner with him.' Maya put down her teacup and leaned back into her wicker chair, which was surprisingly comfortable considering its age and slightly wonky leg. 'I told you he fell into the river and it's his way of thanking for me jumping in after him,' she said.

'That was wildly romantic,' sighed her grandmother, 'but idiotic and I've already told you off for being so stupid!' she scolded dramatically. 'Your grandfather nearly had a coronary after you called him in from his glasshouse and told him. I've never seen him turn such a funny colour. You could have hurt yourself.' Maya took her grandmother's hand and squeezed it. For all of her nutty behaviour and bravado, she worried about her grandchildren and her daughter and son-in-law for working abroad in hard conditions.

'I'm a strong swimmer, Gran,' Maya soothed, taking her hand. Her gran's eyes glittered with unshed tears, which made Maya's stomach tighten with worry. It wasn't like her gran to get over emotional.

Maya hadn't mentioned Noah yet, and wondered how to drop into conversation that he was the guy she was 'dating'. She'd only seen him once and although she had accepted the invitation to his garden party, she wasn't sure if she wanted to mingle with the same people from his last one. Plus, if Noah announced her as his girlfriend, would Tabitha set her sights on her? That was something she'd considered before, and the thought didn't sit well with Maya. It was a constant niggle. She didn't like mean girls and had dealt with more than her fair share of them at school once the kids had found out that her parents had effectively dumped them and gone abroad.

'I've jumped off of *Bertha* and into the river a thousand times over the years and broken nothing.'

'You swung off the trees in the garden into the river enough times too!' her grandmother stated, tutting again. 'The amount of times your grandad and I told you to be careful when you were younger!'

'Arthur, Romy and I spent half of our lives swimming in the river at the end of your garden, so I knew what to do to stay safe. You and Grandad taught us well.'

'You were all a bunch of water babies,' her grandmother smiled finally at the memory and Maya tried to relax a little. 'You and Arthur always had river weed in your hair.'

'We loved living by the river with you both. Coming here from our little square house in London to place with big rooms and an enormous garden by the river, with so many trees to climb and places to explore, was heaven.'

'You were all hoodlums,' Ettie joked, love shining from her eyes. Maya grinned because they were all pretty well-behaved children and the section of their garden that they jumped into the river from was quite safe and in a little inlet from the main riverbed. Her grandmother knew this very well, but was over-dramatising as usual.

'I was very careful. I saw where he fell in and *Bertha* was protecting me from oncoming boats. It was fine, Gran.'

'Plus, you and Joe got to meet Noah Benedict?' her gran asked, clearly already knowing the answer.

'He'd already bought one of my artworks,' said Maya, deftly guiding her grandmother to a safer topic and setting the scene for their fictional meeting. 'It was hanging in his guesthouse.'

'His guesthouse! When did you go in there?' Maya

cursed under her breath and sighed. Her grandmother should have worked for MI5. Nothing got past her.

'He let me quickly shower and change because I was soaked. I was only in there for a few minutes.' She crossed her fingers behind her back. Her grandmother leaned back to see what she was doing and raised that dastardly eyebrow in question again. 'Okay... I was in there for a while.'

'What a coincidence,' her grandmother said slowly with intrigue.

'Not really,' Maya winced. 'He's the guy I've been dating...' Her grandmother's eyebrows shot into her hairline, but she stayed quiet for once and waited to hear more. 'We met when I was walking by the river one morning and he bumped into me, knocking my coffee all over me, but after a few dates it fizzled out because he's away a lot and that's not what I'm looking for.' Maya carried on quickly before she changed her mind. 'After I jumped in the river by his house, we reconnected and his next film is in London, so he'll be home more.'

'I see,' said her grandmother, 'how fortuitous!' Now she knew her gran was over compensating for her underwhelming earlier response. Maya grit her teeth because she wasn't sure if she heard sarcasm in her grandmother's voice. 'Is he the right man if he's that busy?'

What? Maya had gone to all of this effort to make up a boyfriend and now even the fictional one didn't make the grade. 'He's really making an effort now he's home. He came round to see where I paint.'

'Good for you,' Ettie said, winking and grinning as she got up to get them fresh tea. 'Finally some progress with your love life.'

Chapter Fourteen

Maya sipped her coffee, which had grown cold and grimaced. There were several news articles about Robbie across the celebrity section of the papers with images of him declaring his love for the woman who saved his life, apparently!

Newspapers constantly photographed Robbie with different women, and his ex, Amethyst, was very vocal about how she felt about that. They were invariably publicly feuding or desperately in love with one another. Maya daren't pick up her phone to check the amount of texts that her family and friends would have sent, and she wondered how this would make Noah feel because they had just begun telling everyone they were dating. This was more than embarrassing and complicated everything. She picked up her phone and called Noah.

'Hi!' she said breezily, even though she didn't feel fresh or that happy.

'Hi,' he responded, slight amusement in his tone, so she heaved a sigh of relief.

'You've seen the newspapers?'

'Yep! It scuppers our plans, but we were thinking of waiting until my party to announce it more publicly. Unless you and Robbie...'

'No!' she shook her head vehemently, even though she was alone. 'Definitely not.' She heard him chuckle, and she smiled in response, some of the tension leaving her.

'Can we meet up for a quiet dinner somewhere private tonight?' he asked and a shiver of excitement ran down her spine.

'I'd love that.'

'I'll pick you up at eight.'

She got up and threw the dregs of her coffee in the sink. Her hands were shaking slightly, and she turned the tap to cold and splashed her face with water.

When she opened the door to Noah that evening, all of her worries floated away. Noah was dressed in dark jeans, a white-collared t-shirt and a casual jacket. Maya fidgeted for a moment and then reminded herself that this was fake and they were just friends. Maya leaned in to kiss him on the cheek in greeting but he seemed to have other ideas and wound his hands into her hair, their lips touching, sending flames of fire down her spine, making her groan as he pulled her closer to deepen the kiss. When they parted both were panting slightly and then he slipped his hand in hers and grinned. 'Well hello!'

'You look beautiful, by the way,' he added, taking in her light summer dress that crossed over her chest and was fixed at her waist and had little ties at the elbows. It had green ferns and pale pink flowers all over it. The design felt flirty and cute. Noah wasn't her actual boyfriend, just a film star who needed a fake girlfriend to ward off a manic ex, but she definitely didn't mind kissing him! She guessed that was a perk of the role and if she got in a lot of practice, maybe she'd be ready for a real relationship afterwards?

Noah guided her to his car, which was sleek and black and she greeted the chauffeur with a big smile and a nod of thanks as he opened the car door for her. When they arrived at a little bistro that had fairy lights strung across the court-yard outside and tall potted palms either side of the entrance, they were taken inside to a sheltered table at the rear of the restaurant, so she finally gave a sigh of relief and decided she might as well enjoy herself, as the setting was warm and inviting. There were low vases overflowing with flowers on every table and plants trailing lazily from colourful pots on racks that ran along the walls. Each table had embroidered tablecloths with scattered flowers all over them which Maya would hate to see damaged by splashes of food, but as she drew closer she was relieved to see each table top had a glass covering and she sat down and studied the hand-sewn flowers which were works of art!

'How was your day?' he asked, taking her hand across the table. She looked down at their hands and didn't know what to feel, but she was definitely feeling something, which was worrying her slightly. His welcome kiss had been a revelation and now her hands itched to slide up his arms and pull him closer, the way he had at the door. He as acting as if they were a normal couple and she shuddered at her own stupidity because he was an award winning actor! He was probably just prepping her for the role, like he'd mentioned in her kitchen. They needed to be able to kiss naturally for people to believe them. It didn't have to mean anything...

'Just lots of press interest in Robbie, but the phone calls stopped after a couple of hours.' She retrieved her hand and slid it into her lap. She looked at the menu, but suddenly wasn't that hungry. The restaurant was intimate, the perfect place for a dinner with your lover. Maya daren't look at Noah in case he saw the tiny shift in how she felt about him, which would be mortifying!

'Sorry about that. He just doesn't think about the chaos he causes sometimes.'

Neither do you, she thought, but turned and ordered a gin and elderflower tonic from the serving staff who greeted them with a smile and plate of tempura flowers! Maya immediately picked up the delicacy and examined the zucchini blossoms. Next to it were acacia flowers on an elegant white latticed plate that gave it the appearance of fragile lace.

'I thought you'd like it here. You're always drawing flowers and this place uses them in the food.'

'It's stunning!' She wouldn't quite meet his eye, but the fact he'd thought about her preferences warmed her heart a little and softened her mood.

Noah was looking at her over the floral masterpiece at the centre of the table and she offered him a tentative smile. 'Have I upset you in some way?' he asked.

'Not at all!' she overcompensated. 'I just think we need to really talk about our pact if I'm definitely going to introduce you to my family soon. Tell me more about Tabitha.'

'Are you sure you're ready?' he chuckled, the atmosphere lightening as Maya returned his smile. 'We met at a film festival abroad where we were appearing in different films. I'd heard that she wanted to meet me through a mutual friend, but I was there to work, so she began appearing at venues I was at. I didn't think much of it at first because we are both in the same industry, but then, I guess...'

'You were flattered?' Maya teased and he rolled his eyes and grinned.

'My ego isn't that big,' he chuckled when she clearly didn't believe him. 'I guess I got used to seeing her around and eventually we said hello. That was my biggest mistake,' he sighed.

'What happened?' Maya was enthralled.

Noah looked off into the distance for a minute then his focus came back to her. 'She made friends with my friends. Then she got herself invited to intimate dinners and barbecues. It was hard to miss her and she was attentive and funny. I'm pretty sure now that she'd researched me.'

When Maya frowned he clarified. 'You know. My favourite bands, movies, places to travel etc. You can pretty much Google anything about me these days.' Maya's mouth formed an o and he shrugged.

'I guess I *was* flattered,' he finally admitted, giving her a sheepish look and she patted his hand in sympathy that stunning women found him interesting enough to find out more about him... she rolled her own eyes and he took the hit and sat back in his chair, playing with the stem of his wine glass, which fixated her attention for a moment because she could imagine his fingers touching her own skin. 'It was fun for a short while, but I soon realised that I was useful to her for my contacts and ability to open doors to casting directors. I helped her at first – hence her job on my latest film – but that was never enough.'

'What happened,' asked Maya, picking up her own wine and taking a sip.

'She wanted lead roles. I couldn't provide those quickly enough, so we separated. We'd only be casually dating anyway and I was helping her as a friend.'

'Wow! That's tough,' Maya sympathised and he sent

her a sad smile that did something funny to her hormones. She wanted to scoop him into her arms and soothe his problems away with kisses. Lots of kisses.

'Thanks,' continued Noah, oblivious. 'Her own artistic talent was the only thing that could ever secure her a job. I tried to distance myself, even though I believed in her and it got nasty.'

'Hence the fake dates?'

'Hence spending time with you to ease both of our problems,' he added firmly and his eyes sparkled with mischief finally and the mood lightened. 'I enjoy your company,' he admitted, his eyes gazing with intent into hers until she looked away.

They paused while a huge ceramic platter arrived full of fragrant rice, white fish, fresh tomatoes and blue cornflowers that had a spicy, clove-like taste. 'This is incredible,' said Maya as she tried her first forkful and almost went cross-eyed in bliss.

After their plates had been cleared, Noah took her hand again and this time she didn't pull away. It seemed he liked PDAs, even when no one could see them! 'Would you like dessert?' he asked and her stomach fizzed with possibilities that were mostly inappropriate. 'Maybe we could share one?'

Maya nodded her consent and they decided on an ice cream sundae with whipped cream, fresh mango, poached peaches and lots of indulgent chocolate fudge sauce, which they took their time dipping their long spoons into and licking their lips in anticipation of the next bite. Noah filled his spoon with chocolate and cream and offered it to her and she had to lean forward and accept before the sauce slid off and onto the table. He watched her lick her lips and his eyes darkened, capturing hers for a moment, but then the waiter drew near and asked if they needed anything else and the spell was broken.

'The food here is amazing. I can't wait to tell my grandad about it,' Maya said hastily, dabbing her mouth on the napkin to hide her blushes.

'You're going to tell them then?' he asked.

'They know we're dating,' she admitted. Maya's heart fluttered at his words and she hated the fact that she actually wished that this was true.

'That's great news! So what about your past?' he asked, signalling for a couple of lattes as he knew she had a penchant for those.

'I guess I need to tell you about my ex?'

'The guy that broke your heart?'

'That's him.'

'Do you want to talk about what happened?'

'He's my ex for a reason,' she decided. 'I'd rather leave him in the past if that's ok?'

'Of course,' he reassured.

Her heart had finally mended, but now here she was, sitting in front of Noah, and she was afraid that cracks had appeared in the carefully constructed wall around her heart. Surely this guy could only bring more trouble?

Chapter Fifteen

S pending a night tossing and turning after dreaming about kissing a sexy movie star wasn't conducive to looking your best at dinner with his best friend. Noah had walked her to her door after their meal the night before and kissed her thoroughly at the front door but then a flashbulb had gone off in their faces and they'd turned round in horror to find out that a member of the paparazzi had clearly been following them. Noah had broken away and immediately gone to speak to him and Maya had shivered while the guy looked over Noah's shoulder at her and then nodded his head.

'He's leaving?' she'd asked in a shaky voice. 'He knows where I live...' Noah hadn't gotten too close to her again, but had tilted her chin up with his fingers, so she'd had to look into his eyes.

'I've offered him an exclusive on my new girlfriend,' she'd gasped and he'd given her shoulder a reassuring squeeze that didn't feel that reassuring. 'I've asked him not to print it yet and he's agreed. As long as he gets the full story first. We will want people to know at some point. It was all I could think of to hold him off.' Maya closed her eyes and pinched the bridge of her nose at the memory, trying to stave off a headache that had been looming all day.

Stepping out of the red sports car Robbie had picked her up in, she finally felt some tension float away. She'd spent ages trawling the internet for the photo from last night, but it hadn't appeared. He'd kept her laughing the entire journey and when he handed the key to the valet who was outside the restaurant, she was glad she'd worn a dress. It was still her usual style, but was fit for a glitzy restaurant like this. Robbie hadn't asked her for her preference in food or location, but she was more at home in a local eatery than a sleek and industrial looking all-white restaurant. It looked beautiful though, and she could see some exotic plants inside that she was already interested in looking at. Her granddad would have rolled his eyes about them for being a decoration, but she felt they were more than a nod to art with their formal white blooms and wide green leaves standing tall in glossy white plant pots.

Her fitted dress was woven with different shades of blue fabric. The tones were so subtle that she'd noticed people stopping and looking at her, as the colours changed as she moved. The dress had thin straps on each shoulder and the skirt ended just above her knees. She'd teamed it with tall dark blue heels, but she much preferred wearing flip-flops, if she was honest. She sent up silent thanks to her grandmother for insisting that she had a decent wardrobe full of clothes for every occasion, even though she rarely went out.

Robbie took her hand as they weaved their way through the restaurant to their table. She looked around with interest. This was the kind of place Blake liked to frequent when they had been together and before they could really afford it. He'd said they needed to be 'seen' in the right places.

The simplistic lines and design of the restaurant should appeal to her tendencies towards cleanliness and order, but she found it cold and shivered slightly. She craved more softness and texture from some cushions or an abundance of atmosphere and colour, like the bistro that Noah had taken her to the night before. He was great company, she had to admit and they'd spent most of the meal chatting about their respective childhoods.

It was beautiful here, but the murmur of conversation was muted and as they reached their table, her old self would have felt she stood out for all the wrong reasons with her colourful dress. But the Maya of today didn't care. People could take her as they found her or leave her alone. She had found her confidence growing as her little business became more successful and she didn't shy away from experiences that she'd have put off before.

The waiter held out her seat for her and handed her a drinks menu. It didn't have prices and that would have made her heart flutter with anxiety a few months ago, but now it just made her sigh. She ordered a cool glass of Sauvignon Blanc and zoned back in to what Robbie was saying.

'You look beautiful,' he said appreciatively, with a flirtatious smile.

'Thank you.' She felt her skin flush and fiddled with the clasp of her handbag. 'Have you been here before?' she asked as he picked up the menu and glanced at it.

'A few times. Thanks for agreeing to join me.'

They waited while their glasses were filled with sparkling water. 'Can I take your food order?' asked the attentive waiter.

'I'd love the scallops and the sea bass drizzled with herb butter sauce,' requested Maya with a smile as she handed the menu back.

'I'll have the oysters with smoked uni butter,' added Robbie. 'Then the classic lobster thermidor for main course,' he said as he snapped the menu closed with a flourish and focussed back on her. 'The wine based sauce is to die for,' he grinned at her and she smiled back. 'You can try some of mine,' he winked and she couldn't help but shake her head at his antics.

Maya sat back and enjoy being wined and dined by one of the nation's favourite comedians. 'Thank you for saving my life,' he said, serious suddenly. 'I can't believe you were there at that exact moment. I was clearly being funnier than I thought because Tabitha found me so hilarious that she nudged my chest and I lost my footing.'

Maya thought it to be more of a shove, but it had actually been the high-pitched laugh that had drawn her attention. 'You don't have to keep saying that. You've already sent me enough food to feed a football team, and it was nothing, really. I always jump off of boats into the river to get asked for dinner. It's my go to move.'

Robbie spluttered into his wine and the couple at the next table looked their way before returning to their meal. 'How did Noah convince you to pretend to date him?' Robbie asked candidly. 'I can't say it's ever happened before and we've known each other for years. Noah rarely has to make up relationships. He's a bit of a catch.'

She felt there was an underlying tension to his question. 'I'm quite enjoying it now,' she said carefully. She gazed around the restaurant and watched the other diners for a moment. She wondered if any of them were concocting such schemes to stop people from bothering them. 'I'm sure I'm not his usual type, so how believable can we be?' She pictured Tabitha's sleek red hair and tall, lithe body.

'You're more his type than you realise,' said Robbie as he

sipped his wine. 'It's Tabitha who isn't, but she wore him down. Noah appreciates creativity and individuality and you have that in spades, plus you're beautiful,' he added and she felt her cheeks grow warm in embarrassment. 'Tabitha wants to control every aspect of his life.'

Robbie sat back in his seat and linked his hands on the table, looking serious suddenly. 'I've been telling Noah that he needs to remove Tabitha from his life for ages. When he told me about your plan, I admit I was sceptical at first.'

Maya rubbed her temples. 'It was a joke. I said we should date to get our families to leave us alone... or he did. I can't even remember the details, as it was so silly. I wasn't serious. Why would I ever think Noah Benedict would want to date a stranger?'

Robbie frowned and leaned forward to stare at her. 'To be honest, I was astounded that he'd just met you and confided in you about Tabitha, as he can be pretty closed off emotionally.'

'Because of his parents?' she asked, her stomach grumbling, so she rubbed it with her hand under the table.

'He told you about them too?' Robbie seemed flummoxed. 'You literally know about as much about him as half of his friends!' he joked. 'Fame hunters have hurt him one too many times.'

'Me too,' she grumbled and then wished she hadn't.

'You too?' he queried, frowning, as he waited for an answer.

'Umm... not fame hunters, but my ex treated me pretty badly. He's been trying to get into contact lately after seeing us together in the press and I could really do without it.'

Robbie groaned and held his head in his hands. 'I'm so sorry.'

'Don't be. He's always been celeb-obsessed.'

'Was he awful?'

Maya pictured a kinder Blake, who had been tender to her when they were first dating. 'No. He just had sex with another woman in our bed.'

Robbie almost choked on his wine and he signalled they needed another bottle.

'We'll get a taxi home... Tell me everything,' he added. Their appetisers arrived and the aroma of charred scallop and toasted pecans made her stomach rumble. She wondered if he'd think her rude if she stuffed the whole plump morsel in her mouth in one bite. It was the only thing on the plate apart from half a lettuce leaf.

'Why did you ask me to dinner?' she wondered out loud, then wished she hadn't, as she wasn't sure she really wanted to know.

'Didn't you know that we're already soul mates because you saved my life?' he asked. 'Some cultures believe that we have a karmic connection with certain souls that are brought into our lives by destiny.' He smiled into her eyes and she was mesmerised for a moment. She could see how he held stadiums of people in rapt attention to his words, even though he was usually telling them jokes. He was a born storyteller. 'It's not always about lovers...' he waggled his eyebrows at her and she laughed. 'It's the idea that people come into your life for a reason.'

Maya felt her cheeks grow warm and looked away before turning back to him. 'I'm lost for words.'

'You jumped into a freezing murky river to save me – someone you'd never met - without thinking twice. Plus, I enjoy winding Noah up,' he grinned suddenly and sipped his wine with mirth, winking at her.

'Why would us having dinner wind him up?' she wanted to know, but began fidgeting in her seat.

'Because he has his own interest in you,' he laughed, as if she should know that already. 'He told me about the coffee incident, that he'd seen you on a steamboat on the river a few times and that you were painting. It's why he tried to find your art, hoping to meet you.'

'He knew it was my art when we met?'

'Of course! He probably couldn't believe his luck that I fell in the river and you dived in to save me.' He held up his hand to show he was joking, and Maya's stomach clenched. What did Robbie mean? She thought back to when Noah had said he'd sent his interior designer to find more of her work and she faltered. She'd forgotten about that. Noah had said he'd seen her on the boat, but she hadn't connected the dots. Now she was confused.

'You're wondering if me jumping into the river by his house is a coincidence?' she asked, frown lines filling her forehead. 'I had no clue he'd bought my art. Penny – the owner of the café – didn't tell me.'

Robbie seemed appeased by that. 'Maybe she didn't know?'

'Noah said he sent his stylist,' she recalled. 'If I'd have known he was trying to get in touch and wanted to meet him, I would have asked her to give him my number. Surely?' she tilted her head at him and he held up his hands in surrender at her flashing eyes. 'Much simpler that arriving soaking wet and covered in river weed. I'd have at least had time to brush my hair,' she added sarcastically and he winced.

'Sorry,' he apologised but actually looked like he was enjoying their sparring, which annoyed her further. 'I'm also wondering how you really feel about Noah? Women often latch on to him for a certain lifestyle.' He shrugged and waited for her response.

Maya fumed as she straightened her skirt and sat further back in her seat. How presumptuous. This 'date' was more like an inquisition now. So this was why he'd invited her out! 'You think I'm a gold digger?'

She placed her glass down before she threw it in his face, wondering how the evening had so quickly turned sour. 'I need nothing from Noah, or you,' she said firmly and Robbie stared at her thoughtfully as if he was making a judgement call. 'Noah and I aren't dating for real, so how can he affect my lifestyle? In fact, I don't want him to. I'm content as I am,' she added, eyes flaming.

Robbie could clearly see her anger rising. He refreshed her wine rapidly. 'I obviously didn't mean you!' he back-tracked. 'He's definitely had his share of fortune hunters in the past. It's hard for men like him to trust.'

'Men like him, or men like you?' she asked, her eyes narrowing, and he shrugged.

'Both of us, I guess.'

'Do you always take Noah's 'friends' out to dinner to check out their credentials?'

'No,' he admitted, gravely. 'I can tell someone like Tabitha a mile off and I wanted to get to know you better, especially if you and Noah are really doing this hair-brained scheme! I'm sorry for the ambush but I needed to be sure Noah wasn't getting himself into an even bigger mess. To be fair, now that we've spoken properly, I think it might be genius,' he grinned cheekily, and she felt some of the tension in her shoulders ease away and her indignation settle.

'Are you sure that you and Noah can just be friends?' Robbie asked suddenly. 'He's been pretty keen to see you again after he met you at the bridge, even though he was being chased by an angry mob.' Maya sipped her wine and tried to ease the sudden butterflies in her tummy. She tried to think of signs from Noah that he 'liked' her – other than their practice kisses - but although a furnace burned in her body every time he was near and excitement flowed through her veins whenever he texted her, she really didn't trust her instincts where men were concerned.

'Wow!' said Robbie after she took so long to answer, leaning back in his chair and crossing his hands in his lap. 'Noah really needs to get his signals right,' he laughed and she couldn't help but giggle at his gentle teasing, even though she was still cross at him in case he thought she was after Noah's money. She didn't need anyone to finance anything on her behalf. She'd literally gone from losing everything to becoming quite wealthy again.

'From your reaction to my questions and the look on your face when I mentioned his name... I think maybe we could drop the fake part? You two would really complement each other, even if it was just for fun,' Robbie grinned, as if he'd sorted everything out.

'What does that mean?' Maya threw her hands up in exasperation.

'He's a pretty loveable guy. You might fall for him for real,' he grinned.

'I won't,' she responded firmly. 'I've got enough of my own drama without courting more by falling in love with someone famous.'

'Who said anything about falling in love?' said Robbie with a grin. 'Maybe it's time that both of you slipped the restraints and had some fun?'

Maya liked the sound of that. Could she spend time with someone with such magnetism as Noah and not develop feelings? She wasn't sure. Robbie's words weirdly didn't dent her ego because the likelihood of her and Noah falling in love was about ten million to one, but finally she let herself enjoy the evening and not take everything Robbie said to heart.

'Have you been dating Amethyst recently?' she asked innocently, picturing Matt's wagging finger at her prying, even though he'd be the first to ask for the gossip.

'We were. We were dating on and off for a long time, but it didn't work out.' He gazed off into the distance for a moment and his demeanour grew serious. She must have inadvertently hit a nerve.

'What went wrong?'

He paused and rubbed the bridge of his nose. 'I'm not sure I even know the answer to that,' as if it was a question he pondered often. 'We date, then we don't, then we fall back in love and get back together, then she hates me again.'

Maya frowned. Love and hate were strong words. 'I can't imagine that she hates you,' she said, making his eyes twinkle suddenly.

'Tell me about her,' she said, and she scooped the last forkful of rice into her mouth while she settled in to find out about the woman who, it seemed, had already captured Robbie's heart. *She must be a saint*, Maya thought, because he was annoying as hell!

Chapter Sixteen

'Darling girl! You deserve this and a young woman must look her best when she's surrounded by other diamonds,' her grandmother had almost sung as she spoke. Maya had run her fingers through the rows of textured fabrics and beautifully designed dresses before her in her grandmother's dressing room. It always felt decadent to be in here because Maya knew of so many famous faces that had been fitted on the exact same spot she'd been standing on. The room had a golden era glamorous feel to it with rich fabrics draped over an ancient dressmakers table and a full length scrolled wooden mirror that was expertly lit to show the gowns off to their best advantage. Not that anything her grandmother made ever looked bad. Ettie had been overtly ecstatic when she'd casually mentioned Noah's garden party on the phone and she'd insisted that Maya came round for a fitting because she had the perfect outfit in mind for her, apparently. Maya had shaken her head at her gran's thoughtfulness and carefully lifted up the hand-sewn garment she'd chosen and held the dress up to her body and gazing at her reflection in the mirror.

'Gran... I don't know what to say!' Maya had moved her legs, and the fabric swished around her knees and made her grin from ear to ear. 'It's beautiful,' she'd touched the deep blue fabric that was often used in everyday wear in wonder. The versatile denim had been transformed into a masterpiece.

'It had to be understated... but knockout,' her grandmother had advised. 'I wasn't so sad to hear that you dumped the other guy,' Ettie commented and Maya had to smother a laugh at her gran's forthright words. She might be fake-dating Noah, but because of the pictures of her and Robbie on *Bertha*, the tabloids thought she was his latest squeeze, which her sister, Romy, thought was hilarious. She'd had to set her family straight. Maya had thought Robbie to be annoying, but after a whole evening together, she'd discovered his softer side. There was no way she'd date him though!

'I read he was on - off, dating a girl called Amethyst,' she'd said haughtily and Maya had sighed and diverted the conversation to her brother and sister for a while, which always worked with her gran. 'Have fun, my darling.'

Maya controlled her nerves before she stepped off of her boat and onto the wooden jetty next to Noah's house, bracing her legs as it moved slightly on the water. Clearing security and opening the gate that connected to the wooden and glass balustrading that now surrounded the whole jetty at the end of Noah's beautiful garden she admired the flickering lighting that he'd installed all along the walkway, giving the garden an almost magical aura. There were staff carrying trays of food and drink everywhere and clusters of people laughing and enjoying the early evening sunshine and breeze from the river which blew across the rose bushes that were planted along the edge of the garden and filled the air with the sweet fragrance from their petals.

She was wearing the dress her grandmother had offered her. It was made from the softest deep blue denim that matched the colour of the river right now and the fitted fili-gree, almost sheer white lace top underneath had a deli-cately laced collar. It was fairly short, so she'd teemed it with matching inky blue platform shoes with sexy straps that made her ankles look cute.

Maya took a calming breath for courage. She knew she looked good.

People were gazing at her with interest as she made her way up the path, as she supposed many knew each other or worked in the same industry. She heard one lady comment on her outfit, wondering to her companion who the designer was. Fortified by that one comment, Maya decided she might as well embrace who she was and enjoy herself. A waiter handed her a glass of crisp sparkling champagne from a tray of crystal flutes that he was carrying around the grounds and she stopped by a gigantic tree and looked around, taking a sip and composing herself.

There were twinkling lights strung between the various established trees in the garden, and the deck area in front of the house had huge outdoor heaters blazing with flames. Glowing lanterns hung from the canopies of the trees and small tables were snuggled beneath some with crisp white linen, more lanterns and overflowing vases of lush roses with big fat petals that filled the air with their sweet scent. Each table had chairs dotted around it, with plump green cushions on each one. It was still light and early evening, but the sun was dipping below the horizon, leaving the air feeling warm, sensual and almost electric. People were milling around in groups of beautiful people and she recognised many of them, feeling star struck. A couple were actually recent clients, but they wouldn't know that because she kept her personal identity hidden. There was a buzz of conversation and her stomach growled when a waitress walked by with plates of delicate canapés. Maya quickly swiped one and savoured the mini crispy sushi rice cakes with seared tuna and smacked her lips, wishing she'd taken two. The lime zest on the top was inspired and her stomach rumbled again, but this time she guessed it was more from nerves.

As she came out of her hiding place by the tree and walked past Tabitha and a group of fashionable women, she heard them bitchily comment about letting 'the public' into a private event. Noah was standing further up the garden in smart lightweight trousers and a deep blue shirt, which was rolled up at the arms. She paused as it looked like they'd planned their outfits together and she hid her smile behind the rim of her glass. His face broke into a wide grin when he turned and saw her. He touched his companion on the arm to let them know he was leaving and headed her way, his companion's line of sight following him with interest. Noah's eyes danced in the early evening light and when he saw whom she was standing near, he slipped his arm protectively around her waist and pulled her close.

'You look beautiful.' His eyes wandered over her appreciatively. 'Thank you for coming.'

'I'm glad to be here,' she said, and he grinned as she was clearly lying. He laughed and tightened his arm around her as if he was worried she'd make a dash for it and throw herself into the river again.

'How was your date with Robbie?' he asked casually.

Maya eyed him steadily as they had spoken by text since then and he hadn't brought the subject up.

'It wasn't a date... it felt more like an interrogation,' she chuckled.

'He needs to up his game,' he said looking smug.

'He said the same thing about you when I said we'd been to visit a restaurant that cooked flowers,' she tried not to laugh at his frown.

'Would you have rather gone somewhere different?' he asked, more frown lines appearing on his forehead.

She put a hand on his arm and smiled, her eyes dancing. 'No. I loved it! I've been nowhere like that before and it was one of the best nights I've had in ages,' she admitted and he visibly relaxed and he grinned a cheeky grin at her that made her heart flutter. 'My grandad now wants you to take him.'

He threw his head back and laughed out loud.

'And you know that Robbie and I are just friends,' she chided, nudging his side and enjoying the solid feel of it.

'Good,' he said seriously.

'Good?' she repeated, surprised. She enjoyed spending time with Noah – it was relaxing in a very un-relaxing kind of way because her skin literally sizzled when he was close and she dreamt of running her hands along his firm shoulders and pulling him closer all the time now, which was mightily frustrating and not something she was looking for... was it?

'I didn't like it,' he admitted bashfully, but she couldn't be cross with him when all she wanted to do was kiss him. She was also incredibly flattered.

'Robbie is a bit of a flirt,' she chuckled, 'but was actually protecting your heart by finding out if I was a gold digger,' she shrugged as Noah's eyebrows shot up into his hairline.

He rubbed his hand in his hair and then the back of his neck, her gaze following the movement a little bit lustfully.

'What the hell?'

'Don't worry. He apologised after I'd thrown my wine in his lap,' she quipped and Noah's shoulders relaxed. 'I need nothing from you except for a few fake dates and a meet and greet with my family,' she added.

Noah paused for a fraction of a second too long and she began to feel pensive. 'That I'd like to have seen,' he said referring to the wine.

He ignored the fake date comment, so she carried on. 'He's smitten with Amethyst. They just need to stop provoking each other and talk about how they feel,' she said, and he seemed surprised at her insight. Before they spoke further, Tabitha had strutted over in her long flowy white dress with a group of friends trailing behind her and joined them. Maya tried to work out why Tabitha was there, but guessed she'd wormed her way in again. Poor Noah. She leaned in to him and gave him a reassuring smile, as they all greeted each other and Noah introduced her to the group without saying who she was to him, which made Maya frown and a few of those nerves return - as surely that was the whole point of her being there?

Tabitha's eyes slowly perused Maya's outfit and then they narrowed as she grabbed Maya's hand and examined the delicately sculpted ring on her finger. 'Is this a No.1 Ethereal Lane piece?'

Maya swore under her breath. She'd worn the ring for confidence, as it was one of the first pieces she'd ever made, but now she wished she'd left it in her jewellery box at home. She forgot how well known and easily recognisable her own brand had become over the past few months.

'Tabitha!' scolded Noah. He tried to draw Maya's hand

away, but she had it in a vice-like grip and was studying it rudely. After an agonising moment she clearly realised what she was doing and she let Maya go.

'Sorry,' she said, giving Maya what she guessed was supposed to be a winning smile. 'I'm a huge fan of that brand and I'd love to chat to you about it... Later, maybe?' she sipped her champagne and observed Maya.

Maya looked at Noah but he seemed at a loss too. 'Is it a charity piece?' asked Tabitha, her eyes fixed back onto the ring. Maya swapped the hand that was holding her glass of wine and slipped the hand that the ring was on into Noah's hand.

'Tabitha! Enough!' censored Noah, as he drew Maya further up the path.

Maya wished she'd thought about the ring before she'd arrived but she often used it as a kind of lucky talisman and had a habit of wearing her own jewellery out, but only tiny unassuming pieces that she'd thought no one would recognise. Just her luck that Tabitha was a super-fan it seemed. She did make pieces for charity, but not something as unassuming as this. The whole point was for them to stand out.

'Are you okay?' asked Noah. She turned to see worry lines on his forehead. She gave him a reassuring smile.

'It's okay. The ring is pretty, and she's right. My friend gave it to me. I often forget just how big that brand has become and I probably shouldn't wear it out in public.'

'Surely it's made to be worn?' he said with a harassed glance over his shoulder, before he paused and sighed. 'It looks beautiful, as do you.' She flushed as he gazed appreciatively at her outfit. 'Thank you for joining me tonight. I didn't know that Tabitha would be here. I was hoping to ease you into my world gently. She arrived with someone else and I couldn't really turn her away without making a scene, which she probably banked on,' he said, shaking his head in disgust. 'I think she's also tipped off the paparazzi about the party. I've seen people hiding in the bushes across the water. They don't usually bother me at home.'

'Noah... it's okay,' she reassured again, winking at him and making him smile finally. 'We knew this might be tricky because our lives are so far removed from each other, but we *can* do this. The whole point of us being together is to keep Tabitha away and my family off my back, so maybe it's good she's here and sees us together as soon as possible?' She nudged shoulders with him and he nodded and led her up towards the guesthouse, still holding her hand, which caught a few curious stares from his friends. He looked divine and smelt delicious with a deep musky aftershave tingling her senses. It would be very easy to fall for a man like him, so she had to keep things friendly to protect her heart.

As they approached the guesthouse, Noah said he'd find them some food, and she nipped inside to freshen up. As she approached the pool, she stopped in her tracks when she overheard Tabitha and her cronies talking in not so hushed voices.

'We need to make friends with her to find out who gave her that ring,' hissed Tabitha. 'Then we might find out who their contact is and be able to get on the No. 1 Ethereal Lane waiting list.'

'I've been trying for two months and haven't found out how to get on that list. It seems they have a system and only the ones in the know find out how,' replied her friend.

'Whenever I scroll now, I see a viral post about that brand. It's literally everywhere when no one had heard about it at the start of the year. It's so exclusive that everyone I know wants to be in on it. Influencers keep posting hoping to be noticed as a client, or a model,' said Tabitha, jealousy showing in her tone. 'I want in! Maybe she stole it?' they all cackled with laughter and Maya felt bile rise in the back of her throat.

'Let's find the woman who jumped in the river to get an invitation. Perhaps she needs the money and is desperate to sell?' said Tabitha in sudden excitement.

'Do you think that's why she wore it?' asked her friend. Maya back stepped quickly and sighed in relief when she saw Robbie and Noah heading her way. They had tall cocktail glasses in their hands with what looked like mojitos stuffed with mint.

Noah handed her a drink after Robbie had hugged and kissed her and exclaimed about how gorgeous she looked, which made her blush and return the compliment. Noah took her hand again and introduced her to his guests as his girlfriend, which made her face grow warm. Her hand was linked with his and she wondered what the hell his friends would think about her being there, but they all seemed more curious than suspicious. Robbie got into a raucous debate with a friend about whether knocking his head on the boat had made him funnier, so they left them to it. After a few pleasant chats, Maya turned, and her body froze as she came face to face with Blake who moved forward to shake Noah's hand and then stood in front of her. Her body went rigid for a moment before she forced herself to smile.

'Hi Maya. How are you?' he said, his eyes taking in every inch of her and then noting her hand in Noah's. He frowned fleetingly, but she saw it.

Noah looked between them with interest. 'You know each other?' he asked.

'We used to date,' said Maya before Blake could expand. 'A very long time ago,' she added, as Noah slipped his arm protectively around her waist. She smiled gratefully at him, and he turned back to Blake. It was like a punch to the stomach, seeing him again after so many years. His dark hair was shorter, and he had a few more lines on his face, but otherwise he was just as handsome as ever, which was annoying.

Blake smiled at Noah politely then once again focused on Maya. He lifted a finger as if he was going to brush a stray hair out of her eyes, like he'd always done when they were together, but then he dropped his hand. 'I saw Joe's boat in the local paper when I was visiting a client recently. I wondered if you'd had anything to do with the revamp. Then I saw a photo of you and Robbie on Instagram and wondered if you were dating. He looked at Noah's arm around Maya again and his brow furrowed. Do you live here now?' Blake asked her, an edge to his voice.

'No,' answered Maya simply, and Noah frowned. Technically, they were at Noah's house and she didn't live there. 'I'm just visiting.' She could see the moment where Noah realised which ex Blake was and he didn't seem happy about the fact that he'd invited him to his house. He knew how Blake had treated her, albeit a long time ago. Maya had just never mentioned his name. It hadn't seemed important.

'How are your family?' Blake asked, as he had known them well at one time.

'Fine, thanks,' she smiled sweetly at him. 'How's Portia?' she asked. 'Is she here with you?' she gazed around the garden but couldn't see the tall blonde. It was surprising how little it meant to her to stand face to face with Blake, or the woman who had helped him to destroy her life. The adoration and love she'd once felt for him was nowhere to be found. She'd assumed that her feelings would come flooding back along with the excruciating pain of betrayal when she did finally see him face to face, but... nothing.

'Um... No. She's not here,' he said, pulling the collar of his shirt away from his neck as if he was hot suddenly. 'Portia's in London,' he said cordially, his eyes never leaving her face. Maya felt relief for a fraction of a second and Noah stroked his fingers along the base of her neck to let her know he was with her, so she tried to focus on that. Blake watching her so closely unnerved her a bit, but he'd always tried to get inside her mind and she was firmly shutting him out.

'You're still together, then? Well, wish her luck from me,' she said sweetly, and Blake grimaced.

'I will,' he replied smoothly. She refused to bite, even though she'd love to throw her drink in his smug face. Her stomach somersaulted, and she took a sip of her cocktail to ease her suddenly parched throat.

Her brain was whirring with what to do to make Blake go away but he seemed to be was enjoying himself now. 'I can't wait to see your next collection,' she beamed up at him before turning to Noah who was glancing between them with a pensive expression. Blake looked afraid suddenly and rapidly changed the subject to the music that the band were playing from the patio.

'Do you two know each other well?' Blake asked, his eyes darting between her and Noah. Blake seemed surprised to find her there, as if she was the last person he expected to see that day, but then most of Noah's guests probably felt that way. Noah tightened his arm around her and eased her into the side of his body.

'Yes. Very well,' he said simply, leaving Blake to make of that what he would.

'Maya, we need to talk,' said Blake, glancing apologetically at Noah.

'We don't,' she said, looking at Noah and giving him a reassuring smile. She wished she could slip her hand into the back of his jeans and shocked herself at her thoughts, but her past life was getting in the way – yet again. 'That boat sailed a long time ago, Blake. I'm happy for you... really.'

Robbie jumped in and almost frightened the life out of her before swinging Maya into his arms and planting a kiss on her lips in front of everyone, making Noah step back. 'Rob,' he ground out. 'No more kissing my girl,' a warning tone came into his voice, which seemed to amuse Robbie as a mischievous glint came into his eye and Maya groaned to herself, but a warmth spread through her body at Noah's protective stance. She quite liked it!

'Sorry Noah, but you know how much I love Maya, even though she's your date,' he teased and winked at Blake, making him look even more uncomfortable. She hadn't in her wildest dreams imagined her first meeting with Blake involving Robbie planting a smacker on her lips, while Noah had his arm around her. After that he looked like he couldn't get away fast enough, but she knew that wouldn't be the end of it now that he knew she was here and was mingling with the stars, even though he'd clearly been invited to the party too.

As they bid Blake farewell and moved up the garden towards the bar and a huge group of people, Noah stopped Rob in his tracks with a hand to his chest. 'I meant it about kissing my girl, okay?' Maya's eyebrows shot up into her hairline and she paused mid stride in shock. This was a very public display of... she didn't know what.

'Sorry Noah,' Robbie batted his eyelashes at them both.

'I forgot how besotted you two are with each other now,' he shouted and they all turned and almost walked straight in to Tabitha, who had two angry red patches on her cheeks. Maya gasped and plastered on a smile. Had Noah's comment been for show, she wondered, wincing.

'I didn't know you two were dating? Surrey you barely know each other?' Tabitha said frostily.

'Oh, Noah's been trying to catch Maya's attention for ages,' Robbie smiled, saccharin sweetly at Tabitha. 'She's an artist, and he's been secretly trying to buy more of her art to make her notice him after they bumped in to each other in town. He calls her the siren of the river because her smile captured him.' Rob was out to cause trouble and Maya bit her lip, but stayed silent. Surely that wasn't true? Her head felt like it was spinning and she almost missed her footing and tripped into Noah. He grinned sheepishly and took her hand to steady her, linking their bodies side by side.

'Sorry,' he hung his head bashfully and butterflies took flight in her stomach. 'It's true. Plus, I wanted to buy you another coffee.'

'To think that Tabitha 'accidentally' pushing me into the river actually helped you both realise how suited you are!' cooed Rob dramatically, clasping his hands together in glee and smiling at Tabitha whose face had drained of colour. 'It was obviously meant to be.' He grabbed Tabitha's arm and drew her away, muttering about lovebirds needing time alone. She stared over her shoulder at them as Robbie drew her away and Maya let out the breath she'd been holding. Noah led her to a quiet corner and shielded her from the rest of the party with his body.

'Apologies,' winced Noah. 'That wasn't the way I planned on introducing you to my friends and colleagues, or the way for you to find out I really was trying to meet you again before all this,' he rolled his shoulders and stood up straighter. 'Your art is stunning, but I was even more interested in the artist... It's embarrassing. I didn't know if you were single, so I was trying to find out more about you. You're a bit of an enigma,' he grimaced and she couldn't help but smile as she knew that to be true, more than he could ever know. Noah had wanted to get to know her, even before the river incident. It was overwhelming, and she was bewildered how they'd ended up fake dating, if that was the case.

Was he testing her to see if she was like Tabitha? She wouldn't stand for that. She didn't mind helping him out, but she wasn't about to be used as a plaything for his amusement. Maybe he regularly picked up random women he saw out an about and got his assistants to organise dates for him? The thought didn't sit well with her.

Maya tried to calm her racing pulse and the uncomfortable doubts in her mind. Tabitha had looked like she'd wanted to scratch her eyes out. 'It's okay,' she said, masking her own feelings. 'I'm glad we met. I've learned quickly that Robbie is a force of nature and he does exactly as he pleases, whatever the cost.'

'His heart is in the right place. He was probably just preventing either of us from backing out.'

She looked down at their entwined hands. 'Did you want to?' she asked honestly

'No. I've been looking forward to seeing you. I've missed you. We've both been busy.'

She had to ask... 'Do you usually search out random women you see on the river and try to date them?' He looked wounded suddenly and turned to face her fully.

'I rarely date at all. After Tabitha, I threw myself into my work and tried to avoid the press interest in my love life, but when I saw you again and you were painting on the boat, I wished my life could be simpler. I kept hoping that I'd glimpse the beautiful artist again. I'm sorry for not telling you sooner. It just felt weird to say I'd been kind of stalking your art to find you.'

Maya felt heat rise in her cheeks and smiled finally. They had gotten used to speaking most nights on the phone now to have background knowledge about each other for their fake-partner scenario, but mostly it ended up with them chatting about their days and hours flew by without them noticing. 'I've missed seeing you too,' she admitted. 'Why the fake dating then? You could have just asked me out?' Noah's jaw dropped open and then his eyes grew darker and he moved closer, making her breath catch.

'I could?' She nodded shyly. He licked his lips and cupped her face in his hand, which made her brain go fuzzy for a second. She thought he might kiss her, but he frowned and moved back. 'We've both been hurt, and it seemed like a good plan to get to know each other without expectations.' Maya looked at her hands for a moment and then faced him. She'd hoped for a moment that he might have still wanted something real, but it seemed not now that he knew her better. Just her luck!

'Probably a good idea,' she smiled at him, even though she suddenly felt like crying. 'I've sorted out a date for you to visit Bertha if you'd still like to? No problem if you don't have time, or want to call this daft idea off.'

'No. I'd love to,' Noah assured, as the temperature between them cooled. 'Did you just ask me out on a date?' he teased, taking her hand and leading her towards the key party with his hand on her waist, making the heat rise again.

'I did,' she grinned back, and he leaned in and kissed her softly on the lips. She was stunned to silence, then caught sight of Blake in her eye-line and realised that it had been for show. She flushed and grabbed a fresh drink from a passing waitress. The circles he found her in clearly surprised Blake, and didn't look too happy about the kiss. She gave him a cheerful smile and let herself be led away by one of the nation's hottest men.

Maya slumped into a chair hours later and Noah flopped into the one opposite her. They had worked the room all night and now all of his guests knew they were dating. Everyone had gone home except for Noah's staff and he picked up her feet and rubbed them, making her groan in bliss, then blush at the intimacy and tuck her feet under her bottom.

'It would make it more believable if you stayed the night,' grinned Noah, his smile devastating. 'Do you have to get home tonight? The paparazzi might still be outside and everyone else has gone home. They can't see this far up the garden but will have sight of the docks, which was why most people had left by car.' Maya blinked and then tried to calm her beating heart, as this wasn't real. It was the weekend, so she could easily stay over and she was frazzled so she could literally fall asleep while standing up, but this was a very desirable man, asking her to stay the night. 'Purely platonically,' he added hastily. 'You could find out how good the sunrises are from my guesthouse. It's a gigantic bed, so we can take a corner each,' he smiled cheekily and her heartbeat sped up. 'We can work out a plan of action for Tabitha and Blake, but I think we did pretty well, considering we didn't expect either of them to be here. I can't believe that your ex is Blake McBride.'

'Me either,' she grinned and then tried to cover up a yawn.

'Come on. Let's go to bed,' he said, scooping her up into

his arms and carrying her into the guesthouse and upstairs, placing her carefully in the centre of the vast bed. 'I promise to behave,' he kissed her softly on the lips and she sighed in bliss. 'We'll just sleep.'

'Okay,' she decided. Maya rolled over and propped herself up with one arm while she watched him pull his shirt over his head as if she wasn't there with him and then walk into the bathroom for a moment. She had to regulate her breathing to not pass out at the sight of his muscled chest. He came back in wearing a low-slung pair of grey cotton branded pyjama bottoms, and her mouth went dry and her mind blank. Her head was fuzzy from all the wine she'd consumed, but suddenly she was wide awake. She couldn't stop staring at his toned abdomen and the dip just below his waist, tempting her to ease them lower. He came and sat next to her on the bed and smiled at her. 'There's some of my pyjama short sets and t-shirts in the bathroom drawers. Help yourself.' She smiled her thanks and edged herself out of the comfort of the bed and the danger zone of being so near a half-naked Noah Benedict, who was currently making himself comfortable on the pillows next to where her head had just been. 'Do you like to be wined and dined?' she asked as she reached the bathroom and paused, her hand on the door.

'I don't know,' he smiled back and her heart fluttered. 'It's never happened to me. There's always a huge expectation for me to perform a miracle and to entertain on a date, or to be like one of my movie characters, which is exhausting.'

'Perform?' she giggled, then grew serious. 'I can understand that. Not being able to be your true self must be tiring,' she said sadly, realising that her own secret life was taking a toll on her too and that all the subterfuge was maybe not as necessary as she'd thought.

'Not that type of performance,' he rolled his eyes and then waggled his eyebrows at her theatrically. 'I'm told I'm pretty good at that type though,' he grinned and the hairs on the back of her neck stood up. 'My dates always seem to expect me to excite them, but I've never thought about them not interested in impressing me,' he frowned. 'I'm more of a low-key guy. I enjoy simple things and less fuss if it's not something I have to do for work.'

She ducked into the bathroom and quickly pulled on one of his t-shirts and didn't bother with anything else. It felt nice to be in his clothes again and she snuggled into the warm fabric and then hurried back to the bed, feeling shy suddenly and half-naked. He was looking at her appreciatively, and he took her hand and pulled her into a hug. Too soon he pulled back and was looking into her eyes, his own growing darker as the mood in the room changed and the air sparked with electricity. 'Join me in the shower?' he asked. 'I'll happily get undressed again...'

'Tempting...' she answered honestly, wondering at her own powers of restraint. 'But this is...' she looked around the beautiful room and then at the handsome man in the bed in front of her, 'fake. It's probably easier for both of us to keep it platonic.'

'I'm happy to up the temptation,' he flirted, kissing her hand and then trailing kisses up her arm, making her body tingle all over so that she almost passed out or gave in.

'Too complicated,' she pouted with genuine regret. Noah looked disappointed and as if he might try harder, but he nodded and leaned in to kiss her cheek.

'You're probably right,' he said with his own sigh as he

pulled back the covers and beckoned her to join him. She gulped and got in.

Maya remembered a comment that Robbie had said earlier and frowned, turning to face Noah. 'You said that you'd seen me on the river and wanted to meet me again. Was that just because we had an audience?'

Noah turned her way and grinned. 'No. I'd seen you on the boat and thought you might have seen me too.'

'Perhaps,' she flushed.

'My assistant was tasked with finding out where you sold your art, because I really wanted to find you. At the very least I wanted to apologise again for bumping into you and rushing off.' She stared at him incredulously and he held up a hand in surrender. 'I loved your paintings or I wouldn't have bought one, but I still hadn't thought of a way to contact you. Then Tabitha intervened, and here we are.' Maya frowned. Once again, the question arose... If he'd really wanted to meet her in real life - why the fake date?

He could see her confusion and she could see he was warring with how honest to be. 'When you had the fake date idea, I knew you were joking, but thought it was a good way for us to get to know each other without the pressures of actual dating. I didn't want to scare you away with my crazy lifestyle. Plus your own love life seemed as complicated as mine. I didn't know I'd like you so much!' he threw that bomb into the room with a grin and then pulled the covers up to his chest. They both lay next to each other in silence for a while, staring at the huge vaulted ceiling, then she heard his breathing regulate as he dropped off to sleep and it took all of her strength not to turn round and slide her arms around him.

Chapter Seventeen

Maya was sitting outside her house on the private dock, with her toes swishing around in the river when Noah called to ask her out to dinner. She'd been drawing Water Figwort with their tiny pink flowers and tall Willowherbs which she'd love to reach out and touch, but she was of cautious of tumbling into the rushes. Maya grinned into the phone and looked out at the view of the river, watching a few boats sail by. 'Okay. When?'

'Tonight?'

'I can't tonight. I've got a birthday meal with a girlfriend. Sorry,' she genuinely was. She hoped Noah could hear the regret in her voice, but it was Leah's birthday and Matt had gotten them a table at Leah's favourite restaurant in town. Maya had arranged an extravagant cake to be delivered to the table after the meal and Leah had been talking about nothing else all week. Noah had helped her out with Blake, but her family all wanted to meet him and she needed to let Matt and Leah know what was going on as well.

'It was a long shot that you might be free,' she could hear

the genuine sadness in his tone, too. 'I enjoyed waking up with you in my arms last weekend,' he said huskily, and it did something to her heart. What was it with this man and her hormones? The lines were definitely becoming blurred because they'd woken up in each other's arms in the guest-house and spent ages kissing and running their hands over each other's minimal clothes, which had almost blown her mind. Nothing else had happened, but she'd kind of wished it had. She'd had to drag herself out of there for her own sanity.

Later that evening, she sat at a table with Matt and tried to drop into the conversation that she'd been dating Noah. The restaurant was buzzing with conversation and the décor was so beautiful that Maya had to keep pausing because she'd noticed something new. They sat in a central curved table with plush white cushions, high-backed banquet seating and green scatter cushions made it even more comfortable. There was an actual tree in a huge urn next to their table that trailed branches above their heads that were hung with flickering lanterns. The backlit bar had soft orange bar stools lined up along the edge with more green plants in copper pots and low lighting gave the restaurant a sexy edge, which was excelled by all of the beautiful people milling around. The air was sizzling with excitement. It felt like they'd stepped into paradise and she could see why it was Leah's favourite.

She knew Matt and Leah would both explode with questions and she'd never hear the end of it, but it was better than a million questions about why she hadn't been able to produce the high-flying exec who always travelled. Leah had just excused herself to go to the ladies' room, so Maya tried to steady her nerves. She loved spending time with Leah and Matt, but she also needed to tell them about the garden party at Noah's and bumping into Blake. It was something that she'd been putting off. Both of them would want to protect her and would go into bossy mode, which she could do without when her usual laser like focus on life and work were a bit wobbly because of the huge sexy, Noah shaped distraction, to her days now. She tried to enjoy the delicious meal in front of her, but her body was too tense to appreciate the spicy flavours of the jalapeno and pineapple salsa or her skillet enchiladas.

Matt frowned as she paused mid-bite. He looked around to see what she was looking at and they both watched Noah stroll through the restaurant towards the exit, with a group of very glamorous looking friends. He was wearing a smart blue shirt and dark grey trousers and looked every inch the movie star. His hair was swept back and his piercing blue eyes noted her, her companion and then widened in surprise. Matt was looking at her in confusion and Noah turned and quickly spoke to his friends before turning her way. She put her fork down and looked at Matt for help. 'Why the hell is Noah Benedict looking at you like he wants to eat you alive and why is he headed our way?'

Maya felt her knees begin to shake and panicked, looking at the rest room and wondering where the hell Leah was. Why hadn't they invited more people to her birthday dinner? She knew it was because they hadn't seen each other in ages and Leah had a family party the following week for her birthday, but Noah might think she was on a date! She smoothed her hands along her sage green silk dress but then lifted them up because her palms began to sweat. This looked so bad! Where was the birthday cake when she needed one! 'Umm... we've been dating...' Matt's mouth hung open for a second and his head flicked back and forth between them as Noah approached.

'You've been dating Noah Benedict? Since when?' he compelled her to answer. Then turned with a smile as Noah came and said hello to them both, kissing Maya on the cheek and shaking Matt's hand.

Noah was looking into Maya's eyes and his own had questions in them. Maya became flustered and didn't know what to say, so Matt took charge. 'I'm Matt. Maya has only just mentioned that you two are acquainted.' Maya winced and could have kicked him. 'Would you like to join us?' Matt indicated a spare seat at their table. Noah seemed to register that there was a third place set and although he didn't seem happy his featured softened.

'Thanks for the offer. I'd love to, but I wouldn't want to impose on a birthday surprise.' That seemed more of a question than a statement and Matt grinned suddenly. Maya wanted to kick him again. Where the bloody hell was Leah? 'I'm here with friends, so I'd better get back to them.' With that he kissed Maya's cheek again and bid them farewell, leaving her senses reeling and the scent of his spicy after-shave making her want to run after him.

'Well,' said Matt, sitting back in his chair and watching Noah go. 'That was enlightening. He clearly isn't sure if this is business or pleasure. Should I be flattered?' Maya threw her napkin at his head, but he caught it and waited as Leah re-joined them.

'Noah Benedict was just here,' she hissed, fidgeting in her seat and straining to look over the other diners for her prey. 'It's all anyone is talking about. It took ages in the toilets because I had to wait to hear all the gossip. Apparently, he is dating someone new. Some unknown.' Matt spluttered with laughter and Leah looked between them in confusion.

'You literally just missed him,' he laughed.

'What, here? Do you want to tell me what's going on?' she demanded, her prettily painted nails tapping the table in irritation and not even glancing up as her three-tiered birthday cake arrived. Maya used this moment to diffuse the situation and she told Leah to make a wish and she looked tenderly into Matt's eyes as she did this, everything else forgotten and Maya's heart squeezed with love for these people.

'Noah Benedict is dating Maya,' said Matt helpfully a few minutes later, bursting her equilibrium and she did wonder how he'd managed to stop himself from blurting it out for all of five minutes. 'Although it seems she hasn't told him about us because he just thought she was on a date with a well-known supermodel,' his eyes were dancing with mischief as he pointed to himself in jest and Leah darted glances around as if Noah might still be there.

'What the hell are you talking about?' asked Leah, indignation showing as her eyes flashed fire. 'Of course Maya isn't dating him. We'd know if she was.' Maya flinched and Leah turned to face her, two bright spots of red on her cheeks.

'I'm the unknown,' said Maya, trying not to cringe and sink further in her seat to hide from Leah's wrath. 'I'm sorry I didn't tell you, but it's not real.' She just couldn't keep up with this pretence to her two best friends. 'He went for a stroll and got mobbed by some fans which sent him barrelling into me,' she admitted. 'I helped him get away. He knocked my coffee all over me and then brought me flowers after I saved Robbie and we've been talking ever since.' She heard Leah gasp and felt awful. 'I'm so sorry. It's not real,' she reiterated. 'One of us joked we should pretend to date to appease our families and Noah persuaded me to try it. It seemed like a good idea at the time.'

'Why fake dating though?' asked Matt. 'From the way he looked at both of us, his feelings are genuine. He was not happy to see you sitting in this gorgeous restaurant with me, that's for sure.'

Maya wriggled uncomfortably in her seat and flushed. Oh, the embarrassment! 'We have kissed...' she watched Leah's jaw drop open and smiled finally. 'He asked me to dinner tonight and, and I was already busy. I guess he has loads of options,' she thought about the group of friends who had accompanied him to dinner and how beautiful the women were in their designer clothes and perfectly coiffured hair and her stomach sunk to a new depth. She knew dating, fake or otherwise, a guy like Noah, could only bring fresh problems. She already hated the women in his group and they were probably perfectly nice!

'You should have cancelled,' said Leah, aghast. 'What the hell were you thinking?'

'I'm not changing my plans for my best friend's birthday dinner for a man.'

'Not even for Noah Benedict? Are you crazy? You've been single for two years and you made up a boyfriend to shut us all up.' Leah yelled in frustration and Maya looked around for a place to hide from her fiery friend. Her hair was standing up on end in places where she'd run her hands through it in exasperation and her face was showing how appalled she was at her friend's decision, however well meant. Maya felt that she'd made a terrible mistake.

'I wanted to see you both to tell you what's been going on,' she explained. 'I'm sorry I lied. Everyone thinking my love life was such a dismal failure upset me, so I made a boyfriend up.' Maya hung her head in sorrow, and Leah tutted loudly, but gave her a conciliatory hug.

'You literally see us every day! You could have told us

any time.' Maya furtively glanced around as if everyone would know of her stupidity and wondered why she hadn't been more flexible her plans. She could have easily invited Noah to dinner or seen him afterwards. Maybe she was afraid to be alone with Noah now because their friendship had shifted to something more... for her, anyway.

She knew he didn't want a long-term partner after the number Tabitha had done on him, but the pressure from his agent meant they had to work together as Tabitha had just managed to get signed there too, which had made Noah even more uncomfortable because she'd used his name and their 'relationship' as a referral. Finding out about it after it was a done deal hadn't helped. It had pushed him to find a drastic solution to stop her messing up his career with her malicious stories and Maya wasn't about to open her heart to be hurt again. 'You idiot,' sighed Leah, taking her hand and giving it a supportive squeeze. 'Not every relationship has to be the love of your life, Maya. You can just date a man for fun and have lots of fantastic sex!'

'I think she might already be past that point,' said Matt insightfully and Maya suddenly found her wine glass really interesting.

Leah quickly got up to pull Maya's chair out so she nearly fell on the floor and then grabbed Maya's handbag and shoved it into her hands. 'Why are you still here?' she asked with a cheeky grin. 'We promise to save you some cake.' She pointed to the exit. 'Go and get your man.'

Chapter Eighteen

Was persuading a film star to have wild and abandoned sex with you reason enough to borrow a boat, she wondered, then decided it was. Maya eased the vessel from under her house and steered up the river past *Bertha* and towards Noah's house. She didn't use the boat often because it was expensive and not hers. This was an emergency though, and the owners had said she could use it whenever she liked.

She anchored by Noah's jetty and stepped into his garden, only to come face to face with a half-naked Noah, who was pulling a t-shirt over his head. He'd obviously slept in the guesthouse again and his hair was mussed up and sexy. 'You set off the silent alarm,' he told her, pressing a button on the control panel in his hand. 'What are you doing here?' She stood looking at him and felt foolish now. She'd refused to be rushed away from the meal with Matt and Leah at first, but they had insisted and then she'd gone home with *two* huge slices of gooey chocolate cake and procrastinated for a bit. After imagining spoon-feeding Noah the chocolate cake and licking crumbs off of his chest, she finally shook off her funk and plucked up the courage to see if Noah was okay after bumping in to her and Matt. She knew she didn't have to explain herself, but she wanted him to trust her, which was a weird feeling.

'Can I come in?' She gestured towards the guesthouse and felt the burn of humiliation as he paused and seemed unsure. 'I wanted to tell you about Matt *and Leah*, my dinner companions tonight,' she said, stumbling over her words and cursing under her breath. 'It literally devastated Leah that she'd missed you when she got back to the table. She's the friend I told you about who runs the flower shop. She's a bit of a fan and it's her birthday,' she looked under her lashes at him and he was observing her. 'She sent you some birthday cake,' she added as she held out the huge, now slightly squashed, slabs of cake in front of her, which made his eyes twinkle and the edges of his mouth tug upwards, but he still seemed wary. She put the cake on a nearby wrought iron garden table that had been left over from the garden party. 'Matt and Leah are a couple and my best friends.' Noah's shoulders relaxed, and he held out his hand for her to join him, before leading her back inside, the cake instantly forgotten.

'I'm sorry,' he hung his head suddenly and turned to face her on the threshold, dropping her hand, which made her stall for a moment. 'I got jealous. That man looks like a bloody model!' He threw his hands up in disgust.

'He is a model,' she quipped, and they both grinned, locking eyes. She remembered the first time they had walked up to his guesthouse after being pulled out of the river and that was the day that things changed for her. She'd always had a hold on her emotions, but this man seemed to make her want to free them to run wild. Before they stepped into the guesthouse, she tugged on his arm to make him stop and pressed her body into his so that he sank back into the wall facing the house. Their lips met, and he groaned out loud and pulled her into his arms. She slid her hands into the back of his joggers, like she'd been dreaming of doing for ages, and he growled and sunk his hands into her hair, urging her closer still. He moved back slightly, looking into her eyes and she grinned and took his hand, leading him inside and up to bed.

Maya stretched her aching muscles the next morning and took a moment to enjoy the view... not of the river, but of the gorgeous man whose bed she was in. They'd spent hours touching and tasting each other's bodies and she'd trailed her nails along his thighs and made him groan and pull her body into contact with his own. They had finally taken that shower together, and he'd washed her hair while he stood behind her and lathered her body with scented suds while his slick hands roamed freely over her curves. She'd called out his name as he'd turned her around and pressed her back under the torrent of water with his firm body, making her gasp as the cool tiles touched her warm skin and her pulse pounded as he lifted her up to wrap her legs around his waist and finally claim her as his own.

Noah's energy surpassed hers and each time she'd tried to drift off to sleep, she'd felt him kissing his way up her thigh or his breath in the sensitive place at the base of her spine and his fingers and tongue urging her to ecstasy as he reached for another condom. She'd woken up to see the sun rising over the river and then Noah's hand had slipped around her waist and pressed their cores together and his lips had sought hers again and his hands had urged her closer as if he couldn't get enough of her. The man was insatiable, and she was in heaven! She pushed away niggling worries about feelings for now - she was having too much fun. Leah had been right, and it was time for her to throw off the old habits and enjoy a casual relationship with a delicious man. If that meant having lots of sex with a red-hot passionate guy like Noah, then she was all in, for however long it lasted.

She kissed Noah's shoulder as he woke and smiled into her eyes, before kissing her stomach and working his way up to her breasts, stretching like a panther about to pounce as she squirmed in delight. Just then his phone rang and his expression changed instantly to one of dread.

'What is it?' she asked clutching the covers to her chest and sitting up.

'That was my housekeeper. My parents are here!' He was already getting up and looked around for clothes in a genuine panic. 'They never come here!'

Maya felt mortified that she was there and so were his parents. She was a complete mess! *Could she hide and sidle out when they were busy?* She touched his arm to regain his attention. 'Noah. It's okay. They are only your parents. They can't be that bad... I'll hide until I can get back to my boat. Just distract them.' His head whipped round, and he froze.

'You can't leave! I need you to meet them. The pact. Remember?' Maya's heart sank. She'd hoped that the night before might have obliterated that stupid fake date pact, but it seemed not. She let her hair fall over her eyes and her shoulders slumped.

'I'm not dressed for that!' she said, looking down at the flirty little green dress she'd worn out to dinner the night before, which was discarded on the floor with her underwear, where he'd slid it off of her and kissed his way down her body. 'I'm not doing the walk of shame in front of your parents the first time I meet them!'

'Please Maya,' his gave her a puppy dog look. 'You can grab anything out of the wardrobe. Just put a t-shirt over the dress. The dress looked amazing by the way,' he said, looking at her appreciatively and she flushed. They hadn't had a minute to discuss what had happened the night before, but then maybe that was actually for the best. Being with a man like Noah was unlike anything she'd experienced before and she just wanted to keep running her hands over his toned backside and abdomen and would have happily stayed in bed with him all day before they'd brought the pact up again. Now she didn't know how to feel.

The panicked look on Noah's face made her heart melt and she went and put a hand on his arm. 'It's okay. I'll stay if you really want me to.' He sighed in relief and captured her face in his hands to kiss her sweetly on the lips, before turning and hurrying down the stairs and into his house to greet his parents, pulling on clothes as he went. She bit her lip and thought back to if she'd ever been so stressed about seeing her own parents, but she'd always rushed into their arms whenever they turned up, announced or not. She couldn't imagine not being pleased to see them and hurried to the wardrobe to find something to get her out of this mess she found herself in. The last parents she'd met of a man she was 'dating' were Blake's mum and dad, and she'd loved them dearly.

She pulled out a soft sage green cashmere sweater from the wardrobe and slipped it over her dress after swiftly stepping back into it. The sweater actually complimented the swishy soft fabric of the skirt of the dress and she puffed her cheeks out to regulate her breathing. This wasn't how she'd expected to have to spend her Saturday, but then she also hadn't expected to have mind-blowing sex with a guy like Noah, either.

He'd been gentle and caring and then passionate, hot and sexy. He'd brought her to the brink, made her wait and then touched her again until she'd begged him for release. It had been a revelation and he knew exactly how to please a woman, but everything she did seemed to bring him to his knees too. That could certainly become addictive. Maya hadn't gone there with the intention of a one-night stand, but he was hard to resist and she was trying to learn how to let go of her incessant need to control every aspect of her life and let her wilder side roam free. It had been caged for a while and she wondered if it would reflect in her work. Maya stopped and grinned suddenly. It felt good to do something out of the ordinary, and she squared her shoulders and headed down the stairs and up to the main house. She hadn't been in there before, so she didn't have a clue where to go.

As she drew closer, she felt some of the tension leave her as Noah had guided his parents out onto the terrace behind his house and sat them at the beautiful outdoor table and sofa set he had there that was surrounded by cream urns of light yellow roses. He caught sight of her and he smiled reassuringly, waving and calling for her to join them. His mum and dad politely stood up as she arrived and held out a hand to shake hers in greeting. His mum's inquisitive blue eyes looked at her, but they were friendly and didn't hold any suspicion who this strange girl was in her son's house. Noah had taken hold of her other hand as he introduced them and Maya noticed his mother taking that in, too. They all sat down and Maya fiddled with the hem of her skirt and smiled a bit manically as Noah said he'd grab them all some coffee and croissants and his dad asked to see his new car. Maya sent him a pleading stare, but he just shrugged his shoulders, as there wasn't much he could do.

Noah's mum was wearing a beautiful deep blue dress that flowed over her knees and cute mid-heeled black boots. Her blonde hair was softly flowing around her face and Maya could see the resemblance to her son. She was a striking woman. She smiled reassuringly at Maya. 'Sorry to drop in on you like this. It seems to be the only way we get to see our son these days. He's always so busy,' she sighed and leaned to smell one rose that was ambling over the low wall that separated this part of the garden from the lawn.

'I'm sure he's never too busy to see you?' Maya frowned. His mum smiled sadly and shrugged.

'His career takes precedent, and we worried he didn't make time for anything else, but we are glad to see that perhaps we were wrong?' his mum added and smiled cheekily at Maya who flushed, seeing so much of Noah in his mum.

'Does he know you feel that way?' asked Maya, intrigued.

His mum placed her hands in her lap and thought for a moment. 'He thinks we disapprove of his choice of career, but of course we're so proud of him. It's all consuming, and it takes him away from his family, so we worry.'

'So you'd like to see him more?'

'Of course! We see his brother and his family all the time, even though he runs a successful business. Noah can't seem to make time for us in his world, or for a relationship, but again, maybe that's not so?' She regarded Maya with interest. Noah's mum wasn't as cold as Noah had built her up to be when they'd spoken about his family. She was a mother missing her son.

Noah came back with a tray stuffed full of big plump croissants, fresh jam, and coffee. Maya's mouth watered as they'd been too busy to eat breakfast this morning. He seemed tense, and he darted glances between his mother and Maya because their chairs were pulled closely together. Maya sent him a reassuring smile and stood up to help him with the food and drinks. He kissed her on the lips briefly in thanks and then froze as he realised what he'd done in front of his parents, but they were happily chatting about the boats on the water and Maya pinched his bottom when they weren't looking and he almost jumped out of his skin in shock and then grinned, touching her leg under the table as they sat down.

'What do you do Maya?' his dad asked with interest.

'I'm an artist,' she replied. 'I also help my grandad's best friend run his steamboat business on the river, when I can. You should visit for longer next time and come aboard for a ride.' She glanced at Noah who was white with shock at her words, but she ignored him. 'Joe is the best tour guide on this stretch of the river,' she said proudly and Noah seemed at a loss for words that she'd just invited his parents back *and* to stay for longer.

'I'm sure mum and dad don't have time for that,' said Noah defensively. 'They hardly ever visit me,' he added and his mum looked crestfallen, but then a glint came into her eye that Maya recognised from Noah. Sheer force of will to get their own way.

'We'd love to!' said his mum, smiling happily and taking Maya's hand across the table, which almost made Noah fall off his chair. 'We are never sure when Noah's home and hate to disturb his work, but took a chance today which I'm so grateful for, as you were here too Maya! Hopefully we will see you again when we come back?' Maya's skin warmed up, but she couldn't quite meet Noah's eye because who knew where they would be by then.

'She will if I have any say in it,' Noah said, smiling grudgingly now as he pushed her half-eaten croissant back in front of her and encouraged her to finish eating. She smiled as they had both worked up an appetite, but she was a bit too nervous to eat. Her stomach felt like it had shrunk in the last hour and she definitely needed more coffee after being thrown in at the deep end like this. Noah was gradually relaxing, and he seemed happy that his parents wanted to visit again. After an hour more of chat about Maya and her family, Noah's parents hugged them both goodbye and bid them farewell, mentioning how much they'd like to see them both again soon.

'What the hell was that!' asked Noah. 'They are never that nice to me usually.' He ran his hands through his hair and she wished she was confident enough to soothe the worry from his brow with kisses. He walked to the sideboard, pressed a button on a remote control and sultry soul music filled the air, which seemed to relax him a little as he wasn't growling as much.

'I think you're getting mixed signals from each other,' she said simply. 'They don't dislike your career - they're very proud of you. They just think this choice of work means they don't get to see their son, because the travelling to film locations means he doesn't have time to visit his family. The want to see more of you!'

'Wow,' he seemed dazed and sat down, picking up the fresh coffee that his housekeeper had just brought out. 'You got all of that from a two-hour ambush?'

'Your parents are lovely. They just worry that you're not

making time for them, or for love,' she waggled her eyebrows at him suggestively and then looked round for somewhere to hide when his eyes darkened, his smile becoming predatory. He caught her hand and pulled her to him, making her gasp and her pulse speed up as he dipped his head and kissed her as she wound her hands into his hair, pulling him closer.

'Not making love enough?' he ground out. 'I think we can do something about that,' he laughed and swung her up into his arms, she giggled and hid her face in his shoulder as he carried her indoors and upstairs to his bedroom.

'Time for love...' she reiterated. 'They said nothing about making love!' she almost panted in anticipation as they reached a bedroom door.

'I need some practice,' he winked and then paused, growing serious suddenly. 'Stay with me today?' he asked. 'My staff have all just gone home for the day. We've got the place to ourselves.'

She nodded and kissed him full on the lips, linking her arms around his neck to pull him in close. He and growled in pleasure and slid her down his body onto her feet. He backed her up against the wall, holding her arms above her head while he trailed ardent kisses down the sensitive part of her neck, making her groan with pleasure. 'I think you've just persuaded me,' she grinned, grabbing his hand and pulling him towards the bed before placing her hands on his chest and pushing him back onto the soft, silky covers. She stood in front of him as his eyes darkened with arousal and, ever so slowly, eased layer after layer of clothing from her skin, until she stood before him, quivering with anticipation, wondering fleetingly when she'd become so daring.

He moved forward on the bed until he was sitting up and then captured her in his arms, his hand trailing down to touch her curves and pull her body into contact with his own, still fully clothed one as he stood up. His eyes were fixed on hers as he unbuttoned his shirt and slid his jeans from his hips and then swung her up so that her legs wound around his waist. Together they tumbled on the bed, Noah grabbing a condom from his nightstand and covering her body with his while he rained scorching kisses on her face, lips and breasts, that left a trail of fire, making her gasp in pleasure and arch her body towards his mouth. He ran his fingers along her spine, while she touched the firm muscles on his backside and thighs and urged him closer still. As his lean hips met hers, heat filled her body and her legs began to tremble with pleasure. The scent of his skin filled her senses, and she finally opened her eyes and looked at him. He was watching her as they moved together and he took her on a rollercoaster of pleasure that she'd never experienced before. Feelings she'd locked away broke free and she felt a deep connection growing between them, which scared and excited her at the same time. Fireworks exploded in her body, making her groan out loud and bite down on his shoulder. He linked their hands above their heads as he whispered seductive words in her ear, telling her how beautiful she was and that she was his, as he claimed her mouth for another searing kiss.

Chapter Nineteen

Matt and Leah were sitting with their heads bent over the desk, eyes glued to the laptop screen in front of them. Maya came in and peered over their shoulders, munching on a chocolate biscuit. 'Well?' she asked, straightening the sunglasses that were perched on the top of her head as it was a scorching hot day outside. The perky little short red sundress she wore that day made her feel sexy and powerful, and she'd almost strutted to the flower shop. She felt like she'd shed her skin and the old anxious Maya had been peeled back and a sparkling new and more confident woman was emerging in her wake.

'Hmm,' said Matt, standing back and waiting for them all to do the same. 'Later - we want gory details about your dirty weekend with Noah Benedict, but you were right about Gio's potential as a No. 1 Ethereal Lane model and business comes first.'

'Yes!' crowed Maya. 'I told you!' Matt grinned and Leah began dancing around the room and waving her arms in the air to the low hum of the music that was playing pop songs in the background.

'It's incredible!' she sang. 'We were wrong, and you were right. There are social media posts literally everywhere we look and people are podcasting and raving about Gio and your brand. He's your most popular model...' when Matt gave her a withering look, she hastily continued, 'excluding Matt, of course – but he's an entity of his own. Gio has taken the world by storm. You are literally making people's careers by picking them as part of your brand, Maya. Nina - the model with him, looks like she's already fallen under his spell - as have half of the population. The way he's handing her the necklace as if she's the only woman in the world, gives me goosebumps. I know Nina's already popular with your other brand clients Matt, but bringing in Gio and No. 1 Ethereal Lane has made them both stratospheric. It's incredible!' she breathed and then flopped in a chair for a moment, as if she'd worn herself out.

'Everyone is trying to book Gio to model for them now. Have you spoken to him?' Leah stopped twirling her chair and paused for a moment. Clearly speaking and spinning at the same time was exhausting, as she was brushing her wild hair out of her eyes and tying it into a ponytail with the ribbon she sometimes kept in her pocket when she was working.

'Uh, huh,' said Maya, as she was still in a daze about her latest campaign success. 'Obviously, he doesn't know I'm his employer, but we met for a coffee because he can't believe he's been "randomly" selected out of everyone in the world when he's got no modelling experience. I explained that I'd read in the newspapers that No. 1 Ethereal lane, have talent spotters everywhere. We spent hours chatting about it, and I convinced him to take the job, thank goodness! He's really come out of his shell since he's been at Mason's art class on the boat and Phil, Bobby and Margot have become some of his closest friends.

'Does Bobby still have a crush on him?' Leah asked.

'Yes, but he thinks there's no way Gio will notice him now he's famous, so he's heartbroken,' winced Maya. She was trying to help one friend, but another had been caught in the crossfire. She suspected Bobby wasn't alone in his crush, though. Maya had seen the way Gio's eyes followed Bobby around the boat when he thought no one was looking. Maybe she could do some matchmaking there?

Matt rolled his eyes, but she could see he was finally on board with her idea to use the very timid, Gio, in her latest jewellery campaign. Matt still modelled occasionally, but he enjoyed running his new agency too much to deviate too far, especially now he and Leah were thinking of starting a family, which Maya knew would fulfil the secret wish that Leah had made when she blew out her birthday candles. Life with Leah was never dull. Maya had recently sought out a local legal team after her mistakes with Blake. She'd been burnt before and knew she needed the right trusted advisors to guide her newfound wealth.

'Gio's just so dreamy!' added Leah. 'You've got to admit that he's making most of the population swoon,' she looked at Matt with an eyebrow raised, as he'd been the one who'd thought Gio too shy for the role. He grinned finally, holding his hands up in defeat and filched a biscuit from the packet Maya had just taken out of the drawer. She'd hidden them there earlier to stop herself from eating too many.

'That first photo in the series you set up of him sitting on a step with the branded jewellery box in his hand and looking off into the distance is a winner. The main consensus online is that he is thinking of the person he's

delivering it to. Lucky them!' Maya remembered seeing
Gio sit on the bench on *Bertha*'s deck during an art class
and noting the wistful gaze in his eyes. An expert photographer had fulfilled her vision, and the result was breath-
taking. Gio was now a star. The following images with
him handing the necklace to Nina had been marketing
gold.

Matt sat down and swung his feet up onto his desk,
which made Maya tut, but he ignored her. This was his
domain, even though she was now his biggest client.

'The issue might be that Gio will be pretty wealthy soon
and people have preyed on him on for his gentle nature
before,' said Maya with a frown. She had thought of this
previously, but her urge to help him had outweighed it.
Now the gnawing worry was back. Maya settled back into
her own seat, watching the press mentions of her brand and
Gio, on the screen of Matt's computer.

'A bit like Blake did with you,' added Leah, making
Maya wince and Matt give her a censorious look.

'He's suddenly a lot more interested in me now he
thinks my connections are worth having,' admitted Maya
after a short pause. 'He's been texting me.'

'I hope you haven't responded!' said Leah, appalled.

'Of course not! I've ignored his calls as well.'

'Block him,' suggested Matt pragmatically and Leah
frowned about why she hadn't already done this.

'Back to Gio,' she said quickly, pointing to the image of
him on the screen to distract them both. She knew Leah
would have more questions later, but for now she was
letting the subject go.

'We don't want to overwhelm him before he's ready and
it's a change of a career path for him, but one he's happy to
follow, it seems,' said Matt, clicking his own mouse and

checking the latest booking requests for Gio and Nina, on his computer.

'He's already talking about moving into a small flat in the centre of town near to where Penny lives. By next year he'll probably be able to afford his own place if he invests wisely,' commented Leah with a laugh, brushing biscuit crumbs from her work trousers and checking the time and video feed of her shop. 'He's totally gorgeous,' she said again, fanning her face and pretending to swoon, until Matt poked her in the ribs and she yelped and jumped away.

'He's going to be swamped with fans wanting to get to know him now, but we're used to that for our models now,' added Maya. Matt raised an eyebrow because hardened fans from out of town still squealed and ran over to get his signature when they saw the original No. 1 Ethereal Lane model. It was just the locals who left him alone, outside of that he was quite well known. Maya pulled a face and stuck her tongue out at him. Maya knew he secretly enjoyed the attention, so he wasn't complaining. He was a bit of a peacock, but she loved that about him. Leah was always grumbling that he took more time to get ready than she did, which made Maya smile.

'At least Gio is smiling every day now and he has an extra spring in his step,' said Maya. 'It's good to see him grow in confidence. There's no way he'd date a guy like his ex now. He knows his own worth.'

'You can't help everyone, but you can help me' said Matt, batting his eyelashes at them, as he always did when he wanted a cup of coffee and was too lazy to get it himself.

'I know...' responded Maya, 'but I can help a few and you can get your own coffee, lazybones.'

'So...' said Matt, changing the subject because he clearly wasn't getting any coffee and Maya knew she couldn't put off this conversation any longer. 'How was your weekend with our resident film star?'

Maya smiled a secret smile and Leah squealed and jumped up and down, clapping her hands. 'When are we going to meet him properly?'

'I don't know,' said Maya, her hands suddenly feeling clammy, as this was something she'd thought about a lot recently. 'Romy wants to meet him and we talk most nights about how we are both getting on, but she's as busy as I am. Her tea boat is taking off and she works on her own, so I need to visit her there, but Noah would cause chaos if he tried to step aboard.'

'That I'd like to see,' joked Leah and Maya sent back a sarcastic smile.

'The reason we haven't all met up is just as much Romy's fault as mine. Arthur wasn't impressed when I mentioned my new boyfriend, either.'

'How come?'

'Ever the protective brother, he'd read the stories in the papers and had his own questions about Noah's character.' Leah didn't seem that surprised by this and Matt didn't either. Arthur was usually pretty easygoing, but not when it came to the happiness of his sisters where he became a bit growly if he wasn't impressed. He was definitely still dating other women to get over Joe and Olive's granddaughter, Daisy, who he'd been in a relationship with for a while, but then pushed her away when even bigger feelings had become involved. That was his own stupid fault because he'd run away from commitment with her as soon as she'd become serious about him. Then she'd met her husband, had a baby, and the rest was history because he'd persuaded her to move to France. Maya didn't like Daisy's husband,

Harrison – at all - but luckily, Maya didn't have to live with him.

Now her friends and family wanted to meet Noah. She'd made the pact to shut them up, but in a way, it had made matters worse because nothing was real and now she was scared that she wanted it to be. Spending the night with him had changed everything for her, because however much she'd joked to Leah about being able to 'love them and leave them' it had been a lot harder than she'd expected to pretend to Noah that this was just a convenient fling for her. The words he'd said in the throes of passion that she was his, hadn't been mentioned again. He probably didn't even remember saying it.

'Gran and grandad want to meet him too,' Maya explained, 'except they think he's my actual boyfriend and now I'm worrying they might scare him off with their over the top behaviour,' she added, anguish showing on her face. Noah had sneaked into her thoughts when she was working and her work had become softer and more fluid somehow. She didn't want another man to influence her work, and the idea of letting her barriers down again terrified her, so she definitely wouldn't be doing that. It was easier to be alone than vulnerable, she decided.

'But surely it's not as fake as it was...' asked Leah with a frown. 'You're starting to like your new 'fling' aren't you?.' She looked at her best friend shrewdly and Maya couldn't quite meet her eyes. 'You spent the entire weekend there and met his parents!'

'That was an accident, and it scared the hell out of him,' sighed Maya. 'I ended up asking them to visit again soon, even though he's not my actual boyfriend and I had no right to invite anyone to his house!'

'Eek!' winced Leah, but she was trying not to laugh.

Matt shook his head and sat back in his chair, regarding her thoughtfully.

'I guess we'll see how good an actor he is when he meets your family... Ouch!' he said when Leah jabbed him in the ribs. She gave him a fiery look, and he held his hands up in surrender. 'Sorry, Maya,' he added, 'but you're the one who said this was all make believe.'

'Why are men so stupid?' asked Leah as she threw her hands up and grabbed Maya's arm to make her follow her back to the flower shop because a customer had just walked in. 'Sit there,' she motioned to a stool behind her wooden counter. 'Let me just serve this customer, then we will work this whole thing out.' Maya appreciated the gesture, but while Leah was busy behind arms full of tall pink and purple stock stems that filled the air with their heady scent, she slipped out of the front door and headed for home. She had to finish a jewellery commission and if she wanted to keep up the momentum and not fall flat on her face, she needed to forget hours of passion with a movie star and concentrate on continuing to build her brand. Maybe if she jumped fully into the role of pretend girlfriend and stopped stressing about feelings, then Noah could become a good friend. The problem was that they had already become lovers, and she'd never had a lover who simply reverted to being her friend. She'd always admired people who could do this, so maybe this time, her and Noah could come out of the other side of this mess unscathed...

Chapter Twenty

'I'll pick you up at eight o'clock when it's getting dark. Wear black,' she added and a secret smile lit Maya's face.

'Wear black?' Noah chuckled, and she loved the sound of his deep voice. 'Are we going to rob a bank?'

Maya grinned and her eyes sparkled. 'That's for me to know and for you to find out. I'm taking you on a date.' She didn't want them to be noticed because she'd seen from the press articles that going out with Noah could cause a furore. She'd asked Joe if she could borrow *Bertha* for an evening and she'd spent the day fizzing with excitement. They didn't run tours at night very often, as there wasn't much to see except the stars in the night sky! She'd already sorted out fairy lights, plump cushions and rugs that she'd found in a box of storage items under her rented house she guessed the owners used when they took their boat out. She'd made a picnic of crusty French bread, mature cheeses, pickles and she'd added a bottle of rich and fruity red wine.

In the end she'd called Leah and apologised for bolting out before they chatted about her dilemma with Noah. Her best friend had scolded her for ruining her first chance of some fun in years. It had made Maya realise she was still feeling the pressure from her family about having a proper relationship and had put unrealistic expectations on what was happening between her and Noah. She could spend time with him and not fall under the spell of those baby blue eyes, she'd decided, after giving herself a stern talking. She was a grown woman and the love pact idea between her and Noah could actually give them both space to breathe without the constraints of a relationship. That was the idea, anyway. It had made her hatch her plan to bring in some fun and to wine and dine her date, Maya style. She'd popped some Ragged Robin and Cuckooflower stems in a few jam jars and dotted their pink and lilac blooms around, which made the setting a bit too romantic, so she'd pared them back a little.

Since that night in his guesthouse, things *had* changed. She might be confused about what was for show and what was real, but was equally determined to enjoy the moment and not ruin it by overthinking. Noah was an attentive fake boyfriend and as the family party was coming up soon, her family wanted to meet him now that they knew he was on the radar. She'd put them off at the start by saying that she needed to get to know him herself, but they were all eagerly champing at the bit – except for Arthur. It surprised Maya that her gran hadn't turned up at his house and interrogated him yet, but she had spoken to him briefly on the phone a few times, and that had appeased her for now. After finally agreeing, they could all meet at the family party, the date was getting closer rather quickly!

Maya climbed aboard the boat and finished setting the scene for their date. Noah had mentioned that no one ever did anything nice for him, so she wanted to make him feel special, even if it was just as friends. She'd hung the fairy lights across the bar and set the rugs and cushions up on the floor, as she couldn't risk drawing attention to the fact that there was someone aboard as Alex and Luca would fly in to protect any of the boats if they were called by a worried neighbour who lived by the river.

When Noah jumped onto her boat and kissed her in welcome, her knees almost buckled, so she had to sit down and get on with guiding the boat back along the river, the slight wind whipping her hair around her face and making her eyes water. She steered past several other boats that were moored along this stretch of water and avoided the ever-present ducks and swans that floated up and down the waterways while they slept with their heads tucked under one wing. 'Are they actually asleep?' laughed Noah in surprise, clearly fascinated by the sight.

'Yes. It's safer here than on the river bed, unless they are nesting and protecting their eggs,' she smiled in response. 'It keeps them away from foxes and other predators.'

Noah was dressed simply in a fitted black jumper and black jeans, but her mouth salivated at the sight of him. His hair was slicked back and his eyes shone when he looked at her. He seemed happy to see her and excited about where they were going. He grinned when she pulled up by *Bertha* and used the torch on her phone to get them inside as swiftly as possible but putting her hands on his backside to help him up as he climbed on board via a rope ladder.

'Are you taking me somewhere dark to have your wicked way with me?' he chuckled as she hurried him towards the bar. He didn't look too scared at the prospect and her cheeks flushed in pleasure. She opened the door to the bar and his eyes went wide with wonder as he looked around at the snug paradise she'd created. 'You did this for me?' he stood stunned for a moment and then whisked her off her feet and swept her into his arms, with one hand going to the soft curve of her hip and the other to cup her face and bring her lips close to his. When he released her, flustered, she licked her lips and couldn't string a sentence together for a moment, so she stepped behind the bar to calm her racing heart and make them some drinks. The air sizzled with electricity and she felt shy suddenly. Being in an enclosed space with Noah was lethal as she couldn't seem to drag her gaze or her hands away from him and he clearly felt the same as he followed her behind the bar and began kissing the back of her neck and shoulders while she made the drinks, which sent goosebumps down her spine.

She turned round and handed him a drink, noticing that he had a wrapped parcel in one of his hands. He saw what she was looking at and grinned. 'I brought you a gift.'

'You didn't need to do that, but thank you! This date was supposed to be about you,' she said, her skin flushing.

'It's about us,' he said, handing her the gift. She untied the red ribbon and eased the beautiful floral printed wrapping away and folded it carefully before placing it on the bar. She shuffled backwards a step or two as she picked up her gift and held it tightly to her chest for a moment. It was a hardback book about all the plants that thrived around the riverbed. She flicked through the pages in awe, and then pulled him to her by grabbing a handful of his jumper and kissed him thoroughly. 'You like the gift then?' he laughed finally, tenderly brushing her hair out of her eyes with his fingers and then taking her hand and handing her a glass of the *Bertha* special, a strawberry gin and lemonade.

'I love it! It's so thoughtful,' she flushed, before kissing him again and then leading him to sit on the rugs and cushions she'd placed on the bar floor, alongside a wicker hamper full of tempting treats, like chocolate covered strawberries, fresh bread, mature cheese, chilli jam and black truffle crisps - although Noah himself was the most tempting of all to her. Her heart felt like it might burst with happiness and she wished she could bottle that feeling. No man had ever done anything as thoughtful for her before and she adored the beautiful book. She handed Noah a plateful of food and they ate while they chatted about their week and plans for the next couple of months.

'I've got a huge work party coming up that I'd love you to join me at. It's the year's biggest charity ball in my industry and my agent has reiterated that I have to be there on pain of death. The tickets are like gold dust.' Maya was intrigued and nodded, thinking that she'd happily attend with him without thinking of the consequences. 'I'm still excited to come to your family party. I hadn't forgotten. When is it?' he smiled, tasting one of the artisan breads and cheeses from the plate in front of him.

'When's yours?' she countered. He told her the date, and her mind raced through possibilities in a panic, as it clashed with that of her own family party. Oh hell! She cringed and then plastered a smile onto her face before he saw it.

'This ball is part of my working calendar, but it should be fun' reiterated Noah, his voice animated, his eyes shining in the moonlight. 'Dame Rosalie Alton is hosting and there will be an auction during the ball. She's donating a piece of original No.1 Ethereal Lane jewellery to a local museum and it's going up for auction. This brand has come out of nowhere recently and it's literally everywhere I look. It might be exciting to be part of that...' he hedged.

'Um... sounds great!' said Maya, her voice trembling slightly.

'Plus you already have a piece!' he remembered suddenly and Maya flinched. 'The one Tabitha pointed out. You really should keep the ring somewhere safe now,' he advised, 'it's value must have skyrocketed.'

Maya cleared her throat for a moment and then bit her lip while she thought about how to respond. 'Good idea,' she diverted. Maya had been commissioned to create a stunning waterfall necklace for Dame Rosalie to auction at her illustrious party - as Noah said, the ball of the year. Dame Rosalie was a household name, so when the request had come in, it had been impossible to refuse. Noah was working on his next film with Dame Rosalie and he'd told Maya before how much he was looking forward to it.

Blast, thought Maya. *This was getting complicated.* Maya already understood this ball was a tremendous deal to anyone with one of those precious golden tickets. It almost felt like an invitation to the Oscars. Dame Rosalie and Noah had worked together before, but he was headlining this film. Rosalie had a smaller part this time, but the press adored her and most of the film articles were about her and not the movie. Maya wondered how Noah felt about that, but he didn't seem to mind. She'd spent months working on Rosalie's necklace and she was quite a character, so it had been fun to delve into her life for a while, but the work had been gruelling.

'I'd love to join you,' said Maya, without as much gusto as she'd have liked and Noah smiled and took her hand, turning it over and kissing her wrist.

'You don't sound too sure,' he noted. 'Will it bother you if our photo gets into the press? There will be photographers and journalists there. I know we've avoided it so far because you're shy and hate having your photo taken, although I don't know why because you're beautiful,' he complimented and she softened a little. 'They can't stand me, but I try not to let it bother me too much.' She wanted to ease the frown lines from his brow, but nibbled on a bit of bread instead.

'Journalists don't hate you at all! They adore you. One newspaper writes trash and we both know why that is.' She looked at his imploring eyes and her heart melted. Could she face being splashed all over the front pages for him? She tried to calm her breathing and decided that she could. 'I'll come with you.'

Noah pulled her into his arms so that the food was soon forgotten. In the end, they took the rug and blankets outside and Maya rested her head on his arm and snuggled into his side while they watched the stars twinkle in the inky night sky. She put off mentioning her family party again because talking about that would now have to wait, so she gave him a fake date, which was ironic, and made her grin to herself for a moment. She wouldn't have let Noah go to such an important night in his life alone when he wanted her by his side. A warm feeling spread through her body and she decided that she'd do almost anything for this man, even if it meant her family was grumpy for a while and even if they just ended up as friends.

After a while she leaned up on one arm and looked at him. 'Tabitha called me,' said Maya regretfully. 'She keeps asking me out for coffee and seems quite insistent. Blake's been texting me lately too,' she added quietly. 'He wants me to meet him to talk about our past and to try to be friends again.'

Noah frowned and grew serious, sitting up and turning to face her. 'Is that something you want?' He didn't look happy, but there wasn't much she could do about that and she kind of liked the feeling that it riled him a little.

'No. Not at all! Blake is my past. He doesn't have a place in my future.' She was resolute on this. Noah's shoulders relaxed and then leaned in to kiss her gently on the mouth. The problem was that this felt more like a proper date and they hadn't spoken about their conversation in the guesthouse since, probably because they both realised it was a tricky topic. For now they were friends who were still fake-dating it seemed but her feelings for Noah were becoming more muddled by the day.

'Does it matter to you either way?' she asked. 'I'm still unsure about what your intentions are,' she said bravely... 'well I have an idea, but I'm not sure.'

'Can we drop the fake date bit and just date?' he asked, taking her hand and gently kissing his way up her arm, making her skin heat to a million degrees.

Noah pulled her onto his lap and wound his arms around her, his hands slipping up and under her black shirt and touching naked skin. She shivered, but not with the cold and his lips captured hers and plundered them until they were plump and glossy. She ran her own hands over his hard muscles and almost forgot where they were. When he released his arms and she leaned back to look into his eyes with her own glazed ones, he grinned wolfishly and kissed her once again. 'Does that make it clear how I feel?' he asked. She nodded and leant in for another searing kiss, her hands snaking into his hair to pull him closer. He groaned and pulled her so that she was straddling him, deepening their kiss and squirming on his lap so that he had to take hold of her hips, or lose control. She felt like rockets full of glitter were exploding in her brain and she had to pull back to keep hold of her sanity. This man would be her undoing. 'I think we'd better take this back indoors before anyone sees us,' she said shakily, taking his warm hand and guiding him back into the bar, where he swung her up onto the bar, kissing her again, leaving her breathless.

'I was unsure what your situation was with Blake,' he said as he linked his arms behind her waist and dipped his head to steal one more kiss, before setting her back on her feet. 'Is what you had really over?' he asked. 'You said he broke your heart and that scares me a little.'

Maya took his hand and leaned her hip against the bar, mirroring him. 'I got over my heartbreak when I met you,' she looked up at him and his featured softened suddenly.

'Whatever was going on at my garden party seemed pretty intense from what I could understand, and the way he couldn't take his eyes off of you made me feel cautious,' he admitted bashfully, snuggling her under his arm protectively. 'Sorry.'

'Cautious or jealous?' she asked gently.

'Both I guess,' he admitted truthfully. 'I didn't want to end up with my own broken heart.'

Maya moved behind the bar again to pour them both a glass of light and fruity Pinot Noir wine and to stop herself from fainting with shock at Noah's admission. She needed sustenance after being so close to Noah and after talking about Blake. Noah had been jealous and thought she had the power to break his heart! She tried to still her beating heart. Would every significant moment in her life be over-shadowed by Blake, though? She handed Noah the glass of wine and enjoyed the frisson of heat shooting up her spine as their hands touched again. He sat on the freshly uphol-stered velvet banquet seating that Maya had bought and patted the seat next to him for her to move closer. She shuf-fled until their thighs were touching and he put his hand on her leg, as she turned to face him. 'I'm not so mad about you being jealous,' she smiled shyly. 'Blake hasn't been part of my life for a long time. Any feeling I had for him died the day I found him in our bed with Portia.'

'Portia?' Noah frowned. 'I didn't realise the full extent of her involvement. I'm sorry.' Maya brushed her hair out of her eyes, burning with embarrassment suddenly. Maya felt uneasy about the fact that both Blake and Portia floated in the same circles as Noah, but she couldn't do anything about that.

'I really don't know them that well,' Noah said, as if reading her mind. 'I only met them recently. Portia knows Tabitha from a photo shoot they did together last year.' Well, that explained a lot, seethed Maya. She already knew that Tabitha wasn't her type of friend, or acquaintance, so she wasn't planning on inviting her round for dinner anytime soon.

'Blake and I met at art school and then ran a jewellery design business together for a while, but it didn't work out. Portia was one of our models – that's how they met.' Maya tried to gloss over the subject and move on.

'I didn't know you used to design jewellery,' said Noah, interest sparking in his eyes. 'Blake's current brand is pretty popular now, so that must have been awful timing. Maybe I misjudged him if he treated you like that. What an idiot!' he ground out angrily.

Maya quite liked Noah's protective streak but talking about Blake always exhausted her. 'I can't disagree. He's done well since we split up and thankfully he's not a part of my life now,' she sincerely hoped that was true.

She made a quick decision and finally confided in him about what she'd heard Tabitha and her cronies talking about at the garden party. 'She mentioned being annoyed about the public being let in.' She smiled as she could almost see the steam coming out of Noah's ears.

'That's outrageous! How dare she make you feel like an uninvited interloper when you were the guest of honour!' he fumed.

'It's ok,' said Maya holding her hands up and placing one on his chest to calm him. 'I can stand up for myself,' she assured him.

'I told her privately in no uncertain terms that we were dating now and that she had to back off,' growled Noah protectively.

'She's so desperate to be my friend to find out how I got my No. 1 Ethereal Lane ring that she's actually being nice to me now,' chuckled Maya, finally lightening the mood once more. 'She keeps asking me out shopping.' Maya scoffed at how ridiculous the thought of her and Tabitha ever being friends was.

'How did you get the ring?' he asked, linking her fingers with his. She fleetingly thought about telling him the truth that she'd made it, but the mystery around the designer's identity was still rife and she'd trusted and been burnt before. He saw her hesitation and backed off. 'You don't have to tell me.'

'It's okay - Matt gave it to me,' when he paused and rubbed his jaw, his eyes darkened in distrust because he'd already seen them out alone for the birthday meal. She gently reassured him. 'I don't know if you would have seen it in the press, but Matt was the first No. 1 Ethereal Lane model.' She could see the cogs in Noah's brain whirring and the moment when he pictured the billboards with Matt's face on them. 'The jewellery brand had given Matt the ring as part payment for modelling in their first campaign, before the company knew how stratospheric their rise would be in such a brief space of time.'

'You're wondering why he gave such a valuable piece to

me and not Leah?' she smiled at Noah's look of concern and confusion. 'We were friends long before either of us knew Leah. We both grew up here. I actually introduced them. I spotted the job opportunity for him and it was his way of saying thank you for launching his career.'

'You found the first No. 1 Ethereal Lane model and got him the job?' he asked incredulously. 'Bloody hell! Tabitha has just hit a goldmine of information. Never tell her that. She's at all of my work events and meetings and is even trying to be nice to me at the moment because she's dating our producer, Corey. It happened the day after I told her about us. She's acting like we're the best of friends, but it feels like just another way to interfere in my life.' He shook his head in wonder, but didn't look like he trusted Tabitha any more than he had before as his tone was wary when he spoke about her.

'Try not to worry about Tabitha,' she reassured. It felt weird for her to be talking about her actual business with someone other than her tiny team of confidants. She wished she didn't have such trust issues, but was trying to overcome them. Blake had a lot to answer for, but perhaps she'd been over cautious? 'Anyway,' she continued, 'the combination with gorgeous Matt...' she leaned back and fanned her face in jest and Noah rolled his eyes and slid his hand further up her leg to make her skin sizzle and the teasing stop about the fact that he'd thought she fancied Matt. She cleared her throat shakily and continued. 'The brand was dynamite and Matt has become a household name. Hence, he gave me the ring.'

'Wow!' said Noah in a stunned voice. He reached across her and selected a fresh chocolate dipped strawberry from a bowl that she'd placed on the table earlier. He held it tantalisingly, just above her lips and she reached out and took a bite, the sweet juices and tangy flesh filling her mouth and making her groan. She was about to pick one for him, but he pulled her onto his lap instead and she instantly forgot all about work and her mind filled with the delicious man beneath her thighs.

'I think my girlfriend and I should definitely christen the boat in our own way,' he said in a low voice, and his hands ran even higher up her legs as they tumbled together onto the floor and he pushed the fabric of her skirt up to her waist. The last coherent thought she had before she reached for the waistband of his jeans and slipped them from his hips, was that exceptionally hot man in her arms had just called her his girlfriend.

Chapter Twenty-One

Maya was still on cloud nine after that incredible night with Noah and she must have been a bit giddy because she'd finally agreed to meet Tabitha and decided that maybe she wasn't as bad as Maya had first thought because there hadn't been any malicious stories about Noah in the press since the garden party, so perhaps their plan had worked and she was happy with Corey? Tabitha was part of Noah's next film and if Maya could do anything to ease the path to them getting along as colleagues, she would. Maybe they could all get along one day...

Meeting up with Noah was always like planning an MI5 operation and although she understood needing privacy almost better than he did, it was a bit tiring not to be able to wander into a café for a coffee, or to stroll along with someone you fancied, holding hands and staring into each other's eyes. If they did that, a photographer would probably jump out of the bushes pointing his camera their way - like they had after their date night at the flower restaurant, which had almost given them a coronary. Venturing out in public meant the simplest things, like the flavour of ice cream he'd chosen, becoming headline news, which seemed extraordinary, but at least the interest in his love life seemed to have eased off and the photographer had kept his promise not to print the photos of them at her door - so far. Apparently, Noah had given him an exclusive about his upcoming film instead and that had appeased him, but the photos were still out there, which worried her. Maya knew Noah loved his career and didn't mind the press interest because it had made him a household name and he was grateful, but she saw his mask slip and how tiring it was for him occasionally.

Tabitha had insisted that they meet at a beautifully lit bar in Mayfair, London, even though she clearly thought Maya didn't fit in with her own A-list crowd. The bar felt luxurious with dark tones of blue and smoky grey on the plush velvet seating and granite bar. There was soft music playing in the background and the hum of conversation filled the air. Maya plastered on a smile as Tabitha approached and kissed her on both cheeks, almost asphyxiating Maya with her strong perfume. Maya coughed and tried to gulp in some air into her tight airways, her eyes watering.

Tabitha was wearing sunglasses even though it was dark inside the bar and not that sunny outside either! Maya shook her head in wonder. No one was paying them the slightest bit of attention. Tabitha stood out more for wearing the sunglasses, but maybe that was her intention. Tabitha was better known for who she dated than her actual body of work as an up-and-coming actress. She'd been photographed with Noah a few times recently, but only in groups. Maya got the vibe that wasn't Tabitha's choice, though.

'Thanks for inviting me out,' said Maya, hoping to keep the topics neutral.

'I thought it would be good if we could be friends,' said Tabitha with her lips drawn into a tight line as if she couldn't quite bring herself to smile. Considering Tabitha was an actress, Maya didn't believe a word she said.

'Um... Okay,' replied Maya. She had enough friends thanks, but it intrigued her at what angle Tabitha would try to pretend to want to get to know her. She clearly did not know that Maya had overheard her conversation at the garden party.

'I wanted to ask you where you got that divine ring I saw at Noah's party,' she ruthlessly cut straight in. Tabitha didn't look at her while she asked this and waggled her hand in the air, trying to catch the bartender's attention, finally taking her sunglasses off. Maya groaned inwardly. She'd hoped that Tabitha would have forgotten about that by now.

'A friend gave it to me a long time ago,' she said simply, hoping that was the end of that line of conversation.

'Ah,' said Tabitha, looking her up and down again and taking in her slim fitting jeans and neutral jumper with a textured pattern, which was quite tame for Maya's usual taste. 'I wondered how it came into your possession.' A light came into her eyes and she leaned in conspiratorially as the waiter brought them both a tall glass of champagne. Maya took the drink, but caught the arm of the waiter and ordered a caramel latte. She needed caffeine if this meet-up carried on this way. 'I know that there aren't many rings out there and I'm pretty clued up on that brand because it's so current and it's absolutely the hottest thing to own right now,' Tabitha confided, eyeing Maya's unbranded black purse that she'd left on the bar, with disdain, before Maya quickly tucked it on her lap. 'No.1 Ethereal Lane is my absolute favourite and I know they sell out quickly. I thought I'd have heard about this piece on social media. As soon as they release images of their next product being delivered by one of their divine models, it's absolutely everywhere, but no one can buy it because it's already sold,' she studied Maya and sipped her champagne, smiling sweetly and waiting for a reply. When Maya didn't respond, she frowned and rubbed an imaginary chip on her perfect manicure. 'Who donated it to you?' she asked, emphasising the word donate. Her rudeness astounded Maya, but she let it go. 'I think they must have a team of public relations specialists working with the designer by how popular they are. It wouldn't surprise me if a brand like Prada or Gucci were behind it. The marketing is genius,' she added, tapping her long red glossy nails on the bar and waiting for Maya to divulge her contact.

'As I said... a friend,' she didn't elaborate, but loved the fact that Tabitha had just compared her tiny little company to some absolute powerhouses in the industry. 'It *is* a lovely piece of jewellery.'

'It's divine!' hissed Tabitha quietly, as if the ears had walls. 'I'd happily buy it from you, you know. It's worth a good amount of money,' she patted Maya's hand patronisingly. 'You probably didn't realise,' she simpered. 'I'd give you a fair price. Perhaps you could do with a little extra cash right now?' She glanced at the purse again. *That purse was vintage!* Maya seethed.

Maya paused as the barman handed her a sweet smelling coffee and she blew on it to cool it down before sipping it and enjoying the sugar and caffeine hit. She needed it to get through this drivel. She tried not to laugh at Tabitha's earnest expression, as if she was doing her the biggest favour of relieving her of a world-renowned piece of jewellery. 'What makes you say that?' she asked, warming her suddenly icy hands on the tall coffee glass. Tabitha giggled and glanced around conspiratorially.

'Well... you seem to have your sights set on Noah. You know he's quite a catch?' When Maya tried to speak, Tabitha spoke over her. 'You'll need new clothes and honestly a lot of pampering,' She eyed Maya's soft wavy hair and un-manicured nails with a shudder and gave her a false smile. Maya pictured herself trying to create her master-pieces with huge fake nails and almost burnt her tongue on her drink. She felt her eyes water and put it back down to keep cooling. 'Running in those types of circles can be expensive. Our friendship group is pretty tight and we don't get newbies very often, so I'm helping you to fit in now we're best friends.' She took Maya's hand in her own and then suddenly let it go, which almost knocked her off of her tall bar stool.

'Um... I'm sorry, but it's a sentimental gift, and it's not for sale.'

Tabitha's brow creased, and she put her own almost empty drink down. 'But you work on that big *old* boat that sits near Noah's house and paint little pictures, don't you?' She said the world old as if it meant poor *Bertha* was well past her best and useless, when in fact she was looking better than ever and had customers clamouring to steam up and down the river on her. Maya felt her hackles rise in indignation on *Bertha*'s behalf. 'Noah said you sell your pictures from a local café, downstream from his house.' Her brow furrowed in confusion. 'Surely selling the ring will help? We can go shopping and buy you some new clothes.' Tabitha's own style would have fitted perfectly into Blake and Portia's world of glitz and glamour. She was wearing a white heavily branded blouse with an oversized collar that had a weird sheen to it and skin-tight black trousers that made Maya wince because they were a tad too tight on Tabitha's svelte frame. She had a pearl emblazoned blazer with her and a handbag that was probably worth more than the ring. It gave the overall impression to Maya that she could afford the brands but actually did not know how to put them together. Ettie would have a field day with a client like Tabitha. Maya's own outfit was vintage Levi jeans and a gorgeously soft cream jumper that her grandmother had made, that she knew complimented her big brown eyes and sooty lashes.

'Noah and I dated recently,' said Tabitha gravely. 'You know that?'

'I do,' said Maya firmly, finishing her coffee and picking up her champagne again, enjoying the pop of the bubbles on her tongue.

'I think that Noah and I might get back together,' Tabitha blurted out suddenly, trying to grab back Maya's attention as she was checking the time on her phone. 'He's on the rebound.'

'That's between you and Noah, but he and I are dating now... you know that?' she asked Tabitha.

'I think he's doing that to make me jealous,' Tabitha said cattily. 'Sorry to have to be the one to tell you,' she soothed afterwards. 'Does that change things for you? It is still early days if you want to find someone more... available.' Tabitha eyed Maya steadily, but she didn't flinch. She'd dealt with her own share of bullies when she'd had to move home to live with her grandparents when her parents were in a different country. Kids found any way to tease her about the fact that she'd been abandoned, even though she knew her parents were coming back. It had created an unbreakable bond between her, Arthur and Romy and they'd navigated school life and their teenage years together and been each other's best friends, but she did worry that it had scared her younger siblings out of any long term commitment. Both of their love lives were as much a mess as hers was!

Romy had ignored the name calling and Arthur had gotten into a few fights, but sensitive Maya had stuck her head in a book and isolated herself. She found that easier than trying to make friends with people who found her and her family odd. She herself found them to be completely bonkers, but she loved them and was fiercely protective of every one of them. Woe betide anyone who tried to hurt someone she loved. Maya's eyes narrowed in on Tabitha and although she didn't know if Noah was in that category yet, she certainly cared enough about him to want to help where Tabitha was concerned. But what could she do?

She stopped herself from rolling her eyes and instead took another quick peek at the time on her phone. Noah had told her about Tabitha's obsession with his life, but it was weird to see it firsthand. Maya had had her own heart broken, so she had wanted to see for herself that she wasn't stepping on anyone's toes. From what she could tell, Tabitha was looking for status and not love.

'I don't think so,' said Maya honestly, but Tabitha just stared at her with sympathy on her face. 'But thanks for being such a good friend and letting me know...'

'Oh, bless you! Well, we'll see, shan't we? Noah and I are pretty close and you know our next film features Dame Rosalie Alton? Newspapers hound us for stories about our lives. The press tend to put co-stars together in lots of crazy stories, so try not to worry if you see us together.' Maya held her tongue because Tabitha had a bit part and wasn't Noah's co-star and most of the momentum for this new film hadn't built so far. Maya hadn't noticed Tabitha in any of the stories she had seen, so she hoped that wasn't a trigger for her to misbehave. 'Will you not reconsider about the ring?' Tabitha asked again. 'Re-sales can generate a lot of publicity and we could push the article to be about your art as well.'

'You couldn't guarantee that,' said Maya and Tabitha, laughed, a high-pitched tinkly sound that grated on Maya's nerves. Tabitha signalled for the bill but left it on the side, which didn't surprise Maya. She handed her credit card to the barman, and he gave her a look of sympathy. Maya guessed Tabitha and 'friends' were regulars there.

'Oh, but I can! I have a *friend* in the press who is obsessed with me and he publishes anything I tell him to,' she said with a warning tone and Maya's blood ran cold. This was how she was manipulating the stories about Noah. She immediately thought of the power of a story uncovering the designer behind No.1 Ethereal Lane and knew she had to tread carefully or get burnt like Noah had. Maya intended to reveal her identity at one point, but her brand was so high profile now, that it was a bit late for her to say, 'Hi, it's me!' and then explain that she pretty much ran her exclusive business from a laptop and a drew her designs from a bench on a steamboat called *Bertha*. At the moment, the mystery surrounding her was part of why there was so much intrigue and speculation flying around. This, in turn, brought more articles and posts and a wealth of customers buying her jewellery. Her identity, or where she worked, being exposed could bring this all crashing down around her and that wasn't something Maya was willing to risk.

'The ring isn't for sale,' said Maya carefully, finally seeing that Tabitha was actually quite a dangerous person to get on the wrong side of. 'If I change my mind, you'll be the first person I tell, though,' she added quickly, and this seemed to appease Tabitha for now.

'I really think it would be in your best interests to think about selling,' Tabitha said through gritted teeth. 'I'd hate it if negative press stories circulated about that big clunky steamboat Noah said your family run...'

'My grandad's best friend runs it,' said Maya, pressing her nails into her palms to stop herself from jumping to *Bertha*'s defence. There was no way she wanted to bring Tabitha's wrath onto Joe and Olive when they'd just gotten back on their feet. 'But you're right, maybe I should rethink about how important the ring is to me,' she added, ice dripping from her tone. No one had ever threatened her family before, but it wasn't something she'd stand for and Tabitha would soon learn about stamping onto a snake and getting a fang in the calf, if she thought she could simply throw that grenade into the mix and walk away unscathed.

'Why don't you put your name down on the waiting list for a No.1 Ethereal Lane piece? I've heard they are worth the wait,' she smiled, her bones feeling heavy suddenly, and all she could picture was her own comfy bed. She'd spent much more time than she'd expected speaking to Noah on the phone or in his bed. She couldn't seem to get enough of his company, but she needed to back off a bit for her own sanity and to protect her heart. The problem was that she feared it was already too late.

'I've just got on the list,' said Tabitha as if she was a complete moron, 'but it could be years before my name reaches the top.'

'Ah... sorry. I know little about that,' apologised Maya wearily, wondering why she'd been so stupid as to let Tabitha sign up. She'd thought it would stop her asking about the ring, but it seemed not.

'Clearly,' said Tabitha, draining the dregs of her glass and picking up her bag to leave. 'Maybe I should take a leaf out of Noah's book and buy a piece of your art from that café with the blonde server. Although I ate there the other day and got an upset stomach. I've been looking at a way to support the local community now we'll be here filming for a while, but I should let my colleagues know to steer clear of that place.'

Maya's body froze at the veiled threat to her friend Penny's reputation, too. 'That's so generous of you, but they are currently sold out,' said Maya with relief, purposely not saying anything about the clearly false food comment in case it let Tabitha know she cared about Riverside and its proprietor.

Tabitha tutted and pulled on her blazer. 'If I ever decide to go for a *private* river tour on that steamboat, I hope the service is better than that of the café,' smiled Tabitha evilly, emphasising the word private and watching Maya like a hawk regarding its prey. Maya gulped and wondered how she knew that she'd had a private boat date with Noah. 'Noah and I might be having a break from dating, but we are dear friends now and I'm important to him and he confides in me, even if he pretends he doesn't,' she lifted her chin in challenge and Maya frowned. 'How serious are you?' Tabitha demanded to know.

'Quite serious.'

'Hmm. Well, I'm sure Noah would be happy if you helped me to find out more about No. 1 Ethereal Lane,' Tabitha added. 'How do you know Blake? I saw you talking to him at the party. I bet Portia would like to know about that,' she said spitefully, watching Maya carefully again and Maya felt a trickle of sweat run down her spine.

'I don't know him very well.' This was true because she

hadn't seen him for almost two years before the garden party ambush.

'Hmm,' said Tabitha, not sounding convinced. 'The producers of the film Noah and I are starring in have been talking about trying to get a piece of No.1 Ethereal Lane jewellery for the set to generate more press coverage for the film.'

Maya let the star of the film remark fall off target, as it couldn't be further from the truth, but she felt her stomach sinking. 'Um... that's not something I would know much about.'

'It's already a hugely anticipated project, but a collaboration like that would make it stratospheric. Think of the press coverage that a person might get by finding the designer! It could make someone like Noah's career.'

Maya's stomach somersaulted. Noah needed nothing like that, surely? 'He's more than famous already,' she defended.

'You can never be too famous, darling,' Tabitha said with a tinkling laugh as she put her hand on Maya's arm. 'Poor Noah is under so much pressure from our bosses to bring in the bucks. These films cost millions, and this is his biggest project yet. There's a lot of expectation on his shoulders. He needs a smash hit.'

Maya just bit her lip and stayed silent. Tabitha was on a role now and carried on regardless. 'I guess if they can't persuade the No. 1 Ethereal Lane designer to join us for publicity, then they could ask Blake to design them something. He's always looking for an opportunity and surrounds himself with people who help his star quality shine,' she added bitchily, amused by her own insight. 'Maybe Noah could be the next No. 1 Ethereal lane model?' she added with glee at her own idea. 'That would be huge news!'

Maya felt bile rise in the back of her throat. When would she ever break free of her ex? Noah had spoken about the ball and the fact that Dame Rosalie was auctioning the No. 1 Ethereal Lane waterfall necklace. Were they going to use that for publicity for the film somehow? She cursed under her breath and was glad when Tabitha took a call on her phone and waved to Maya that it was private and she should go.

Chapter Twenty-Two

Maya touched the detailed crystal she'd just shaped and blew out a sigh of relief. She'd been working on a new idea for a while and it was gradually coming together. It was called ice cave, and it comprised delicate layers of sculpted crystals, which looked like a necklace of intricate stalactites hanging around the wearer's neck. They reflected light from any angle and it looked like water was dancing across the surface of each crystal. It took five layers of the finest crystals to form one necklace, but the result was breath-taking.

The alarm pealed on her phone and she swiftly put the necklace on its pedestal with practised hands and then into her safe. She made sure she had a fresh mug of coffee from the posh machine in her office and then closed the windows and put the air conditioning on. No one would ever hear her clients' conversations, but she closed the tall windows to the balcony and side windows just in case.

She felt nervous and excited about this client meeting because Robbie was becoming a friend now with playful phone calls to see how his 'soul mate' was doing and he'd told her more about Amethyst being a big part of his history. She loved visiting Noah's house and hoped she could ease the way for him and his parents to see each other more, as she felt that was the crux of the problem of their miscommunication issues. Her own family grabbed any visitors in for a hug and assumed everyone else was like them, but Noah's family was more reserved. Perhaps they'd learnt to be that way because of his career and the stories in the press too, though? It must be hard for them to know who to trust, mused Maya. Noah had said they were cold and unwelcoming, but when Maya had met them, she thought they were friendly and curious, not judgemental. They just missed their son.

She guessed outsiders might think her own parents were unusual, for leaving three teenagers with their parents, but their grandparents cared for Maya, Romy and Arthur and they'd never felt unloved or disapproved of. The wild gardens and glasshouses they'd had the freedom to roam around, had given flight to their imaginations and instilled a sense of adventure. Their grandad spent his days walking in and out of the huge Victorian glasshouses with arms full of Frangipani plants with their knobbly bark, oblong green leaves and overlapping petals that were sometimes considered a symbol of immortality because the plant could flower and produce leaves even if uprooted. Her grandmother was often found sewing something or other, or baking, but whatever it was it was usually bright and beautiful, unless it was the biscuits that she enjoyed making in splodges.

Maya, Arthur and Romy's parents saved lives, and they were needed in crisis situations. Their children did fear for their safety occasionally, but regular online video calls and tales of who they had helped eased the way. It wouldn't have worked for everyone, but it did for them. Maya had never experienced her parents criticising her choices, so that must be hard to bear by Noah, especially when his choices had fulfilled his dreams. She couldn't imagine anyone not loving Noah... she froze for a second and then gulped down some hot coffee, making her splutter and quickly grab a tissue to dab her mouth. So much for a serene start to her meeting!

She felt nervous and excited about this one because Robbie and Noah spoke about Amethyst, her next client, often. Maya had bumped Amethyst up on her client list. She'd never done that before as he meticulously planned everything, but Maya was curious about the woman who clearly still held Robbie's heart in her hands, even though he was too stubborn to see it.

Maya grinned as she changed into a funky green textured dress from the little wardrobe that was built into an alcove by the upstairs bathroom, as her clients never actually saw her face. She still liked to feel that she'd presented herself professionally, and she worried that one day someone would finally see her sitting there through a computer glitch or something, and if she was half-naked, or in her dressing gown, they'd get one hell of a shock! It had become a habit, and she tried to ignore the fact that she was being ridiculous.

Gio had been back to the art group on *Bertha* earlier in the week, and it was as if a rock star had arrived. He was metamorphosing into a confident young man and it looked like he might also be ready to open his heart again by the way he had blushed when he'd seen Bobby and a little bird had told Maya that he'd plucked up the courage to offer Bobby the spare room in his new rented flat. Gio had hugged Maya with excitement and spent most of the session telling them about his new life while they'd sat around in rapt attention. It had been weird for Maya to find out what the effects of her work were in person, but her heart filled with pride and she was glad it hadn't impacted negatively on her friend. Gio had stood next to her at the coffee break time and had hugged her and swung her around and around until she'd squealed and asked him to put her down, which he did with a swift kiss to her cheek and a flushed face.

'How are you coping with your newfound fame?' she'd teased him and he'd grinned shyly and then stood taller.

'It was scary at first,' he'd admitted 'but with every day I'm more thankful for my guardian angel, because I still can't work out why a high-profile brand chose me,' he'd added as he'd scratched his head and shrugged in wonder, then rushed away to get the space alongside Bobby and start unpacking his extra art supplies and fresh canvas.

Maya straightened her notes next to her computer screen and clicked the link to begin the video call to Amethyst. Adrenaline buzzed through her veins and for a second she had the fleeting thought that perhaps she shouldn't interfere in the love lives of her friends, but she didn't have time to dwell on it as Amethyst's smiling face filled the screen and the conversation began.

'Hello Amethyst,' said Maya, with a smile about how excited Amethyst looked. Some of her clients were too affluent to be excited by a piece of jewellery, but many couldn't wait to work with her. The computer changed Maya's voice so no one would recognise her that way. Maya sent up a brief prayer of thanks to her little brother, Arthur, for his tech skills.

'This is so weird!' exclaimed Amethyst. 'I knew I wouldn't see your face. The logo screen, although beautiful and full of enticing images of your designs that I wished I owned, is surreal. I've done nothing like this before.'

'It is a bit like a blind date,' said Maya thoughtfully, and Amethyst burst out laughing, easing some of the initial tension.

'Exactly! I can't tell if you're a man or a woman, but I'm guessing that's the point?' she asked.

'Sorry about that,' said Maya. 'It's part of the company ethos, but I can understand it must seem strange.'

'It's ok,' said Amethyst. 'It's amazing how quickly I'm getting used to it. Okay...' she paused and then shrugged in delight.

'Tell me what you're looking for in your design?' Maya asked.

'It's the intricacy of the design that I love,' replied Amethyst and Maya's heart warmed with pride. 'I'm looking for something fluid and fairly small.'

'Something like this?' Maya responded as she navigated her screen and brought up a few samples of a smaller piece she'd begun working on. The delicate Fen Violet had caught Maya's eye recently because she knew the species was in decline because of the draining of wetland habitats. The leaves of the plant had been molded from sheets of white gold, and the wide pale petals and soft fluffy white stamens were represented in the tiniest diamonds and precious metals.

'Yes!' said Amethyst. 'Exactly that. I love the way the leaves almost look like they're protecting the ethereal flower,' she added and Maya had to stop what she was doing and regroup for a moment because Amethyst undoubtedly saw her vision as clearly as Maya did.

Maya spent the next hour getting to know Amethyst, and she'd spoken openly about the love of her life, which surprised Maya, even though she was clearly talking about Robbie. Someone who didn't know him might not have picked up on the nuances of what Amethyst said, but Maya was an artist and she noticed the smallest things. From the way she spoke about her past heartbreak, Maya could tell she was far from over him. Maya was already sketching two entwined hearts as the conversation ended and she knew without a doubt that these two were meant to be together. She wondered if she could incorporate two miniature hearts into her design, perhaps at the centre of the flower, she mused. She'd dropped in a few hints about being open with those you love and how misunderstandings can grow without communication and then steered the conversation to family and friends, hoping that the titbits she'd mentioned could at some point come back into Amethysts consciousness and that she might pick up the phone and give their mutual acquaintance, Robbie, a call. The meeting made Maya think about Blake again, especially after Tabitha had drawn him into their conversation as well. He'd been texting her again, and she'd actually answered twice because it had been about a few loose ends from them running a business together and one document she still hadn't signed. It was nothing important, but he wouldn't let it go for some reason. He hadn't been able to send her some copies of their paperwork because she'd pretended to disappear abroad, but now he wanted to meet. Signing the document severed all ties between them and made everything final. Bumping into him at Noah's garden party had shocked her to the core, because following his career on social media was one thing, but meeting in the flesh was entirely different. She'd felt nothing at the time, but when she'd arrived home, she'd gotten angry about his impertinent questions about her and Noah. She needed to sign the dratted document and get him out of her life forever.

Chapter Twenty-Three

Noah pulled his boat into the dock under Maya's house and waited for her to join him. Work was all-consuming lately because the movie he had coming up featured Dame Rosalie and she rightly demanded perfection from everyone, including him. Tabitha had been playing up and kept trying to upstage everyone, laughing out loud and touching his arm, or leg, whenever she thought anyone was looking, which was putting his nerves on edge. He kept bringing Maya into their conversations, but Tabitha acted as if they were best friends now and she'd told him more details about her drinks date with Maya than Maya had. Maya had been pretty dismissive and told him not to worry about anything, but he was sure Maya had never dealt with anyone like Tabitha before and his intuition told him she was up to something, even though he couldn't work out what it was. He hoped it didn't involve the film or Dame Rosalie, because that would risk all of their careers.

He might be a household name already, but Rosalie wanting to film with him again had made his year. Working with a legend like her was an absolute joy and a privilege. Rosalie was fierce and funny and he learnt so much from her every time they met. She was hosting a ball in a couple of weeks and Maya had agreed to be by his side, but she had been distant since her drinks with Tabitha. It was nothing he could put his finger on, but he'd thought that they had grown closer lately and dropped the fake relationship part. Maybe he'd been wrong?

He knew she didn't court publicity for her art, but being photographed on the red carpet for this event, which was about as exclusive a party as he had ever been to and he'd travelled all over the world, could help skyrocket her career because he wanted to help her any way he could. Her unassuming nature and beautiful smile had caught his heart, it seemed. Maya never judged him for his opulent and sometimes downright crazy lifestyle, which added to all the other reasons he wanted to see her as often as he could. He'd like to see her more, but they both had busy schedules right now and he worried that might be a problem in the future too.

When she didn't come out of her house or respond to his texts, he left his boat under her rented house and went in by the hidden door on the lower floor. A prickle of unease crept up his back, so he quickly pressed the buzzer and looked around, but it was dark and no-one was wandering by the Riverside café at that time of the evening. Recently, he'd been meeting Maya at night for movies, cocktails, occasional dinner at each other's houses and sleepovers whenever they could tally their diaries. They hadn't spoken about the status of their relationship recently and that troubled him slightly. He wanted a deeper emotional connection, but he could feel Maya holding back, which confused him and he feared that was because of Blake. She'd assured him she was over the man who broke her heart, but Noah wasn't sure that was the complete truth. He still seemed to have some kind of power over her, because she always changed the subject when Noah tried to find out more.

He'd already invested a lot into his relationship with Maya, but he needed her to reciprocate. She was distant at times, and he could sense an undercurrent of something that he didn't understand. It was as if she wanted to share things with him, but wouldn't let her guard down, which frustrated the hell out of him. This relationship had begun as fake, but his feelings were raw and real now and he feared she could crush his heart if he wasn't careful.

After officially dating for a while now, they hadn't had the exclusive talk yet, making his stomach crunch with tension, which was a new feeling for him with someone he was dating. It was driving him crazy, being near her so often now, but his job had made him guarded after being burnt a few times by press hungry women like Tabitha.

Maya opened the door and beckoned him inside, but she hadn't greeted him with a smile, so he immediately frowned and quickly went to see what was wrong. He was protective of her already, even though she was one of the most independent women he had ever met. She didn't seem to need much and never asked him for anything, which took some getting used to and actually put him on edge in case he was reading the signals wrong and he should do more. It was nice to feel needed and although he'd always felt claustrophobic in relationships before, he had recently had a lightbulb moment where he'd understood that he wanted some reassurance and enjoyed being able to do nice things for his partner. Now that he was in a genuine relationship with Maya, she was on his mind more and more, which he kind of liked. Noah missed her when she wasn't in his arms.

He followed her into the lounge and she stopped,

turned to face him, and finally smiled at him before she opened the door. He touched her arm to make her look his way. 'Are you okay?'

'Blake's here,' she grimaced and alarm bells began ringing in his head. Why was that a problem?

'Your ex, Blake?'

'Yes,' she sighed and rubbed her eyes, making him notice how tired she seemed. He could see faint worry lines around her usually sparkling eyes, and her shoulders were slumped.

'Why is he here?' he asked, leaning against the wall and kissing her briefly on the lips to prolong the conversation. Noah could feel the tension radiating off of Maya and he didn't like it.

'Your guess is as good as mine!' she shrugged and pushed the door open, but not before fixing a bright smile onto her face. She entered the lounge and sat down opposite Blake, motioning for Noah to do the same after they had shaken hands in greeting.

'I'm sorry,' Blake apologised, amiably. 'I didn't know you had plans, Maya.'

'You didn't ask,' she responded a bit waspishly, and the room fell uncomfortably silent. 'Drink?' she asked Noah, and he nodded, noticing that Blake didn't have one. When she left the seating area and moved into the kitchen and started opening cupboards in search of wine, the men faced each other.

'Have you two been dating long?' asked Blake, a polite smile never leaving his face.

Noah ignored the question. 'I didn't realise that you two were still in touch?' said Noah, keeping his tone purpose-fully neutral.

'We aren't really,' sighed Blake. 'When I saw Maya at

your party, I'd just read an article about the steamboat and its makeover in a local paper while visiting a client. I guessed Maya might have something to do with it,' he added pompously. 'I know how close her grandad is to Joe.' He paused for a moment too long and Noah frowned feeling slightly off kilter at how well Blake clearly knew Maya's family when they still hadn't met yet. The whole point of the love pact had been to appease her family, but he'd assumed he'd have met them by now and the fact that he hadn't however busy they both were, seemed odd to him. Maya was incredibly close to her family, so was she embarrassed by him, or did Blake being back on the scene have more to do with this that he'd originally thought? His hackles rose and Noah grit his teeth, but made himself stay calm. 'I went to see her at Joe's boat because we have unfinished business from when we used to work together. A guy behind the bar told me to find her here.'

'You mean Roman - unfinished business?' questioned Noah, his mind racing at what on earth Blake meant. The last thing he needed was to get into anything new when the person was still mixed up with their past, but he feared he was already in too deep and just about keeping his head above water. Surely Maya wouldn't look twice at this man after what he did to her... the problem was that Noah knew first loves were hard to forget, especially if they left you feeling that you didn't deserve better. He was lucky that his own first love had been someone he met at university and they'd parted as good friends, but he couldn't imagine what he'd feel if she'd betrayed and belittled him, or how that would impact his future relationships. She still meant a lot to him as a friend, but lovers... no. He drew in a calming breath and tried not to think about how much Blake might still mean to Maya.

Noah turned to glance at the open-plan kitchen area, but Maya had clearly gone upstairs or outside for something, as she was nowhere to be seen. There were three glasses on the counter, but no wine, so perhaps she'd gone to get a bottle from the huge walk-in storeroom by the boats. He knew she occasionally had deliveries and kept them in there, as she liked clean lines and mess-free cupboards.

'We used to run a business together. Didn't she tell you?' Blake smirked and seemed to enjoy this a bit too much and Noah's body was suddenly on high alert, his muscles taut and his legs ready to jump up if he needed to. Noah had always gotten along with Blake and Portia whenever they'd met at social events, which wasn't often, but he was usually a charming guy. Now Noah could sense an undercurrent he didn't like and hadn't encountered before. He knew that Blake and Portia were still together, so why was he really there?

'I knew you used to work together,' said Noah. 'But I thought your relationship was over ages ago, for various reasons?' He looked straight at Blake, who blanched, his smirk sliding from his face.

'We were also engaged,' Blake slid into the conversation.

Engaged? This *was* a revelation and not one that sat well with Noah. Being previously engaged was a pretty big nugget of information not to tell the guy you were currently seeing when you spoke about your past and family and all other kinds of things. That stung and Noah winced, but tried to hide his discomfort by getting up and wandering to the window to look out, forgetting that it was dark outside, so the only thing he could see were the street lights reflecting on the dark river surface. Ouch, his feeling stung - not that he'd let Blake realise and feel victorious, so he smiled and turned back to face him.

Maya chose just that moment to walk back in with a bottle of red Pinot Noir wine, which gave him a flashback to lying naked with her in the bar on the steamboat after they'd enjoyed a glass. She gave Noah an odd look, probably because he was smiling manically, and then she poured three glasses of wine. He immediately went into the character of someone who'd just found out something about the person they were dating, but didn't care, even though his own thoughts were much more tangled than that. He often did this as a defence mechanism and he knew he was hard to read sometimes because of it. She handed a glass to Noah and then Blake, who sniffed the aroma and then sipped it, as if he expected it to be laced with arsenic, or be a really crap glass of wine. His eyebrows shot up when he tasted it and it seemed he approved as he took another sip and sank back into his chair as if he owned the place. She didn't mention that it was one bottle Robbie had sent her with the hamper.

'Our engagement was years ago,' said Maya, making Blake almost choke on his wine, as he clearly hadn't expected her to have come back in and heard his last comment. 'Noah knows exactly why our relationship broke down,' she said sweetly, her eyes flashing, but Blake suddenly couldn't meet her eye. 'How is Portia? Did she get the No. 1 Ethereal Lane modelling job? Tabitha told me she was trying to connect with the brand.' When Blake went puce and no one spoke, she sat down on the single couch opposite both men and continued as Blake seemed to have been suddenly struck mute for a moment.

'You know that Blake and I ran a business together straight out of college,' she said and Noah nodded, 'but we had very different ideas about how it should have been run,' she said conversationally to Noah, ignoring Blake. 'I was inexperienced and Blake clearly wanted to run things on his own terms, which included putting his penis in Portia,' she added with a flourish and both men winced, but humour sparked in Noah's face and she recognised it and her own eyes danced with mirth, some of the tension leaving her face.

'That wasn't exactly...' tried Blake, finding his voice, but Maya's eyes warned him not to lie and he backed down.

'The relationship broke down, so we parted ways.' Noah grinned and wished he could get up and applaud her or swing her onto his lap, the knot of fear about a reconciliation between these two loosening its grip.

'You both formed, BM bespoke?' asked Noah, biting his lip and trying not to laugh at Blake's expression. He looked like he'd just been sucking lemons. He mentioned Blake's brand as she'd already told him about the wandering penis part. Blake frowned and darted glances between them, clearly surprised that his truth bomb hadn't exploded the way he'd wanted it to. Most people thought someone named the brand after Blake McBride, as that was his full name, but Noah guessed it had stood for Blake and Maya. He sipped his wine and regarded them both, deciding how he should play this as Blake was clearly out to cause as much trouble as he could for Maya, but Noah couldn't understand why, unless he'd been jealous seeing her with Noah at the garden party and his intention was to split them up? Just like that the stomach pain was back.

Then he thought of Tabitha and how malicious she was when they'd only been dating for a short while. If they'd have been engaged, she'd have probably killed him and dumped his body in the river by now, or sold another million made-up stories about him in the least. He usually had pretty amicable relationships with ex-partners, so Tabitha's behaviour was something he didn't understand.

He'd tried being friendly, thoughtful and caring of her feelings, but she'd stamped all over him and still wouldn't leave him alone, so he turned back to Blake and was about to be very clear on his relationship status with Maya.

'That's right,' stated Maya, before Noah could speak, clearly tired of all the lies. Blake stood up suddenly and was shifting from foot to foot as he went around the back of the couch and pretended to admire some of the art on her walls. He clearly had more to say to Maya, but he suddenly clammed up when faced with a now, not so amenable, Noah.

'I ran the studio and client lists,' Maya said simply. 'Blake popped by tonight to see how I was getting on, but as I explained to him...' she paused and looked Blake straight in the eye while he adjusted the collar of his pristine pale blue shirt, 'I've no hard feelings about him and Portia now and I'm happy for his success, but don't need any part in it. I signed away my shares and don't regret it.' She nodded towards some paperwork that Blake had brought with him and left on the table. 'I've moved on,' she said clearly as she moved to stand next to Noah and slipped her hand into his, which he squeezed to let her know he stood with her on that.

She put her wineglass down and looked between both men. 'I was shocked to see you at my door, Blake and Noah's been patient enough. It's been interesting... but Noah and I had better head out now.'

Blake placed his glass down on the nearest table, leaving a drop of wine on the surface and Noah watched Maya cringe, which made his heart melt a little. She was such a neat freak, and he loved that about her... He felt winded for a moment, and his body froze. Love? He quickly brushed that thought away. He'd always cleaned obsessively to have a methodical mind for his work. It also stopped him from overthinking every comment that his family made about his job. Unfortunately, the habit was a hard one to break. Maybe they could help each other ease up a bit? Suddenly a picture of Maya naked and in his bed came to mind, and he smiled to himself about lots of ways they could distract each other. He gulped and turned to face Blake again, making a point not to show his growing displeasure at the way Blake spoke to Maya on his face. Blake wanted to score points, so Noah was determined to come out on top. This man wasn't a threat to him... was he? He hoped Maya didn't still have feelings for Blake, but for now he'd have to trust his gut and believe she didn't want him there.

Blake took Noah's outstretched hand, as he stood up and shook it cordially, a smile firmly stuck back on his face. Maya didn't give him much of a chance to say anything else as she grabbed the glasses and quickly rinsed them in the sink, leaving them to drip dry on the integral granite draining board. Noah was bemused by what he had walked into and firmly closed the door on Blake as he left so that Maya didn't have to.

'Good riddance,' she said as she slumped against the wall and he pulled her into the safety of his arms. 'Shortly after we split up, I tried dating a couple of vaguely mutual acquaintances,' she explained, 'but Blake always appeared at inopportune times when I wasn't there and scared them away, even though I'd made it crystal clear there was no hope of a reconciliation. In the end, a family member informed him I'd moved abroad.' She snuggled further into his arms and he rested his chin on the top of her head as she spoke. 'Then he sent ridiculously expensive gifts to my grandparent's house and pleaded for a second chance. In the end, our parting was even more bitter because I had to sign the company over to him to get him to break our partnership clause. I literally walked away with nothing for years of hard work and he let me, to punish me for leaving.'

'After that, he acted like I didn't exist and paraded Portia everywhere. There was no way we could reconcile and work alongside each other after that. My heart was shattered and my confidence was in shreds, but I'm not that woman anymore and I don't have time to waste on the past.' Noah felt his heart melt a little more for this brave and incredible woman. He held her away from him and gently kissed her on the lips.

He led her into the kitchen and sat her down on one of the bar stools and then began milling about and drying the glasses before placing them back in the glass cupboard. She smiled at that and then looked out at the shadowy night sky through the double doors to the river.

'I'm sorry Noah,' she sighed, leaning against the island unit before coming round to stand next to him. 'I should have told you about Blake and I being engaged - but talking about it gives it power.' She rubbed her temples and began rifling through the kitchen drawers for no reason, then stopped and puffed out her cheeks, which made her look cute. 'It meant a lot to me at the time,' she continued, 'but I was clearly delusional to think that man loved me and he crushed any ounce of feeling I ever had for him years ago. I've no interest in seeing him or having him anywhere near my home. That's why he didn't know where I lived. He actually still believed that I was abroad until Robbie pulled his love boat stunt.'

Noah eased her into his arms. She resisted a bit at first because she was so agitated, but then she gave in and laid her head against his chest, her own arms wrapping around him. They stayed that way for a few moments, although he'd have happily done so for hours. He loved the feeling of her in his arms and the rate that she was in his thoughts now worried him slightly.

'Do you want to talk about it now?' he asked.

'Only if you do,' she responded, a bit defensively.

'Not really. The past is the past, and it seems to me like Blake has already taken up enough of your time.'

'Is Tabitha really in your past?' she asked as she paused and looked up at him. 'She invited me out for that drink we had, to tell me you were dating me to make her jealous,' she sighed and Noah's head jerked back in shock. 'It's why I didn't go into details when we spoke about it,' Maya added as Noah felt anger shoot up his spine. 'She tried to convince me to sell her my ring so that I could afford for her to take me shopping to buy clothes to fit into your world.'

Noah spluttered and then shook his head in disgust. He captured her head in his hands and touched his lips to hers, then circled his arms around her waist and rested his forehead on hers for a moment before pulling back and looking deeply into her eyes. 'I've made it very clear to Tabitha that after our very few dates, that we weren't compatible. What else can I do? I'd hoped our dating would make her leave us alone.'

Maya's eyes twinkled suddenly. 'Us?'

Noah grinned cheekily and stole another searing kiss. 'Yes, us. We're in this together now. I'm sorry about that,' he hung his head, although he didn't feel that sorry. Without the whole Tabitha mess, he might not have met the girl of his dreams. He enjoyed having someone to talk to and to share things with. Maya was a skilled listener, even though she herself seemed to hold back. He didn't know what else he could do to persuade her she could trust him, but hopefully that would come with time. 'Shall we go out on the river like we'd planned?'

Noah wanted to run his hands under her jumper and pull her into bed, but he needed to earn her trust and tonight was going to be about him persuading her to open up to him more. He could barely string a sentence together or think of anything but running his hands along her body when she was close, and the sensual scent of vanilla and patchouli that she wore on a date once drove his senses wild. He'd asked her what it was while he was kissing his way up her body and she'd giggled and told him. After finding a store that sold it, he'd sent her a beautifully wrapped bottle, with a note to say that the scent reminded him of her.

'You're wearing my favourite perfume again,' he said, kissing his way up her arm and then forcing himself to stop or carry on forever.

'I love the idea of driving you wild,' she teased, as her cheeks flushed a little.

Perhaps Blake arriving at her door would show her she needed to trust Noah and be more open with him for him to fully let her in, too, he hoped, but then all further coherent thought fled when she reached up and pulled him in for more kisses and he growled with lust when she slipped her hand in to the back of his jeans and touched his warm skin. 'We could just stay in,' she grinned as he caught her hand and then ran his own along her leg, making her shiver in excitement. 'I was going to show you where my grandparents live by the river, but we could do that another time,' she waggled her eyebrows suggestively at him and he laughed.

'So it's a choice between ravishing you in bed or visiting your grandparents?' he asked incredulously. She grinned, and he tried to calm his libido, but he wanted to slip her clothes off of her body and kiss every inch of her skin whenever he was alone with her. She seemed to feel the same way by the way her hand had found its way to his derriere again. He grinned and playfully nudged her hand away.

'Maybe we can go out in the boat and see their house from the river and then you could stay over here for the night?' Noah's eyebrows rose at this as she hadn't invited him to stay before. He grabbed the boat keys and a fluffy blanket off of the back of a chair and practically dragged her out of the kitchen and to the boat. Maya was giggling so much that he ended up swinging her into his arms and placed her into the boat so they could go sightseeing and take a quick photo to send to her family to prove they were having proper dates now, then get back within the hour.

Chapter Twenty-Four

Was it possible to be more pedestrian than this? Tabitha glanced around the Riverside café and saw nothing to inspire or even to cool her down. She fanned her face with the plastic table menu and cursed under her breath. It was stifling hot in there and even with the doors left open and the river breeze tumbling through. Hadn't they heard about air conditioning? The sun was beating down outside and she needed a drink, and fast. She hated being in provincial places like this passably clean coffee shop. They didn't serve her favourite fat free, decaffeinated tomato mint tea, so they could hardly call themselves a real coffee shop. She'd finally decided to meet a friend at the café that was just by the riverboat dock, because she'd heard Noah raving about Maya's little paintings and wanted to find out what prices they went for. Surely she'd need to sell hundreds of them to make up the amount she could pocket from Tabitha for the No. 1 Ethereal Lane ring? Tabitha had fibbed when she'd mentioned to Maya about visiting the café, so she thought she had better see it for herself, but she certainly wouldn't be eating anything, she shuddered.

She'd asked the young woman from behind the counter where to find Maya's work, but had been told that it was sold out, which was infuriating, as it meant Tabitha had endured the walk through the high street and curious glances from the locals, for nothing. Now she couldn't even get a decent drink. Tabitha enjoyed being famous most of the time, but she didn't normally have to walk from a car park to get somewhere. She was used to valet service. The docks had parking just off of the main street, so you could walk up to the admittedly pretty market town, or turn right to reach the boats and this café. It had unnerved her a bit to leave her sleek red Porsche behind and made her wish she'd brought a bodyguard, but her friend, Portia, was pretty famous now too and when she arrived, Tabitha knew she'd feel better. They would chat about their most recent problems and they often came to a suitable solution that would cause them both to come out on top. Nothing else would be acceptable.

She guessed that Maya's art must be dirt cheap to sell so quickly and a bit of digging had resulted in Tabitha finding out that Maya attended art classes for down and outs, so surely she'd decide to sell the ring at some point? The tutor looked pretty dishy from the art class flyers that were by the front door of the café, so perhaps Tabitha could tempt Maya that way and get rid of her for good? Surely that would be a better match than a nobody trying to date a superstar? Tabitha just needed to keep Maya close and then she could make Noah realise he was making the wrong choice in his selection of partner. Maya was a mess, and she didn't seem to have any ambition, so what on earth could they have in common?

Tabitha looked at her expensive watch and tutted that Portia was keeping her waiting. They both had careers that kept them in the spotlight, but Tabitha knew she was the more famous of the two... by far. She sat up straighter and ignored a couple of young women who had been staring at her since she walked in and then scrolled through her phone at the hundreds of dresses she'd bookmarked. She'd bagged a ticket to the ball of the century and she needed to make a statement with her dress to catch the eye of the swarms of photographers who would be outside Dame Rosalie Alton's party. She also wanted Noah to know exactly what he was missing. Sleeping with Corey, her producer, to ensure she had his plus one invite had been tedious and she could tell his attention was waning, which could be problematic. The press occasionally photographed Corey with the cast of their film, so she made sure that she was standing next to Noah each time and smiling up into his eyes, which their fans went wild for.

She eyed the drinks menu to see if they served a chilled glass of white Riesling wine, but alas, no such luck. A framed photo that was hanging on the wall behind the serving counter caught her eye and it sucked the breath out of her lungs for a second. The cogs in her brain whirred, and her cheeks flushed. She knew there was something dodgy about Maya and now she had proof! Noah needed to understand what he was getting himself into and that Maya was clearly a fame hunter, and Tabitha knew she was just the person to help him out and console his pain from the betrayal.

Chapter Twenty-Five

Maya wriggled in her seat in the sleek black limo that Noah had collected her in and watched the plush greenery outside become less dense and inter-spaced with a mixture of buildings and then skyscrapers, as they journeyed towards central London and the bustling, vibrant streets and restaurants of the city. She hadn't been back to where she'd grown up for years, and it felt bittersweet to be returning with a new relationship and fresh hope for her future. She was wearing a floor length dress made by her grandmother that had layers and layers of burnt orange and red chiffon draped across her body. Her movement created the illusion of a blazing flame. It was certainly a statement as the dress moved fluidly around her and clung to her curves in all the right places. There were no straps, just clever drapery and invisible stitching. Maya had baulked at the colour, but her grandmother had insisted. Her family knew about Noah, but they still hadn't met, which was driving them crazy. She'd become precious about her time with him because they were both busy, but she knew she couldn't put it off any longer. Noah had asked when he was going to meet them and she had told him a bit about her past, but omitted how batty her family really was because now she was actually more scared of him meeting them and being scared off!

Maya knew how important this big gala ball was for Noah and his career, as this was his biggest movie to date. Dame Rosalie was a huge advocate for museums and the history they curated for later generations and had donated lots of memorabilia from her films to charities to raise funds to keep them open. Tonight's auction was in aid of a beautiful local museum that desperately needed investment to survive. After Dame Rosalie had performed there when she was a fledgling actress, they had supported her career, so she was returning the favour, Noah had explained.

Maya had designed a stunning No. 1 Ethereal Lane waterfall necklace for Dame Rosalie to auction after a lot of excitement about how much money it might raise for her charity. Maya had worried that she might get bombarded with donation requests after that, but Dame Rosalie was a force to be reckoned with and what she wanted she usually got, Maya had discovered. Her fingers could only create so many pieces a year and she had her own charitable causes now, which were very close to her heart, including supporting local businesses like the refit of *Bertha* and offering materials for the art class that Mason ran on the boat. It had been so rewarding to watch the art class flourish and their canvases sell extremely well at Penny's café.

'What's she like to work with?' Maya asked Noah about Rosalie.

He thought for a moment and then responded. 'She's scary, but an absolute sweetheart. Plus she's the most professional and talented woman I've met in a long time, present company excluded,' he winked and kissed her hand, which made her flush with pleasure. 'I know how hard you work. She's amazing, but growly,' he laughed. 'She keeps trying to set me up with friends of friends, though.'

Maya raised her eyebrow. 'Really?' Thank goodness that hadn't happened.

'Yep. Apparently she knows someone who would be perfect for me, but she doesn't know that the perfect woman already fell into my lap, or the river by my house, anyway,' he grinned and leaned in to kiss her softly on the lips. She smiled, feeling shy suddenly, and she gulped in some air as the car smoothly pulled up against the curb by a red carpet and she took a moment to calm her racing nerves before they got out. She wasn't sure how she felt about the possibility of Noah being set up for a date by someone else.

Photographers and reporters lined the road and flashes of light filled the dark night sky as people stepped out of their cars and walked up the red carpet to the event, which made Maya sit back in fear. 'It's okay,' reassured Noah, who was looking suave in his black tie suit and crisp white shirt. 'I'll be with you the whole time and we only need to stop for one or two quick photos to help support Dame Rosalie and to fulfil my contractual obligations to my bosses.' He winked and grinned. 'They keep saying I've been too busy and my mind elsewhere to promote my next film much,' he laughed. 'Apparently, you're quite the distraction.'

Maya gasped. 'Are you in trouble because of me? ' she asked, horrified. She could suddenly picture Tabitha leaning in and telling a few people on set that Noah wasn't at the top of his game because his current date was distracting him from work. It was just the tittle-tattle that she enjoyed.

Noah shook his head and smiled. 'I was joking. The publicity department just reminded me to get my face out there a bit more, which, to be honest, I probably should do. Are you okay?' he asked. 'I'm sorry for teasing. Bad timing on my part,' he inclined his head towards the bank of photographers waiting eagerly outside and tucked his arm around her for a moment. 'We can do this,' he said supportively. She tried to quell her nerves and nodded, but her hands felt clammy and she gripped onto her sparkly handbag with undue force, which made her wince when the sequins pinched her skin.

Images of the events she'd been dragged along to with Blake flashed into her mind, but she tried to focus on Noah's warm arm around her waist as they exited the car and she smiled mechanically as the flashbulbs went off in their faces and crowds of people called Noah's name. She'd never been out with a superstar before and she tried to hide her vulnerability by straightening her shoulders and standing tall, as Noah led her inside and whispered words of encouragement in her ear, which made her smile for real, finally. This whole thing was terrifying! She had always let Blake preen if they'd seen any photographers about and stayed well into the background, sidling indoors as soon as there was a chance. Now she was walking up the red carpet with an A-list celebrity!

They stopped when they saw the scene in front of them on entering the ball, their eyes wide in awe because it felt as if every surface sparkled. It was like walking into what Maya imagined a palace under the sea would look like, with swirls of ice blue and white everywhere and huge glass pillars reaching from the floor to the ceiling, which were half full of water and topped with huge pink Lotus flowers with their dark green lily-pad like foliage. The vast venue had a swirling curved stage area rising from the centre and the bar tables dotted around had wide vases of water topped with soft yellow Water Poppies with their deeper yellow centres, dark stamens and heart-shaped leaves.

There was an actual waterfall to one side of the room with the water falling into a crystal clear pond beneath it which was surrounded by tall white and purple Water Iris with their three-petalled flowers and tall grass-like leaves. The light bounced off the myriad of surfaces and rippled across the room. Beautifully attired people were standing around in small groups chatting and laughing as waiting staff dressed as water imps wandered around with trays that looked like they'd been sculpted from ice, even though they clearly hadn't and champagne in crystal flutes and morsels of mouth-watering food that was fresh from the sea.

'Wow,' said Maya in awe. Her artist's eye was almost overwhelmed by the beauty of the room. It reflected the waterfall necklace she'd made to perfection, and she felt emotion well up in her throat. Her No. 1 Ethereal Lane logo and images of Maya's jewellery collections were projected over the main stage on enormous screens, and people were looking at them with interest.

'Unbelievable,' echoed Noah, as he took in the scene in front of them.

Rosalie had taken charge of every aspect of her charity ball and Maya had overseen her part in the event and signed it off, but seeing it in person was a revelation. Maya was humbled and at a loss for words. Luckily, the room had the same effect on every single person who stepped inside, as they all stopped to stare around on first arrival. Dame Rosalie was holding court on the stage, which had water flowing from the edges into small rock pools on the floor below. The rock pools seemed to have little diamonds glinting from the bottom of each one and tiny silver fish swam between them.

There were six security guards stationed on or around the stage and Maya knew that there were many more dotted within the room, dressed as guests. Only a few people were being allowed up onto the stage to greet Dame Rosalie as the waterfall necklace was showcased in a glass case at the front, where the auction would be held. There were fully staffed bars all over the venue, including one on the stage to serve Dame Rosalie and guests invited up onto the stage.

Images of a stunning model wearing a ballgown and the waterfall necklace appeared from time to time on the screens. It had clearly been taken at the venue as the glass pillars could be seen in the background, which created an extra hum of excitement. In one of the photos, Gio was taking her hand, looking incredibly handsome in a tuxedo, his eyes alight with happiness. It really was a breath-taking photo and Maya thought back to her first meeting with Gio, where he'd barely spoken a word. This confident photo of an alpha male made her smile, and she hoped he was gradually taking confidence from his new role and enjoying life. Bobby was certainly smiling whenever she saw him now, and living together seemed to work well for them both.

Maya took a moment to enjoy the sparkle and haute couture of the guests' clothes and how much they seemed to enjoy the event from the smiles and hum of conversation. Classical music was being played by a group of musicians towards the ornate doors that led to an outside patio area and Maya couldn't wait to move closer and hear more later. She hoped tonight might be the start of her two worlds entwining and that the fallout wasn't her relationship with

Noah, because he was becoming more and more important to her happiness. She knew she couldn't keep the fact that she'd designed the waterfall necklace from him for much longer, but that she hadn't already told him created its own problems. Would he think he couldn't trust her now? She hoped not, but it was a possibility.

Noah turned to her with wonder in his eyes. 'This is incredible. I know Rosalie is a perfectionist and I've been lucky enough to be invited to a few extraordinary places, but this is cooler than most of the film sets I've been on!'

'It's stunning,' added Maya, trying to take it all in.

'I should bid on the necklace for you,' he joked, 'but that might be forward of me before we have the exclusive talk. I do want that conversation,' he added carefully. Maya looked into his eyes in shock and hoped he didn't bid because this was her highest value piece to date! She knew he could probably afford it, but that was beside the point. She wondered if he was simply joking about either point or if he was serious! Surely not? He grinned at her and took her hand to guide her to a group of beautifully elegant men and women. Unfortunately, one of them was Tabitha, who gave her a tight smile before looking Maya's outfit up and down as if searching for something, then stopping herself and giving them both a kiss on each cheek. Tabitha's own dress was clearly couture as it fitted her svelte body perfectly, but the amount of jewellery she wore with the subtle green fabric was almost obscene. Her heavily jewelled emerald drop earrings and matching necklace were a lot to take in, but the added diamond cuff bracelet, belt and branded clutch bag made Maya blink a few times.

Noah introduced her to his producers Corey and Tom and a couple of other key cast members and they chatted amiably for a few moments, then Corey leaned in to Noah.

'I'm really sorry about the timing, but something's cropped up with one scene. We need to run through a few points.' He winced and looked apologetically at Maya.

'What here? Now?' asked Noah, his face showing his displeasure. 'I can't leave Maya on her own.' Maya's heart fluttered at this show of protectiveness. She touched his arm to let him know she was fine.

'Noah. It's okay. You know what I'm like. I've been itching to look at the plants and the water features since we arrived. Come and find me when you're done.' Noah was frowning as if he really didn't like that idea, but Tabitha was already drawing him away with a firm hand on his arm.

'Work must come before play, Noah,' said Tabitha with a tinkly laugh, her hand still on her arm while she rolled eyes at Corey as if to say, see... flaky. He stood still and refused to budge, turning to lean in and kiss Maya on the cheek.

'Are you sure? I'm not happy with leaving you on your own at an event like this.'

Maya refused to get riled up by Tabitha, so she smiled up at him and a warmth spread through her veins. She'd been so worried about tonight, but it would be okay. 'I'm fine,' she reassured him, darting a glance at a nearby corner that seemed quiet and unpopulated. Hiding there and catching her breath for a minute seemed like an inspired idea. Maya currently felt like she was sleepwalking through her own life and she needed to wake up and enjoy such an incredible experience. She hadn't wanted to be there, but now she was, she was determined to enjoy it.

Maya had wrangled the floristry contract for Leah as part of the deal, so she was excited to inspect her handi-work. Normally she'd step in and help her friend with such a huge contract, but in the end Leah had hired two extra staff, and her team had clearly worked diligently with Dame Rosalie to fulfil her vision. Maya was so proud of Leah she could almost cry to see how far her friend had come. She ran her hands over the green stems and oval leaves of the pretty pale purple Water Mint flowers that were potted in damp soil in wide almost white vases around the edges of the room. These wildflowers grew on the banks of streams and around ponds and were sometimes used for infusions and essential oils, leaving a fresh minty scent on Maya's hands as she touched them. They softened the edges of the room and filled it with colour and texture. It was a total triumph!

Just as Maya was trying to avoid catching anyone's eye and was inspecting a delicate little flower, someone firmly took her arm. She gasped and turned to see the burly security guard she'd seen standing with Dame Rosalie towering over her. He was wearing an immaculate dark suit, and he had an earpiece in his ear. 'Um... can I help you?' she asked, looking around the nearly full ballroom and noticing people turning their way to stare.

'Dame Rosalie would like to speak to you,' he said in a steady voice that she understood immediately to mean that she had to follow him. She winced and bit her lip, her face flushing.

'I was just admiring the plants,' she said, playing for time and realising that she sounded quite whiney. 'Can't I just stay here?'

He arched one eyebrow at her, but didn't release his grip. He wasn't hurting her at all and she could see that they were attracting rather a lot of attention now, so she nodded her head and he led her towards the stage. 'You didn't tell us you were coming,' he growled.

'Surprise!' Maya said feebly as Evan, the head of Dame Rosalie's security, rolled his eyes.

'You know she hates surprises. She likes to be informed of everything.'

'I didn't know myself that I was attending until the last minute,' said Maya. The crowds parted as they walked through and for a split second Maya rested her head on his shoulder and whispered, 'How long did it take her to spot me?' Her captor turned and grinned at that and then rolled his eyes again at her stupidity.

'About five minutes. You aren't exactly inconspicuous in that dress!' Maya huffed, then glanced down at her eye-catching gown and groaned.

As they reached the stage, she turned her head to where she'd left Noah, and the group were all now staring at her with their jaws hanging open, as Evan still had hold of her arm and didn't appear to be that happy. Noah was frowning, and she knew he'd be panicking about what was wrong. She tried to send him a quick, reassuring smile. As Evan led her up the steps to Dame Rosalie, the security guard at the top grinned at the sight of her, his eyes dancing as he leaned in and gave her a kiss on the cheek, which made Noah's frown deepen and Evan smiled finally and let her go. Before she could think of what to do, Dame Rosalie had pulled her into a bone-crushing hug, knocking the wind out of her. Then Rosalie held her out at arms-length to take in her beautiful outfit and then drew her in for another hug before finally letting Maya go. 'You naughty child!' scolded Rosalie. 'You didn't tell me you were coming. Party preparations have been ongoing for almost a year, and last month you said you already had plans! People wait in trepidation to receive one of my invitations, you know young lady,' she scolded haughtily, the light dancing in her eyes, belying the humour in the situation. Rosalie was never cross for long.

Maya hung her head for a moment. 'I'm sorry. You know I'd never miss this, but I had another engagement tonight and at first I didn't realise they were the same party. When I did, I thought it would be more fun to turn up unannounced. You're always saying that nothing surprises you these days,' Maya teased. 'I have another one, but I'm not sure how you'll take it. I've brought a date...'

Rosalie tutted and narrowed her eyes at Maya. 'I know that look. Please, please tell me you haven't let that scoundrel Blake back into your life.'

'Blake isn't here,' assured Maya, seeing the distress on Rosalie's face.

'Thank goodness! Blake would do just about anything for an invitation to an event like this and I wouldn't put it past him to wheedle back into your life now I'm in it.' Rosalie saw Maya's appalled look and grimaced. 'I'm sorry, but the man's a social climber. It's about time you let someone else in. I've got my own ideas about that,' she added and Maya wished she had a drink to down as this was more like the usual interrogations about her love life now. 'Your grandmother didn't tell me you were attending either!'

'She didn't know,' said Maya, as she looked forlornly at Evan who winked at her with a grin. He knew full well how many times her family and friends went on at her about her love life, as Rosalie often spent time with Ettie, who had become her best friend in the past couple of years. 'It was a last-minute decision.'

'With a dress like that!' Rosalie held her away from her again and twirled her around to take in every inch of her grandmother's handiwork. 'Ettie is a genius!' she proclaimed. 'I keep pleading with her to make the outfits for my next film, but she refuses,' she tutted and then glanced around to see they had an audience.

'Gran's retired,' reasoned Maya helpfully. 'You're right though. Blake might have stayed with me if he'd have thought my connections might still be useful,' she rolled her eyes, but her good humour was returning because Rosalie was often right. 'He'd be gutted to find out that you spend more time at my grandparents' house than your own!' Maya laughed suddenly and it was Rosalie's turn to chuckle.

'Pfft,' said Rosalie, before spotting Noah and his group and nodding to Evan to retrieve him, too. He headed off with an enormous theatrical sigh, and Maya giggled. Evan had run Rosalie's protective detail for decades now and was pretty much one of the family, too. He put up with a lot because of her antics with Maya's grandmother, but Maya secretly thought he was having a lot more fun himself, too. When Ettie and Rosalie got together, every moment of their time was spent making mischief.

'Evan's happy tonight,' noted Maya with a sarcastic lilt.

'He's fed up with guarding the jewellery because he'd rather be sipping a non-alcoholic beer from the bar where he can see most of the room.'

'Oops,' said Maya with a grimace. 'How long until the auction? Hopefully, he can rest after that.'

'In an hour,' said Rosalie as they both turned to look at the stunning diamond and white gold waterfall necklace that sparkled on a pedestal on one side of the podium. The publicity for this event had been astronomical because of the host and the auction. Security had been a bit of a headache, but Maya had been given some helpful advice from Evan, who was a pro at looking after something precious.

Before Maya could protest, Rosalie signalled to her security team that they should let Noah onto the stage as he'd moved to the foot of the stairs to see if she needed rescuing. Maya tried to send him a reassuring smile, as she curled and uncurled her hands around her evening bag. She knew what a powerhouse Rosalie was and yet Noah had been ready to jump to Maya's defence, anyway. For all he knew, she might have been trying to steal the necklace, or the plants, but he was there for her, even if it might cause problems for his own career.

Rosalie beckoned to him to join them and he walked up and through security with Evan, in a bit of a daze. 'Noah,' boomed Rosalie, as he greeted her with a kiss on both cheeks. 'This is my best friend's granddaughter, Maya.'

Maya couldn't help but splutter at Noah's shocked face. 'Rosalie is a close family friend,' she explained, her nerves fizzing.

'You know I think of you as one of my own,' scolded Rosalie, giving Maya a stern look, which made her smile.

'I know you do,' said Maya, reaching up to kiss Rosalie's soft cheek as Maya flushed and her lip wobbled. Rosalie enveloped her in a perfumed hug and then stood regarding them both. Rosalie was wearing a magnificent ocean blue dress that skimmed her curves and had a long train behind it that looked like rushing water. The décolletage glittered with tiny diamonds, and the bodice of the dress was a deep blue that faded to a lighter shade as the dress reached the floor. It was quite beautiful. She was also wearing the original No. 1 Ethereal Lane necklace Maya had created for her years ago when they'd first met. Her loyalty touched Maya. 'You're a big part of my family, too. You know I love you dearly... even if you are always causing trouble,' she inclined her head towards Noah. 'Rosalie and my grandmother,

Ettie, spend a lot of time together,' explained Maya. 'I came here with Noah, Rosalie. He's my date.' She pulled an apologetic face at Noah, who frowned in confusion at this turn of events.

'Sorry for not telling you before, but I didn't want my connection with Rosalie to create problems for you at work. I thought that if the press linked us all, they might speculate about you working together again when nothing could be further from the truth. Rosalie wasn't aware that we knew each other until just now.'

Noah still looked flummoxed but smiled finally as he digested this last piece of information. His stunned expression eased, and he reached for Maya's hand. 'How did you meet?'

'Through Maya,' said Rosalie, which made his eyebrows shoot up into his hairline again. Rosalie's eyes narrowed for a moment and then she waved her hand around and caught the eye of the waiting staff to ask for them to bring them all a drink, which happened quickly. Maya sipped her delicious crystal glass of champagne and thought of what to say as Rosalie was clearly waiting for her cue. She was one of the few people who knew about the astronomical growth of Maya's brand and it was also how she'd bagged the best piece for auction tonight. She wasn't averse to the teeniest bit of emotional blackmail when she felt the cause deserved it, and Maya had caved quickly, anyway. Especially when the bone of Leah getting the floristry contract was dangled in front of her face. Rosalie knew Maya was a sucker for helping her friends and Rosalie loved Leah dearly too. The museum that was benefitting from the charity piece was close to her heart and in desperate need of money to renovate.

'Now they cause havoc everywhere they go,' said Maya

with affection. 'They wear disguises and cause all kinds of mayhem!' she laughed and Noah grinned too. She liked the fact that he was holding her hand in public and didn't seem to mind Rosalie's pretty brutal teasing.

'They went for a steamboat cruise on *Bertha* a while ago to celebrate Grandmother's birthday – for the tenth time in a month - and waved half a bottle of vodka around. Gran had a walking stick that she used to point at the seagulls, even though she has never used a stick in her life and Rosalie brought a cake that she forgot was in her bag and almost squashed. Joe and Roman thought it was hilarious, and we all had to pretend we didn't know who they were. No one else noticed them because their disguises were so good and they made such a racket that other customers steered clear!' she added in amusement, remembering the day and shaking her head at their antics.

'I can't wait to meet your grandmother in person. Is she well known?' asked Noah, chuckling at the story and not seeming that surprised by Rosalie's behaviour.

'She's certainly incorrigible!' laughed Maya, and Rosalie almost spluttered her drink before she composed herself. 'She enjoys the drama of the fact that Rosalie gets mobbed if she's seen out in public because everyone loves her so much. Hence why I understood your predicament on the bridge by the river so well,' she added, just for Noah's ears and understanding dawned in his eyes.

Rosalie blushed and shushed her away, but Maya continued. 'They have a huge dressing-up box left over from film sets and they use it to disguise themselves and go out in public because Rosalie is so recognisable. Believe me when I say they are like two delinquent children. They giggle, cause a raucous and leave a trail of destruction behind them,' she joked. Rosalie looked about to protest, but then she grinned and nodded.

'We have a lot of fun.'

'Grandad is just as bad because he drives them all over the place so they can misbehave and encourages them to have a wild time! They've even corrupted Joe and Olive now,' she added. 'Olive's been talking about joining them on their next outing and Joe thinks it's hilarious. Plus, it means the men get a bit of quiet time and a chance to sit in the pub with a glass of cold beer.'

Noah laughed, but seemed unsure if he should be in the presence of Dame Rosalie at such a grand event. They watched the guests milling around in their finery and trays of delectable canapés being tasted by everyone as the band continued to play. Rosalie patted his hand and smiled, her eyes sparkling with mirth. 'It's wonderful when the stars align and you meet your friendship soul mate. Ettie and I don't cause that much mischief...' she glanced at Maya's sceptical gaze, 'but we do like to solve romance dilemmas and encourage people to talk more after we've eavesdropped on their conversations or tiffs.' Noah's jaw dropped again and Maya nudged him on the hip. 'We pretend to be doddery old women who need help and then we butt in on their chat and solve all of their problems,' she belly laughed now. Maya shook her head in mock - despair and Noah couldn't help but grin.

'I've tried telling them to mind their own business, but it falls on deaf ears,' she shrugged. 'They've been meddling in my love life for the past two years and keep trying to set me up on dates with "eligible" men. Hence my fear of relation- ships when we met,' she explained.

'We aren't deaf!' said Rosalie with a grin. 'We have selec- tive hearing about who is suitable and if Noah had listened to my matchmaking earlier, you'd have been together years ago! Your gran said he'd be perfect for you when she saw all that rubbish in the papers.'

'What?' Maya couldn't believe what she was hearing now. 'Gran wanted me to date a cheater?' she felt her skin growing hot and her fists bunching. 'Sorry Noah,' she said as he looked wounded. 'It's just what the papers said. I know it wasn't true, but gran wouldn't have known that.'

Rosalie shook her head at Maya's stupidity. 'Of course not! Your grandmother only wants what's best for you, as you well know,' she scolded gently and Maya shrugged helplessly at Noah who grinned, but ran his finger along his dress shirt and let in some air, as this conversation was getting mightily uncomfortable. At least he'd understand why she'd joked about fake dating now. 'I'd already worked with Noah,' continued Rosalie, 'I knew he was an absolute sweetheart. We thought he'd had a tough time of it like you had and that you would get on.' It was Noah's turn to flush bright red now.

'You're kind of ruining my street cred here, Rosalie,' he joked, taking Maya's hand again.

Rosalie noted their linked hands and frowned. 'I've been trying to introduce you to Maya for years,' she rolled her eyes at Noah and he blanched and then Rosalie shook her head in exasperation as if he really should keep up.

'You aren't serious? I thought you were joking. This is the friend of a friend that you meant?' He looked incredulous, then horrified, and his cheeks went pink. Maya winced and bit her lip again, trying to gauge just how mad he was going to be with her for not explaining her family dynamics earlier. The problem was, that after Blake, she was fearful of fame hunters because of her family, as much as Noah was because of his career and that had been a huge factor when she'd decided to keep parts of her business hidden. Her grandparents were pretty famous in their own right, as was her brother, with his good looks and burgeoning tech business, that had recently made him a multi-millionaire.

'I didn't think I'd be able to make the family party because I'd promised Noah I'd accompany him to a prestigious event. The dates clashed,' she told Rosalie.

It was Rosalie's turn to focus on Noah, and her eyes narrowed. 'So you chose Noah over your family? Interesting...' Maya sighed. She knew they'd all read something into this when they found out she was actually there.

'She didn't choose me over her family...' added Noah in confusion, his face perplexed.

'This was the family party I wanted you to come to,' said Maya sheepishly, looking round for somewhere to hide, but they seemed to have a rapt audience and all she could do was fix on a smile and straighten her shoulders, taking a quick sip of her chilled champagne. 'I didn't know you'd invited me out on the same date, or until later that it was the same event. Rosalie hosts a lot of parties,' she tried feebly to joke, but it missed the mark. 'Half of my family are here.' Noah looked astounded, but then he took her hand again and moved closer to her side, his tuxedo brushing against her arm.

'You'd have missed all this for me?' he asked in awe.

'Umm... you said your event was important to you.'

'It is! But over a big family party? My parents would kill me!' He turned to look at Corey and Maya saw Noah give him a reassuring smile, but he just continued frowning as he put an arm around Tabitha's shoulders, but she threw him off and glared at them. Rosalie, however, was beaming from ear to ear and Maya groaned as she'd just spotted her grandparents further across the ballroom. Rosalie followed her line of vision and grinned.

'We knew you'd be perfect for each other!' Rosalie crowed happily as if she'd personally set all of this up.

'I told you they were incorrigible!' said Maya. 'It's why I needed a fake boyfriend.' Suddenly the conversation went silent and Rosalie's features set into a firm line.

'Fake relationship?'

Noah put out a hand to reassure her. 'Once we met, we had a daft idea to pretend to date to stop our families from worrying about our relationship status. But as soon as we started spending time together, we kind of fell in love...' He looked bashfully at Maya as she gasped and stepped back. Rosalie suddenly looked as if all of her Christmases had come at once, but as they turned, they saw Maya's grandparents heading their way. Maya gulped and Noah blanched because she hadn't seemed that happy about his declaration of love. Maya's stomach swirled, and she needed some air.

'Love?' she asked, as they both took a few steps away from Rosalie and Noah put a protective arm around her.

'Too much too soon? Sorry. I wasn't planning on it, but I just blurted it out,' he said quietly.

'Another act?' she demanded to know. He faced her for a moment, but seemed to realise her response was coming from fear of being hurt again. 'No. From the heart,' he reassured her calmly. 'It's how I feel. Have I scared you away?' he wanted to know.

'I... um... no,' she decided quickly as she smiled shyly up at him. 'Not too soon at all. It was just a shock. We haven't spoken about what the future holds for us both and I have so much more to tell you about my work and upbringing.' Noah brought her hand to his mouth and kissed it, happiness radiating from him. 'You keep creeping into my thoughts until I'm happier when I'm with you.' She felt her cheeks flush and her pulse race even faster. 'This is special and I'm not sure I've ever felt that way,' she said bravely. His eyes darkened, and he swooped in for a swift kiss, not caring who was staring their way. Maya would have loved to have kept kissing him forever, but her grandmother was getting closer and they needed to step away and fast. She glanced behind her and drew him away from Rosalie, both grinning like idiots at their secret. Rosalie seemed thrilled to be in on it, too. This was the last thing Maya had expected to have resulted from tonight, but they were three words she'd never forget.

'Go,' Rosalie urged kindly as they stepped closer to her again. 'Enjoy the party with your *love*,' she emphasised the last word and Maya's face was alight with joy. 'You are just what she needs,' she added to Noah, giving him an 'I told you so' smile of triumph. He grinned back and gave her another swift kiss on the cheek, before whispering in her ear that she'd been right and beginning to lead Maya back to the group he'd been standing with. Robbie and Amethyst had just joined them and they were greeting each other with kisses and hellos. Maya was happy to see them together again and hoped she'd played some small part in that. As she turned back to the stage, Maya just had time to watch Evan guide her grandparents up to greet Rosalie. She could see from her grandmother's face that she'd seen the entire performance, but was choosing to let Maya escape for now.

They walked around a few groups of people who glanced at them with open curiosity, but then went back to their conversation. Noah nodded at some people he knew and Maya admired the bejewelled gowns and smart suits the guest were wearing. She noted a few of her own jewellery pieces being proudly worn and loved the way the riverside was brought into the event with each scroll of silver leaf, or glittering diamond petal. Maya knew that a popular band would play a concert for them after the auction, but she wasn't sure how much more drama she could take for the moment.

'What the hell was all that about?' asked Tabitha within twenty seconds of them reaching their original group and catching their breath. Everyone turned to them, waiting for Maya's response.

'I didn't realise, but this is also a family party,' said Noah, his eyes twinkling with mirth. He had his arm around Maya now and he seemed to find the whole scenario quite funny.

'Whose family?' demanded Tabitha, stamping her feet in impatience, clearly expecting to be the most informed in the room. 'Are royalty here?' she asked, as if this was a distinct possibility at a party of this grandeur and decadence.

'Maya's family,' said Noah simply, waiting for the bomb of information to explode.

'Mayas?' Tabitha paused suddenly and looked at Maya as if she was an alien. 'What do you mean?'

'That's her grandmother,' said Noah, nodding towards Rosalie talking to Ettie and Tabitha gasped.

'Dame Rosalie Alton, is your grandmother?' She was incredulous.

'No,' smiled Maya, glancing back towards the stage, as Tabitha let out a tremendous sigh of relief. 'That's my grandmother,' she nodded towards the flamboyant couple who had just joined their host on stage. Ettie was wearing a floor length lilac silk gown with a sequined bodice that shimmied as she moved. She had an intricately laced shawl covering her shoulders in a slightly deeper shade, and Maya knew she was wearing light purple ballet shoes under the dress so that she could dance up a storm later. The dress was subtle at first glance but struck a punch in another, which summed her grandmother up. Owen has resplendent in a deep blue velvet tuxedo with a simple exotic pink bloom tucked into his breast pocket, that Maya was sure he'd snipped from his glasshouse before he'd left for the ball.

'Ettie Milton is your grandmother?' asked Tabitha, her facing looking puce suddenly. 'She dresses half of the Royals!'

'Isn't that the gentleman who filmed the award-winning documentary series with one of the Attenborough brothers?' asked Corey, in a stunned voice as he took Tabitha's hand, but she shook him off.

Maya shrugged. 'Probably. Gramps is always filming something or other about exotic plants. It's his speciality. I'm really sorry,' she said to the crowd, 'but Noah... now that my family knows we're here, would you mind meeting my brother and sister as well? They are probably propping up the bar.'

'Brother?' asked Noah, straightening his shoulders and pretending to quake.

'Arthur Lopez,' added Maya with a beaming smile.

All of the colour drained from Tabitha's face. 'The millionaire tech designer?'

Maya grinned and nudged hips gently with Noah, ignoring Tabitha's shocked face. 'It is my sister you have to worry about. She'll barrage you with questions and probably want to check you aren't a gold digger,' she winked at Robbie, who burst out laughing.

'Touché!' he said, grabbing a fresh drink for Amethyst from a passing server as her glass was dry and receiving a kiss on the cheek in return.

Maya took Noah's hand and led him through the crowd, who suddenly seemed to offer her smiles of interest instead of the earlier suspicion and angst. 'Joe and Olive are probably here too,' she quipped. 'Olive's a huge fan of your movies, so be prepared to talk endlessly about film sets while Joe regales you with his latest stories about *Bertha*. He's been wondering out loud if there should be a film written about a certain steamboat on the Thames that had a makeover and became a star!' she winked.

Chapter Twenty-Six

T
he last thing Noah had expected from tonight was pretty much everything that had happened so far. Swirls of emotions were flowing around his body and he felt like he'd had too many drinks when he'd only sipped one glass of bubbly all night.

He was astounded that it was Maya that Rosalie had been trying to introduce him to and he might have missed the whole Tabitha debacle if he'd only listened to her! He sighed and rubbed the bridge of his nose, which was pounding like mad, so he swiped a glass of water from the bar and gulped it down his parched throat.

Maya had just popped to the bathroom, but what he could hear from the whispered conversations all around him was that she was the talk of the night! He wasn't sure if that was a good or a bad thing and in the middle of it all, he'd blurted out that he was in love with her in front of Dame Rosalie, who he now knew she was as good as related to! He recalled their conversation in the car on the way there and the playful questions she'd asked, but why hadn't she said she already had a party invite and knew the host well? Was this all an elaborate charade at his expense? Was she a bored socialite who played with guys like him for her own amusement? He was so confused. Noah didn't like the heavy feeling of dread that thought brought with it, because he'd never considered her a liar. He hadn't been introduced to Maya's brother, Arthur, yet, but Noah knew he was watching him from the bar and it unnerved him a little. Tabitha had described him as a playboy, whatever that meant.

Why did Maya spend her days sitting on a steamboat on the river when it seemed she had fame and luxury in the palm of her hands? She said she didn't court the press, but he'd just heard from Tabitha… who wasn't the most reliable of sources that Maya and Blake had been the darlings of the jewellery world and splashed across all the front pages at one time, so that was probably the real reason she didn't like being photographed now. She'd already told him she'd left that relationship with nothing, so Blake must have betrayed her even more if he'd kept their profitable business, too.

His fingers had itched to Google Maya's history, but he was loath to do that. Who knew what was real or fake and he understood from his own experience how judged he felt from untrue stories. Maya said that her relationship with Blake was over years ago and he had to trust what she said… He didn't like the feeling of unease that she was still keeping something from him, but he'd had to let it slide. He was still in shock that Dame Rosalie Alton's charity ball was just a family party to Maya.

The auction had been a resounding success and Maya had tears in her eyes for the astounding amount Rosalie had raised. Rosalie had sought Maya and Noah out afterwards and she'd raised a glass to them both.

'To you,' she'd said, hugging Maya over and over until her grandmother had stepped in and saved her ribs.

'Well done,' said Ettie as she turned and faced Noah, his body tensing at her piercing green eyes. Maya's own eyes were shining with unshed tears and he assumed she was just happy for Rosalie and the success of her auction and party, but once again, Tabitha had been in his ear suggesting that Maya had clearly been lying to him for months about her family, so what else was she hiding? Had Maya helped with preparing the party or something? He wondered, vulnerability settling on his shoulders like a dead weight. 'So, Noah,' said Ettie, 'we finally meet in person...' which made Maya cringe because the fact that they hadn't met yet was her fault, not his. 'I've heard about you. Which version is accurate?'

'Gran!' said Maya, almost dropping her drink in shock.

'Well, you haven't brought him round for me to make my own opinions,' scolded her grandmother, swishing her long purple dress around her ankles. Noah felt a genuine grin unfurl finally. Maya was so like her feisty grandmother and it actually felt good to meet someone Maya was related to at last.

'I'm sorry about that,' said Noah solemnly, going to kiss Ettie's hand, which she accepted gracefully. Maya's grandad joined them and introduced himself to Noah with a firm handshake and a slap on the back as her siblings arrived too. 'We should rectify that immediately,' he added to Ettie. 'What would you like to know about me and I'd love to extend an invitation for you all to join Maya and I for lunch at my place by the river, if you have time?' Ettie took her time in answering, then her face softened and she smiled at him. Noah could see the family resemblance to Maya, as they both had big inquisitive eyes and a beautiful smile.

'Well, that's settled then,' she grinned. 'I've wanted to see inside that guesthouse since Maya mentioned it and I do like a swim,' she winked at him.

'Gran!' squealed Maya. 'Honestly. I can't take you anywhere.' Maya slipped her arm around his waist and moved in so that their sides were touching, a movement noticed by her grandmother's eagle eyes. She gave him a mischievous grin, and he laughed and let some of the tension go.

'You're more than welcome to use the pool,'

'I've heard the view over the river is astounding,' she winked at Maya and she threw her hands up in exasperation and Rosalie snorted a laugh.

'Ettie, Owen,' she said to Maya's grandparents, 'I think we should leave the youngsters to chat. Poor Arthur is champing at the bit to annoy his sister and Olive and Joe have already bent his ear for the past half an hour. The poor boys just agreed to read Joe's scribbled notes about a screenplay,' she chuckled.

'Sorry Noah,' said Maya. 'I forgot to introduce you to my brother and sister. This is Arthur and the gorgeous blonde in the red dress is Romy.' Noah turned to see a tall, good looking man in smart evening dress, with sandy blond hair and piercing dark eyes move forward to shake his hand. He didn't seem like someone who was easily won over from the wary look on his face, and Romy's expression was even worse. Maya gave them both a pointed stare, and they smiled genially enough, but it wasn't the warm welcome he'd been hoping for. When this had been a fake-date situation, he could have become anything Maya wanted him to be, but now that his feelings were genuine, he wanted them to like him for himself. He remembered Maya telling him that Arthur was a tech guy and Romy had brought a run-down boat and moored it opposite *Bertha*'s dock, which had caused a stir amongst the locals, especially the Bowen brothers who owned the glossy cruise ships that sat next to *Bertha* on the river. Noah tried to summon up the charm that usually came easily to him, but he actually felt a frisson of nerves shoot up his spine. These were two very important people to win over, so he guided them to the bar and offered to refresh both of their drinks, hoping that they took pity on him and eased up on what he guessed would be an interrogation.

Chapter Twenty-Seven

Maya and Noah slumped into the back seat of the limo a couple of hours later and sighed in bliss. 'Well, that wasn't how I thought that night would go,' he said honestly, and she pulled a face.

'Sorry!' she said, wriggling her feet out of her shoes and looking out of the window for a moment, collecting her thoughts. 'You told me how important tonight was for you, so I knew you couldn't miss it. When I found out what and when my family party was, I didn't know what to do,' she sighed, her bones feeling heavy. 'If I'd have told you beforehand, I was worried you'd run for the hills and get in trouble at work,' she finally admitted. 'My family are such a handful, as you found out by the way my siblings fired questions at you for an hour.' When Noah didn't disagree, she bit her lip, and he tilted his head and looked into her eyes.

'They are a lot to take in, but they're welcoming, friendly and loveable, after the first hour,' he winked, and she finally laughed.

'Were they too much?'

'No,' he said truthfully. 'They are amazing and they're all just looking out for you.'

'The same way your family and friends are for you...' she added, and they both went silent for a moment.

'I don't need your family to further my career,' he clarified and she nodded. 'I didn't even know about them!' Then he frowned suddenly as a thought struck him. 'Was that why you put off me meeting them? Did you think I'd use them for publicity?'

'Of course not!' she reassured, but he didn't look convinced. 'You don't exactly need my contacts. You're doing pretty well on your own.' She nudged his hip, and he softened a little and put his arm around her.

'Would you like to stay the night at mine?' Maya asked as she snuggled into his arms as the car sped through the moonlit streets. Noah kissed her firmly on the lips and her world tilted sideways, as it always did when he was near and she didn't hear his reply.

When they pulled up outside her place, he told the driver he could go home and they went inside, Maya sliding her arms around his neck and pulling him in for a kiss as soon as the door closed behind them. Noah growled and swung her up into his arms, but she buried her head in his chest and put her hand on his arm to make him wait before he climbed the stairs to her bedroom.

'There's something I still haven't told you' she said, her heart racing. Noah frowned and her stomach somersaulted as he put her back on her feet. She moved closer to him and went up on her tip-toes to kiss his lips softly. She saw him hesitate and took his hand, leading him upstairs. When they got outside her bedroom, for the first time, she didn't stop and led him towards the top floor.

'What haven't you told me?' he asked, confusion filling his face.

'I need to show you the real me.' The colour drained from Noah's face and she unlocked the door to her workroom and stepped inside, asking him to follow her.

'What is this?' he asked, looking around and then moving to peer out through the window to the balcony and river.

'It's my studio.'

'Your art studio? I thought that was downstairs? It's pretty neat for a studio,' he said, noting her beautifully crafted work desk and sideboard with a coffee machine and neatly stacked glass coffee cups. On the walls were images of her No. 1 Etheral Lane models and jewellery in slim silver frames. The latest one with Gio had pride of place and Noah frowned at that because he'd only just seen a copy of that image at the charity ball. 'I know you like things to be in order, but this is beautiful,' Noah said in wonder, inspecting the posters. 'Did Rosalie give you these?'

Maya went to the wall and opened the safe, removing her latest design, which was half finished. Noah stood rooted to the spot, and he noted the No. 1 Ethereal Lane logo on the platinum tag. He turned to look at the work she'd just placed in the centre of one desk and then back at the advertising images and it seemed he was lost for words.

'It's you?' he asked incredulously.

'Yes.'

'But... why? Why not tell everyone?' Noah moved closer to the half finished ice cave necklace and bent to touch the crystals, then stopped to check if it was ok. She nodded, and he ran his fingers along a sculpted crystal and pursed his lips in wonder. 'This is stunning. I don't know what to say, Maya.'

'I'm trusting you with my life here, Noah. My whole marketing ethos revolves around the mystery of the designer. It started off as two fingers up to Blake, to prove I didn't need to attend the right places or know the right people to become successful, but the mystery behind who makes the jewellery caught people's imagination and now I can't tell anyone who I am. I've boxed myself in,' she admitted finally.

Noah rubbed his neck and then ran his hands through his hair, making it mussed up and sexy. His black tie was undone and so were the top buttons of his shirt now and he could easily have been one of her models. She recalled Tabitha mentioning that, but shook the thought away. He sat down on the couch at one end of the room by the windows and patted the couch next to him for her to join him. Maya opened the double windows to the balcony and let the evening breeze cool them and hopefully the conversation. She'd known he'd have lots of questions when she finally told him, so she sat next to him, their legs touching. 'I was fed up with everyone knowing my business when I split up from Blake because it was all over the papers for a short while and the Portia debacle humiliated me. I felt like people were looking at me wherever I went, which they weren't of course. He made me feel worthless and then he used my designs for the continuation of his own brand, which infuriated me, even though I'd signed my partnership away because I was stupid about that too and didn't seek legal advice.'

'Oh Maya,' he sighed, taking her hand and warming it with his own.

'I wanted to hit back and prove I could find success without him. I didn't know the company would go viral and explode from a little idea to a worldwide brand within a couple of years.'

'But what does it prove to him if he doesn't know that it's you?' asked Noah, sitting up and cupping her face in his hand. She leaned into him and he pulled her onto his lap, his arms keeping her close.

'That's what my family says,' she said as she snuggled into his chest, 'but in the end the mystery made the brand what it is.'

'Your designs make the brand what it is,' soothed Noah.

'But what if everyone's disappointed that it's me?' she said, her voice quivering.

'No one could ever be disappointed in you, Maya,' Noah said, pressing a gentle kiss to her lips which lit a fire in her belly again.

'I have a feeling that Blake knows it's me, but he's never revealed it. He knows my deigns better than anyone.'

Noah faced her, his demeanour tense suddenly. 'But it's all over the press that Blake is probably the No.1 Ethereal Lane designer. It's giving him even more exposure and publicity.'

'Noah, I have a healthy bank balance now. I don't crave fame or attention, and my business is growing beyond my wildest dreams without any of that. My life is quiet... or it was before I met you and I liked it that way.' Noah flinched and she saw her words stung, but there was truth in what she'd said that made her feel slightly uncomfortable. She had enjoyed sitting on the bow of Joe's steamboat while the worries of the world floated by. She'd also been missing something though and Noah crashing into her life brought excitement, unpredictability and love.

'I'm sorry I'm such an inconvenience.'

'You know, I didn't mean it that way. I just don't court the press.'

He raised an eyebrow in question, and his face was set rigid. 'You think I do?'

'It's part of your job. You have to be in the public eye. I don't.' Noah's shoulders slumped, and he pulled his tie off and shoved it in his suit jacket pocket.

'Most of what you've told me has been a lie,' he ground out through gritted teeth. 'I can understand you needing some level of secrecy, but this has made my head spin. You could have trusted me earlier.'

Maya felt sick and put her hand out to a couch to steady herself. This wasn't how she'd thought he'd react. She imagined him swinging her up into his arms and then making love to her on her workroom floor, but his eyes were flashing fire at her. Intimacy looked to be about the last thing on his mind. She wanted to reach out and soothe his worries away, but vulnerability had burnt her before. All she could feel was alarm that she'd revealed her deepest secrets and now the truth was about to ruin everything they'd built up together.

She took his hand in a panic and he didn't shake her off. 'Lets go back downstairs and talk about it over a glass of wine. I promise you that this isn't about Blake or me wanting to hide things from you.' Noah rubbed his jaw and let her lead him back downstairs, flinching as the locks slid into place as she put the necklace back and closed the safe.

'I've told you everything there is to know about me,' he said gravely 'Is there anything else I should know?'

'No. I promise you. This is it,' she said as she grabbed the wine, but he shook his head and made them both a cup of coffee. So much for his earlier declarations of love at the charity ball. That felt like a lifetime ago instead of a couple of hours. Now it seemed like love couldn't be further from his mind.

'It wasn't as easy as I've made out to have my parents living abroad,' she admitted finally, weariness making her eyes sting, but she refused to cry.

'That must have been tough.'

'It was, but it wasn't. Mum and dad worked long hours at the hospital and Gran and Granddad spent most of their time with us by then, anyway. The kids at school teased us about it mercilessly, and it made me become quite introvert-ed,' she wrapped her hands around her mug and sighed. 'I guess I started keeping secrets then, but I didn't realise. I told no one what I was going through because it was hard for Arthur and Romy too and I was the eldest.' She hung her head, and he gently lifted her face and brushed the hair out of her eyes before letting her go. Her eyes misted over and his stance had softened now. He urged her to drink her coffee, and she sipped it and felt the warmth seep into her bones and give her a little extra energy.

'I do sometimes worry that it curbed Grans career,' she admitted. 'She has told me often enough that's nonsense. She was quite famous in her own right, but had been rest-less for a while with demanding clients. I wonder if she'd secretly quite like to work with Rosalie on something, though.'

'That would be amazing,' said Noah, warming his hands around his own coffee mug. 'You could too, you know. We need a jewellery centrepiece for one scene that Rosalie is in. Your designs would work beautifully and it could open new windows of opportunity,' he clearly saw her face become guarded and hastily added, 'not that you need them.'

Maya bit her lip and watched him over the rim of her coffee mug. What he'd said resonated with something

Tabitha had mentioned about Noah needing publicity for the film and him saying his producers had asked him to up his game and do more public appearances. She tried to shake the feeling off, but years of distrust were ingrained and she wasn't about to be used by a man for his own gain... ever again. When he came round the island unit and pulled her into his arms, she wearily complied because that was one of her favourite places to be. The usual feelings of warmth and safety were missing and as she rested her head on his heart, she hoped with all her might that she hadn't made the same mistake twice.

Chapter Twenty-Eight

Maya woke up the next day with a stony heart and an empty bed. The charity ball and family meeting with Noah had all gone as well as it could have, but as soon as she'd confided in him about her real life, everything had fallen apart. At first, he'd been understandably upset by all the lies, but he had given her time to explain and not stormed out. Staying the night and talking things through hadn't left her feeling much better, and they'd fallen into an exhausted sleep where she'd tossed and turned all night. After all the protestations from her friends and family and trusting a man again, finally bringing a new person into her circle left her raw, exposed, and uncertain. Noah had listened for hours while she'd told him everything, and he'd explained more about his own childhood and upbringing. It had brought them closer together, and she'd fallen asleep in the safety of his arms, but in the cold light of day the bed next to her was empty and as she glanced around for a note and listened out to hear if he was downstairs in the kitchen, the room was deathly quiet.

She pulled the duvet cover off and shivered, even though it was another gloriously bright day. Summer was almost over now and the colder nights were setting in, but there was still sunshine and blue skies to be found and today was one of those days. The brilliant blue made her eyes hurt, and she squinted as she peeked out of the windows around her thick white velvet bedroom curtains. Her eyes darted around in search of Noah, but she didn't know why, as it wasn't as if he'd be strolling beside the river with a coffee. He couldn't do that without being mobbed by fans, which was grating on her nerves a little and was another reason she'd shunned the limelight.

Had she done the right thing in confiding in him? She wondered. Maybe she should have discussed it with Matt and Leah, or her family, first, but she was a woman in love and had felt the time had come. She was fed up of the deceit and Noah had been right to be upset, but then he was the one who had wanted to lie to everyone about dating each other in the first place! Maya had hoped that Noah might be excited or impressed, but certain members of the press hounded him and he didn't want that for her when they found out, if they ever did.

'I understand why you hid your identity from everyone else,' Noah had said the night before with hurt in his voice. 'But it leads me to believe that you don't trust me, because you waited until now to let me know about your family and your business.'

'I know. I'm sorry,' she'd replied. 'Hiding my business has become ingrained this year and Blake taught me not to trust anyone outside of my family.'

'I'm not Blake,' he ground out and gone to get them both a glass of water from the kitchen. That should have reassured her, she guessed, as Blake would only have considered himself, but she wasn't used to letting a man care for her because she'd never experienced it before. Where the hell was Noah?

She padded on the soft carpet over to her bedside table and checked her phone. There was no text from Noah, so she sighed and then scrolled down, which made her scowl. Tabitha had messaged her, asking to meet and saying that she only had an hour that day to do it, typical dictator style. Maya fleetingly thought that perhaps she'd leave her alone for good if they met, but she wasn't changing her plans for anyone. She'd been lax in her drawing and painting time recently and needed to get back onto *Bertha* and create some new designs. Quickly sending a text to Tabitha, Maya said she'd meet her but that Tabitha would have to join the steamboat cruise, then cursed as she clearly hadn't thought that through because it meant being stuck on a boat for an hour with Tabitha and the only way to get rid of her would be to throw her overboard. She shook off the annoyance because she finally had a good man in her life and if she'd learnt anything from last night; it was that he put her first – even if he'd left without saying goodbye or where he was going. She gulped as a knot of fear hit her stomach. Tabitha couldn't hurt them now...

Maya wrote a text to ask Noah where he was and then paused in indecision before deleting it. Noah deserved her trust. If he'd gone out, then it was probably a last-minute work call or a meeting he'd forgotten to mention. She'd shared her biggest secret with him, as well as her heart, and was taking a colossal risk.

She hastily threw on some washed out jeans and a fitted t-shirt with gold, silver and tones of blue zig-zagging across it at all angles. After putting her art supplies in her tote bag, wondering if she'd get a chance to use them that day, she saw a reply to her text ping back and Tabitha agree to board *Bertha*. If she got there a while before the ship departed from the dock, then maybe they would have a quick conversation and Maya could enjoy the journey in peace. What on earth could be so important she couldn't fathom, but maybe Maya could jump off at the racecourse and grab a drink and jump back on *Bertha* when she returned with the next set of guests. That way her time with Tabitha was limited to twenty minutes maximum, she reasoned.

She called Leah and waited for her to pick up. 'Have you recovered from last night?' she teased immediately, and Maya's mood finally lifted. Leah always could make Maya smile, even when she was being pushy.

'It didn't end as well as I'd have liked,' Maya admitted solemnly.

'What happened?' Maya hated the alarm in her friends voice, but she really needed someone to confide in right now.

'I told Noah about it being a family party. He took that pretty well considering...'

'Well what then?' asked Leah, never one to have much patience when waiting for information about Maya's love life.

'I decided the time was right to let him into my studio and showed him some of my designs.' Maya heard Leah gasp and her heart sank. 'Did I do the wrong thing?'

'No... you definitely did the right thing,' comforted her friend. 'Matt and I are the biggest supporters of how you've built your brand up, because your crazy idea worked, but he agrees with me that you will have to trust others with it from time to time.'

'I know,' said Maya, pressing her fingers to the bridge of her nose.

'How did Noah take it?' asked Leah and Maya could imagine her twirling her long red hair around her fingers, as she did this when she was nervous and she'd already picked up on Maya's tone.

'He said I hadn't trusted him and then he was gone when I woke up this morning,' Maya dipped her eyes and closed them tight, refusing to let tears flow.

'Maybe he left you a message? Have you looked?'

'Of course I've looked. He's never left without kissing me goodbye before.'

'Maybe he didn't want to wake you?' soothed Leah. 'Noah's one of the good guys,' she assured, but even she didn't sound as convinced as she usually was. 'Let's meet up later for a debrief and we can dissect your conversation and hunt him down if he even thinks of letting you down,' said Leah with steel in her voice that made Maya giggle at last.

'I'm sure there's a reasonable explanation,' she responded, biting her lip and hoping that was true. Work needed to take precedent that day and she'd just remembered that she'd said Tabitha could join her on a cruise, so she promised Leah that she'd meet her later and closed the front door behind her as she went to find out what Tabitha wanted from her now.

Chapter Twenty-Nine

Hugging Joe and Roman felt so good after the night she'd had, so she held onto them for a moment longer than usual and then went to check on the bar. The new staff had everything under control, and the setting looked as beautiful as it had when they'd done the makeover. The glasses sparkled in the sunlight and the rows of drinks bottles lined the shelves and tempted Joe's customers to try a tipple. Maya ordered a strawberry lemonade and ran her hand along the plush velvet banquet seating as she passed, remembering how much fun it had been to bring *Bertha* back to life. She hadn't known Noah personally then, and she wondered if she'd been happier? She didn't think so, but the confusion of the morning had put her on edge. The thought of meeting Tabitha wasn't helping and when she set herself up with a little space by the bow that was sectioned off for staff, she heaved a sigh of relief, as it looked like Tabitha wouldn't make it on board.

Tabitha's eyes lit up when he saw Maya, and Maya's

heart sank. It looked like Tabitha had visited the bar too because she was holding a half-full glass orange juice. Was Maya doing the right thing, giving her the time of day? She'd been euphoric after confiding in Noah and the unburdening of her secret felt incredible at first, but now Tabitha was in front of her again and she turned towards her and sent her a wide grin, Maya's stomach flipped and she suddenly had a terrible feeling that she'd made the wrong choice about letting Noah into her secret just yet.

Tabitha was wearing casual cream trousers and a very expensive-looking blouse and lightweight jacket, but she paused and seemed surprised at the pleasant river view and the bustle of other customers, before moving forward and sitting in the seat next to Maya, oversized sunglasses perched on her nose.

Maya shifted uncomfortably in her seat and finally focused on Tabitha. 'Why did you want to meet me?' she asked, thinking it was about time they put their toxic past to bed.

'I wanted to apologise,' Tabitha said with a wobbly voice and Maya frowned as Tabitha removed her sunglasses and her eyes looked red and sore as if she'd been crying.

'I thought you were my enemy, but I wonder now if that's just what Noah wanted me to think.'

'Um... I'm not sure I understand,' said Maya, sipping her drink and then tucking it under her seat.

'Have you seen Noah today?' asked Tabitha, her brow creased with worry.

'Not yet. He had already gone out when I got up,' admitted Maya, not liking the way this conversation had started, or that she was telling Tabitha anything she could use against them.

'That's because he's in an emergency public relations meeting for the film were both in,' explained Tabitha, taking her hand and patting it in a consoling manner that Maya didn't like. She drew her hands away and put them on the bench either side of her legs. 'Our bosses have invested millions in this film and they've told us it has to be a success,' Tabitha sighed and glanced around as if they might be overheard.

'What's that got to do with me?' asked Maya, who waited anxiously for the answer.

'Well,' Tabitha leaned closer as if to confide a secret. 'You know that tabloid reporter I told you about? The one I give story titbits to?' Maya nodded, a ball of dread forming in her tummy but she didn't know why. 'It was actually Noah who introduced us. Noah has been filtering him stories for years. Being portrayed as a love rat, as long as an explanation comes out in his favour afterwards, keeps him current.' Tabitha sniffed and tears filled her eyes.

'I don't understand,' said Maya, picturing Noah's quick conversation with the guy in the bushes outside her house and wondering about the fact that the picture still hadn't surfaced yet.

'He made me fall in love with him, then told other women I was a bit of a stalker,' Tabitha wiped her eyes with the back of her hand and Maya handed her the branded napkin that had come with her drink. Tabitha dabbed at her eyes and sat straighter, looking directly at Maya. 'I think he might end up doing the same thing to you.'

'What?' asked Maya. 'Why would he do that?'

'He needed a fresh relationship to keep the news current. After you jumped into the river to save Robbie, I overheard them talking about the possibility of the film being a flop. Robbie told him to get more press coverage. Now I'm thinking that he might have already had information about your family. They are pretty famous.'

'But Noah said you weren't even invited to those parties?' questioned Maya.

Tabitha rolled her eyes and sniffed again. 'He would say that. I'd told him to stop using me in the press. It's why I started dating Corey. He's really kind,' she added, 'nothing like Noah.'

'But Noah's kind...'

'He's a talented actor,' scoffed Tabitha. 'Plus, he has background checks done on anyone he dates.' She left that spark in the air to catch fire and Maya gasped and put her hand over her mouth in shock.

Maya could feel pain slicing through her ribs. She'd waited for so long to hear Noah tell her he loved her, but it had only happened in front of Dame Rosalie, not in private. Why was that? Had he known about her family all along and played the long game? Had he already known about the family party being the charity ball?

She sighed heavily and puffed out her cheeks, then took a hefty swig of her lemonade, while she digested what Tabitha had said. Maya calmed her mind and folded her hands primly in her lap.

'I tried to warn you when we met before,' said Tabitha, her eyes watching a couple of children run along the riverside and their parents pick up pace to catch them up. They were nearing the racecourse now and Maya intended to get off. She needed time to contact Noah or at least think clearly about what Tabitha had said, but a couple of points could ring true.

'In what way did you warn me?' Maya asked, her eyes closed as she tried to stop the pounding in her head.

'When we met for a drink, I told you how different your worlds were and tried to put you off him to get you out of his clutches. I'm contracted to the movie, so I have to go to lots of the same events. I explained to Noah I don't like the way he works, but our producers told us we have to get on,' she said, confusingly, as this kind of mirrored what Noah said but in a different context.

'Why tell me?'

'Because I want to do the right thing,' Tabitha said. 'The last thing I want is for you to get hurt like I have been by a master manipulator. Plus, I don't want to see your family splashed all over the papers like I have been, either.' Tabitha glanced around again, then seemed to weigh up whether to say more. 'Has Blake been texting you lately? I know you were engaged. Portia told me.' When Maya didn't answer, that gave Tabitha the answer. 'Portia and I are quite good friends and Blake tries to control everything she does.'

'Why doesn't she leave him then?' Maya asked, not wanting to bring back memories of how dominant Blake used to be. 'She thinks he's having an affair and wants to find out the truth first. She loves him... sorry...' Tabitha winced and gave Maya an apologetic look.

'Well it's not me he's having an affair with and maybe how they first got together might have given her a clue to his nature,' Maya added shortly, looking out at the river and trying to focus on a family of Egyptian geese that was trailing happily alongside the boat.

'Noah and Blake are quite good friends, so perhaps Blake told him about you?' Tabitha wondered out loud. Maya's lip trembled. Could Noah have known already?

'But, I thought they didn't know each other well?'

Tabitha gave Maya a sympathetic look and her insides crunched up. Had Blake given Noah a tip about Maya possibly being the No. 1 Ethereal Lane designer and Noah had used that to his advantage to gain leverage with his bosses? 'There's no way Noah could have known I'd jump in the river after Robbie,' Maya stated, trying to claw back some sense of reason, but it was slipping through her fingers.

'He'd already been trying to find you through your art though.' Tabitha dealt the final blow and smiled at a couple of cruise guests who were looking their way and chatting quietly as they'd clearly recognised her.

Maya felt like someone had punched her in the stomach as she'd just confided in Noah about No. 1 Ethereal Lane and confirmed who she was. She collected her things and got up to leave as *Bertha* maneuvered into the second dock. 'I need to go,' said Maya. 'Are you staying for the ride back?'

'No,' said Tabitha as she stood up on shaky legs and put her arms around Maya for a hug and a pat on the back, which Maya took mutely. It felt so weird to be hugged by Tabitha after all this time. 'I've got a driver picking me up at the racecourse. Think about what I've said,' she added before she collected her own bag and joined the throng to exit the boat, her sunglasses firmly back in place.

A few people glanced Tabitha's way, but most were excited to jump on dry land and explore the racecourse. Maya's body was numb as she sat herself back down on the bow and Roman came over to check on her. He was wearing their new uniform and his hair had been cut really short and was growing through again in a dark halo of curls, which made him look even more handsome. 'You okay?' he asked with concern.

'I'm fine,' assured Maya, although she certainly didn't feel it. 'Roman, can you bring me a *Bertha* special with an extra shot of gin?' she asked, and he frowned and nodded, rushing away to grab her a glass. Maya felt her own legs shake as she unpacked her pad and pencils again and stared unseeing out at the river as the boat turned around and headed back to Windsor.

Chapter Thirty

Maya had fallen into an exhausted sleep after the emotional meeting with Tabitha and then a barrage of work emails that she couldn't ignore. She'd tried to contact Noah, but he wasn't answering and in the end she'd given up and put her phone onto silent. She'd drank a couple of glasses of wine while she'd been working to soothe her growing unease about why she couldn't get hold of Noah, but decided she was being paranoid as they went days without contact from time to time when both of their schedules were busy. Surely this was Tabitha being malicious again, but she'd appeared vulnerable and open about her feelings and a few of the things she'd said had rung alarm bells in Maya's head. The timings of this absence of communication couldn't have been worse, but she was a tough cookie and she could cope on her own as usual.

When she woke the next morning, her head felt like it was banging at the gates of hell and her mouth was so dry that she could barely stumble into her en-suite to run a glass under the cold tap. After glugging a whole glassful of water down, she walked over to her windows and gasped in shock. Maya grabbed hold of the curtains for support and quickly ducked behind them as she fell to the floor. All the air whooshed out of her and as she pulled herself up to look again, she noted hundreds of photographers and journalists outside her home, swarming around the front door. Pulling out the earplugs she sometimes wore when she was anxious and needed a good night's sleep, she threw them on the floor.

Maya tried not to hyperventilate and dressed as quickly as she could, shoving a baseball cap over her hair and some dark glasses on her face. The constant dinging of the front doorbell was incessant, so she grabbed her phone without looking at it and didn't switch the ringer back on because her head was already pounding. Throwing a few items of clothing into a bag that she'd left by the door to the dock, she slid her phone in her pocket and swung the bag over her shoulder before slipping out of the door and into the boat stored under her house. Smoothly, angling out of the berth and along the river, she was on her way before anyone thought to look at that side of the house.

Maya breathed a sigh of relief as she left the jetty behind and wondered what the hell had happened? She pulled up at the private dock by her grandparent's house that was partially hidden by an enormous willow tree and slipped inside the house after a quick sprint up the garden, avoiding the many plants in pots that her grandad had arranged haphazardly on the grass. He must be having a glasshouse clear out, but it looked even more like a leafy assault course than usual. Her whole family was already sitting around the kitchen table like a council of war when she stepped through the kitchen door via the conservatory. The air smelt of freshly brewed tea and all the lights were on for some reason. She noted her parents were currently on FaceTime to her siblings, and they all looked her way as she rushed in and darted glances around. Romy jumped up and hugged her fiercely, muttering under her breath about 'bloody men'. Her grandmother waited patiently and then did the same.

'What the hell has happened?' she asked, trying to catch her breath. 'Is it something to do with Noah? I haven't even had time to check my phone. I was so tired from finishing my latest design last night that I passed out.' Arthur handed her a rather full tumbler of brandy that he'd been drinking from. Maya sniffed it and flinched at the pungent aroma, but sipped it anyway to calm her racing nerves.

'You're going to need that,' he said, anger emanating from him as he paced back and forth across the room, running his hands through his tousled blonde hair, his face unreadable. He pointed to the newspapers that were strewn across the huge wooden kitchen table and she leaned forward and started scanning them all with her eyes, before stepping back like they had shot her, with a hand to her heart. There were photos of her with Robbie on *Bertha* where he was kissing her on the lips during his surprise visit, ones with Noah were they were watching the stars at night and were in each other's arms and several with her and Blake, some of which looked like they'd come from the little album she'd made up for him for their three-year anniversary. She didn't even know he'd kept it and had assumed he would have thrown it away by now. She looked like a complete strumpet, or a fame hunter, and stumbled back, winded by what the images looked like. Arthur put his arm around her and pulled her to his side for comfort. The biggest headline was: Secret No.1 Ethereal Lane jewellery designer unmasked! The rest were more of the same. It made it look like she'd slept her way to the top.

'Someone must have tipped off papers,' she said gravely.

'Who would do that?' asked Arthur, his dark eyes watching her closely as she moved back to read more.

Had Noah and Blake concocted this together for their own gain as Tabitha suggested? Did Blake set this up because he was splashed across the papers as well and they had linked his brand with hers, because they now knew she'd designed his ranges too. Now their names would be interlinked forever, she flinched and her heart sank. She had wanted to let everyone know who was behind her brand, but not this way. Now it looked like she'd used her famous connections to make No. 1 Ethereal Lane popular and had flown on Blake's coat tails.

She read on as her grandad came and pulled out a chair for her and urged her to sit down, motioning for Ettie to make fresh tea and bring sustenance for them all. She rushed to put the kettle on and returned with an enormous plate full of homemade biscuits of various sizes, which finally made Maya smile before the feeling of pure dread returned.

There was a press statement from Blake saying that he couldn't confirm that the No. 1 Ethereal Lane designer was Maya. He'd added that they'd worked together in creating BM Bespoke as a team and their brand stood for both of their initials. Nothing about how he'd slept with their model while they were engaged or that he'd profited from her designs without her consent.

One newspaper had printed a photo of her hugging Dame Rosalie Alton at the ball, so now speculation about who she really was, was rife. Some articles said she was an artist local to Windsor, another said she served drinks on a steamboat cruiser on the river Thames. There was a copy of the photo of *Bertha* where she was standing next to Gio, and he had his arm around her. 'Oh, my God! What do I do?' she asked in a panic? 'This makes me look like I'm a pathetic loser who uses my friends for fame.'

'No, it doesn't!' raged Romy, banging the table and making them all jump. 'Your artistic talent made both you and Blake famous and your designs caught the interest of the public, not who you date.' Maya's heart softened at her sister's protective words, but the reality was that kudos behind her carefully built up branding had just crashed and burnt.

'If anyone dares to speak unkindly of my sister, they'll have me to deal with,' Romy added with fire.

'Likewise,' ground out Arthur, coming to stand behind his sister, his hands resting on the back of her chair. Maya put her hand on his and squeezed it in thanks.

Maya turned a page over, hoping to see fresh news, but the next photo was one of her and Matt a couple of years after they'd first met. He was hugging her tight, their faces full of laughter. Maya remembered Leah had taken the photo, and she'd been pulling funny faces to make them smile because she'd said they were both spending too much time in Matt's new office. How had they gotten that photo? Matt and Leah wouldn't have given it to them. That was one thing she was sure of. The thought made a shiver go down her spine and she hugged herself with her arms to get some warmth back into her veins.

'Who would have broken the story?' demanded Romy. 'Who had the most to gain?' Maya's head was spinning and she couldn't think straight, but Arthur moved one news- paper across and pushed another in front of her. Her face drained of colour when she saw it. Noah's movie was discussed in many of the articles that her grandmother had kind of hidden and she stood up and moved around the table to read them all. Rosalie was in one image, at the ball, holding up the waterfall necklace and then later, hugging Maya, with image after image of Noah and Rosalie's upcoming movie being mentioned. Maya was pictured with Noah as they smiled into each other's eyes as they left the event, and she remembered how happy she'd felt in her vibrant dress with a man who'd just expressed that he loved her. She squeezed her eyes tightly shut and refused to let the tears flow. The image made her blood run cold, and she quickly picked up her phone and tried to scroll through the million messages on there, then gave up and handed it to Arthur, who did the same.

'They're asking if Noah might be the next No.1 Ethereal Lane model or if you might design for his movie,' said her grandmother, taking a biscuit and handing it to Maya who ate it without thinking and then winced as her stomach pushed back and refused to take it in. She gulped down the whisky and then grimaced at the bitter taste.

'There's also this...' said Romy, ignoring her grandmother, who tried to snatch that article away. She dodged it and went to stand next to Maya, handing her the article and putting an arm around her shoulder for support. The image was of Noah and Tabitha the previous evening. He had his hand around her waist, but she looked wary and uncomfortable as they left a top-end restaurant. So much for being snowed under with work! Had they both played her for their own gain, or had Tabitha been right? She certainly didn't look happy in the photo. Maya sobbed and pushed away from her sister to run to the bathroom and fall to the floor while she curled up into a ball and howled, her body shaking at the injustice of it all. She'd done it again. Trusted the wrong man. When would she ever learn?

'It has to be Noah or Blake or someone who hates her enough to want to destroy her life,' said Romy, her teeth barring and her fists bunching, as Maya finally pulled herself together and return to the kitchen after washing her face several times, using eye drops to mask her tired eyes and giving herself a stern talking to about standing up people who thought they could control her, or her life. She'd survived before and she would do so again. Maya hadn't known what her life would look like after Blake, but she had more choices than she'd had last time, including a home, money in the bank, and her friends and family. Her smile wobbled when she heard what Romy had to say, but she couldn't disagree with her sentiment. Someone was clearly out to tarnish her reputation or add to their own career. There was still huge speculation about the exact location of No. 1 Ethereal Lane in pretty much all the articles and although some voiced the opinion that it was a fictional place, or just what she called her new studio, others said it must be real.

Arthur handed her the phone where he'd separated the emails and texts into files, and she gratefully received another hug of support from him. He was over six foot tall and towered over her, but he gave the best cuddles. 'Is there anything else I can do?' he asked. 'Want me to beat Noah and Blake with a stick?' he half-joked. Maya tried to summon up a smile, but it fell short.

'Thanks for the sentiment, but the last time you got into a fight, he was twice your size and he broke your nose,' she chuckled but it hurt her ribs where she'd been crying so much.

'Good point, although I was only twelve. I'm more of a

lover than a fighter,' he winked, and she spluttered a laugh at that, which made him grin and ruffle her hair like he had when they were kids, even though she was older than him. 'You'll be okay, sis. It needed to come out at some point, so maybe they've done you a favour?' She raised an eyebrow at this, and he just shrugged and guided her back to sit at the family kitchen table. She looked up as she heard noise outside, which made her quake with fear, but she sighed in relief when Matt and Leah arrived in a bustle of greetings, exclamations of anger and hugs of support. Rosalie was next, but they all did a double take as she was disguised as a grey-haired man with a flat cap, tweed jacket and walking stick, which raised a few smiles.

'How did you all get here without being seen?' she asked incredulously, her eyes beginning to water again, so she sniffed and rubbed her already red nose.

'Noah brought Matt and Leah,' said Rosalie as Maya gasped in shock. Noah was the last person she wanted to see right now. She'd probably shove him in the river and invite Tabitha to watch. 'He knew you'd need support, so he arranged for Matt and Leah to be picked up and drove them here on his boat,' continued Rosalie, patting her hand kindly and then hugging her fiercely.

'We had to hide under a big blanket!' said Leah, but it sounded like she'd enjoyed the subterfuge. 'Noah's in the back garden waiting for you,' she pulled a face, but didn't look that sorry. Maya hadn't had time to tell Leah about her conversation with Tabitha, but when she did, all hell would break loose. Maya's cheeks flushed pink, and she looked at her grandmother for advice, rubbing her sore eyes.

'Take my stick in case you want to shove him in the river,' she advised, echoing Maya's thoughts. Maya was unsure about what to do, but she would have to face Noah at some point, so she might as well get it over with. She pushed herself up on tired arms, kissed Ettie on the cheek and then quickly hugged Matt and Leah before leaving them all to it, knowing they'd have their noses pressed against the conservatory glass in seconds. Evan was standing guard by the door and she gave him a quick kiss on the cheek in thanks. He clearly hadn't let Noah through to the house and her heart swelled with love for her family. Noah was wearing a long-sleeved fitted black top and slim fit jeans that hugged his waist and Maya hated the way her heart soared at the sight of him.

Her eyes met Noah's concerned one and before he could speak, she tilted her head further down the garden to let him know to wait and that they should begin their conversation there. She hadn't picked up her gran's walking stick, but there were plenty of places to stash a body in the river if it came to that, so she grit her teeth and led the way, being careful not to touch him as they walked side by side. 'What are you doing here?' she asked him as they reached a huge glasshouse at the end of the garden that was partially hidden by an enormous willow tree.

Chapter Thirty-One

'How did you find me?' she asked, not quite able to meet his eye. 'This place is at the end of a long, unmade road and only the people who live here can get through the gates. No one knows I'm here.'

'We saw this place from the river on our date and I remembered how you spoke about it.' He looked hurt that she'd forgotten, but she shrugged and waited to hear more. 'I assumed you'd come here after wracking my brain for a while and bothering Leah and Matt.' She looked at him finally and his hair was mussed up and he had bags under his eyes. He still made her heart flip at the sight of him because he was so handsome, but she shut those feelings down quickly.

'Anyone could have seen you come here,' said Maya.

'They didn't. I'm used to this,' he sighed. 'Have you seen the news today? I promise you I didn't tell the press,' he breathed, taking her hand. She didn't pull away at first, but darted a glance towards the river as if a photographer might jump out on them. The protective boughs of the tree hid the glasshouse, but she wasn't taking any chances.

'How do I know I can trust you after what has just happened? My face is splashed all over the media.' She felt tears fill her eyes and scratch the back of her eyelids but she refused to let them flow and scrunched up her eyes, turning away for a moment to brush her hand across her closed eyes. 'You stayed the night at my house and then I heard nothing from you for two days.'

'I left you a note by the coffee machine.' Noah frowned. 'I got called in for an emergency production meeting, admittedly about personal appearances and us stepping up our duties, but by going on chat shows and podcasts, not by who we are dating.' Noah started pacing, and he rubbed his chin that had stubble growing, so unlike his usually clean shaven image.

'I didn't see the note,' Maya pictured swiping her hand across the kitchen surfaces and straight into the bin to clean them. There had been some of her smaller sketches there that she wasn't happy with because of how upset she'd been, so she'd thrown them away, which was unlike her. Maybe Noah had used one sheet of paper for his note? It was possible.

'It said I'd been called in and asked you to text me about meeting up to talk more, but you never replied. I know how busy you've been but I was starting to get worried.'

'Did you need press coverage for your film?' she demanded to know.

'The film is already hugely publicised!' Noah protested. 'I'm just one person amongst thousands of cast members. Dame Rosalie being one of them! She was called to the meeting too.' Maya paused at that and her lip wobbled. 'They want the main cast to schedule in some guest appearances. It's tricky to work out, but we did it. It had nothing to do with you. Why would you think that?'

'I don't know what to believe,' she ranted, her fists bunching as she faced him. He looked crestfallen and stopped trying to take her hand.

'Selling a story about you to the press would be my biggest nightmare!' His eyes implored hers for understanding. 'I've spent years avoiding that for my family.'

'Tabitha told me you gave her that dodgy press contact, and it was you who fed the stories to the press about your relationship with her.'

Noah's eyes went wide with shock and his mouth dropped open, his face growing red. 'Tabitha? When did she tell you this?' he demanded to know.

'She asked me to meet her and visited *Bertha*. She said you knew Blake well and always do background checks on who you date, so probably knew who my family were before the party.'

'That's ridiculous!'

'You deny it?'

'You believed her!' he was incredulous and for the first time, Maya's resolve wavered. 'What would a background check have told me?' he fumed. 'That your amazing grandparents were famous but are retired now? That you used to date Blake, who has a visible brand, but nothing that much interests people in my circle? Sorry...' he hung his head. She couldn't correct him because her BM Bespoke brand was popular with influencers, but she couldn't imagine A-list superstars buying it, although the recent news might make Blake even richer as people sought that brand out. She shook her head to clear it.

'I reacted like a jealous jerk when you told me your secrets and I'm sorry,' he parried and her body sagged in exhaustion. 'I'd just told you I loved you then found out most of what you'd told me was a mistruth.' She watched him from under her lashes and tried to work out all the emotions that she'd had to deal with that day. 'I should have accepted that you needed to tell me in your own time and now this has happened I realise why you wanted to keep your two worlds separate.'

'It's so unfair,' seethed Maya. 'I worked hard for my own success.'

'Your face is everywhere,' Noah added, his own shoulders drooping.

'Yours too,' said Maya in disgust and he flinched.

'I'm sorry. I would never sell a story about the person I care about most to the press. Please believe me,' he pleaded, and she finally looked into his eyes, doubt in her own. Was he telling the truth? He could clearly see her wavering, and he took her hand and kissed it. 'I would never hurt you intentionally, because I love you.' His vulnerability was apparent and she felt her eyes fill with tears again. She didn't pull away as he took that opportunity to pull her into his arms and kiss her ever so gently on the mouth, briefly, in case she kicked him. He let out a tremendous sigh of relief when she didn't and they both gave each other a small wobbly smile, as he brushed her tears away with the pad of his thumb.

Noah finally took a proper look around. 'So this is No. 1 Ethereal Lane?' he asked in wonder as he turned to the glasshouse and noted sun catchers and crystals glistening in the morning light in the windows, sending spirals of colour dancing across virtually every surface. There was a time-worn and much used work desk to the left and a huge drawing board with descriptions and drawings of plants in childish lettering to the right. There were flower garlands strung across the ceiling and fairy lights by the door.

'Yes,' she admitted finally, deciding that she had to at

least try to trust his word. 'My granddad said the place had an ethereal feel to it as it's such a delicate glass structure and I always hung sparkly things in every window, which makes myriads of light hit every surface, so the name stuck. Although the workshop next door where my brother gets up to all kinds of mischief is called The chip shop!' she tried to lift the heavy atmosphere, but she sniffed and couldn't meet Noah's eye. 'Arthur's obsessed with anything to do with tech and microchips,' she joked lamely and he joined in, but then they both grew serious again. Noah turned and saw movement further down the garden by the house.

'What is Blake doing here?' Noah felt Maya's shoulders tense, and he put a hand on her arm to reassure her.

'Helping... finally. All this subterfuge is exhausting,' he answered. 'I thought my life was confusing until I stepped into yours.'

'I know! What's that got to do with Blake? If it wasn't you...' she paused because she still wasn't 100 percent convinced of his innocence in all of this. 'Did he leak my identity to the press?' she asked, her fists bunching. 'I saw the photo of your date with Tabitha last night,' she ground out and stepped further away from him again, and he sighed in exasperation and reached out to pull their bodies back into contact.

'It wasn't a date. She told me she'd discovered who the designer that everyone was looking for was,' Maya gasped and turned to face him.

'What?'

'She wanted to talk to me about it and plan how to use the information, but I told her to leave it alone. She wasn't happy and that exact moment a photographer took a picture. It was another work event. I told you about it last week and I text you yesterday as well, but you didn't reply.'

May thought back and then recalled him telling her he had a work engagement. Her mind was flitting back and forward, trying to piece everything together. 'So Tabitha knew who I was when she met me on the boat.'

Noah closed his eyes to refocus, but pressed his hands together and then looked at her. He looked so exhausted that she wanted to go to him, but she held herself back. 'It seems that way.'

'She was trembling and crying about how you were using us both and she warned me away. It seems she's a talented actress after all...'

'I called Blake so that he could explain face to face what really happened. I thought you might not believe it from me.' They watched Blake have cross words with her grandmother at the door and Evan preventing him from walking through, but then they stood aside and let him in, which made Maya's gawp in shock.

'I'd rather you tell me,' she said wearily. 'I don't have the energy for Blake today.'

'Blake called me when the story broke. I tried to text and call, but you didn't answer the phone. I couldn't turn up at your place because they'd mobbed it. Tabitha made sure they pictured me out with her last night, even though we were with the entire production team. I thought it weird that she said she had to tell me something important outside, but as soon as the flashbulbs went off, I knew she'd suckered me again.' Noah took a fortifying breath and Maya didn't interrupt him. She stood frozen with her arms at her side and didn't know what to think. Tabitha was certainly more than capable of doing what he'd said. She'd done it countless times before.

'Blake said he felt he owed you the truth, but I think he also wanted to get himself firmly out of the blame game,' he scoffed in anger. 'Tabitha met Portia at the café by the dock and saw the photo of you and Gio. The cogs all slid into place and she used Portia to stir up trouble.' Noah took her hands and led her to sit at her childhood jewellery-making desk. He bobbed down on his haunches in front of her and spoke again. 'Tabitha told Portia that Blake had been texting you and persuaded her you were sleeping together again. She tried to convince me of the same thing last night.' Maya rocked back in her chair and Noah put his hands on her legs to support her.

'That way, her own hands were clean when Portia exposed who you really are to Tabitha's source. Portia accused Blake of having an affair with you and went ballistic, Blake said. Now she's licking her wounds at their flat after realising you were innocent of any wrongdoing once again and that Tabitha also set her up. Tabitha thought it poetic justice that Portia ruined your life twice because both have been burning up with jealousy about who you really are,' Noah tried to soothe, but her blood was boiling!

'Blake is fuming, as it seems he's still protective over you,' he shook his head at the lunacy of Blake's logic. 'I'm not sure their relationship will last.' Maya stood up and wobbled on unsteady legs and Noah caught her. 'I know this is a lot to take in, but I promise I'd never hurt you. I have no aspirations of being one of your models and I don't need my girlfriend to find me more work.' He was emanating anger and she finally let go of some of the hurt.

'Do you believe me?' he asked, his eyes dark and watchful.

'Knowing Tabitha and Portia and even the way Blake's brain works, I do,' she said shakily, more tears threatening to flow. 'I'm guessing this is as much of a headache for you now as it is for me?' She rubbed her neck, and he pulled her in for a hug, which she sank into. She raised her face up to his and kissed her as if he'd been dying without her. Her knees trembled, and she wound her arms around him and gave herself to the sensation of being in his arms again, heat flaring through her veins.

'We should get back,' she said finally, when they pulled apart, eyes glazed. 'I should have known Blake would be mixed up in this whole mess somehow. And Portia!' she leaned back into his body and he wrapped his arms around her as they looked out of the windows and towards the boats ambling up and down the river as the sun peeped through the clouds.

'Why has your grandad put plants all over the lawn like an assault course?' he asked with interest, dropping a few kisses to her neck and making her squirm against him. 'I almost tripped over one and broke my neck on the way in,' he smiled.

'That was probably his plan,' grinned Maya finally, taking his hand and leading him back to the house, which was full of people who loved her and would do anything to protect her, she realised. She ignored the fact that Blake was amongst them. She didn't have to face any of this alone, which made the problem seem easier, suddenly.

'I love your family's inventive ideas and I love you,' Noah reiterated firmly, to make himself doubly clear. He was on her side too.

'You still love me?'

'I do. I've told you that before though,' he mock scolded and she admitted she loved him too. 'Finally!' he joked, his eyes blazing with devotion. 'I think I fell in love with you the minute our eyes met after we'd both been pulled out of the river,' he admitted, his eyes never leaving hers.

'Me too,' she blushed and took his hand, while his other one cupped her face.

'We can deny recent stories about us in the press, but I'd rather not. I want us to be a regular couple.'

'A regular couple?'

'Okay. An irregular one,' he laughed, turning her around and pulling her to him. 'No more love pacts unless they involve us agreeing to move in together.'

'Move in together?' she squeaked in surprise.

'I've got a beautiful room with a view of the river that would make a perfect design studio,' he coaxed. 'We both have busy lives, but this way we can spend more time together,' he added, hopefully.

'Sounds perfect to me,' she responded happily, her heart filling with joy.

'Do you think we can jump in the boat and get out of here before the rest of them notice?' he asked cheekily.

Maya kind of liked the idea, but knew she needed her family and friends around her right now. 'I think they might kill us both and hide our bodies in the river if we did that,' she joked, urging him forward. 'I'm guessing Blake will have told them what has happened by now, because he loves an audience,' she rolled her eyes and then went up on her tiptoes to kiss his nose. 'so we'd better trounce that by announcing our own news and see how that flies,' her eyes sparkled with mirth and Noah looked scared suddenly, but then grinned and swooped down for a proper kiss, picking her up in his arms and striding towards the house and the heart of Maya's family with the woman of his dreams in his arms and a triumphant smile on his face.

Order book 2 today: The Windsor Love Connection.

Acknowledgments

A big thank you to my friends, family and readers - you mean the world to me.

Huge appreciation goes to my incredible writer friends, including my local writing group, Emma Robinson, Carrie Elks, Lorna Cook, Lizzie Page and Julie Haworth. Heidi Catherine, Isabella May, and Chris Penhall are my constant support and I feel so lucky to count you all as my friends, alongside Susan Buchanan, Donna Siggers, Deborah Klee and Alice Cullerne Bown. I appreciate you for listening to my story ideas, never telling me to stop writing and for being an amazing group of people.

Thank you to my agent, Nicky Lovick, who supports my writing journey and offers endless encouragement and great advice.

Thanks to my wonderful advance readers, supporters and street team, including: Valerie Findlay, Fiona Jenkins, Claire Rowlands, Sue Baker, Lyndsey King, Cora Ryan, Grace Power, Ritu Bhathal, Hilary Mackelden, Rie Allen Linton, Meena Kumari, Maureen Bozowske, Pinar Tarhan, Emma Jane Lambert and Belinda Missen. You are all rock stars in my eyes.

I wanted to add thanks to the Facebook group members from Lizzie's Book Group. To Sue Baker and the members of Riveting Reads and Vintage Vibes for the group's brilliant support of all authors. The friendly Book Nook for great content and support and to The Global Girls Online Book Club and Jenny Colgan and more great books, for amazing bookish communities.

To my incredible readers. Without you I wouldn't be able to keep writing. I appreciate you for picking up my books, for telling your friends and for the amazing reviews you write and share. From Lizzie. X

About the Author

International bestselling author and award-winning inventor, Lizzie Chantree has been featured on television and radio. She discovered her love of writing fiction when her children were little. She now writes books full of friendship and laughter, that are about women who are far stronger than they realise. She lives with her family on the coast in Essex. Visit her website at www.lizziechantree.com or follow her on X @Lizzie_Chantree

Sign up to Lizzie's newsletter for a FREE pdf book tracker where you can record your favourite reads, reviews, characters, wish list, swoon rating and more. Plus a monthly monthly prize giveaway! www.lizziechantree.com

If you liked reading my novel, please consider leaving a review. Many readers look to the reviews first when deciding which book to choose, and seeing your review might help them discover this one. I appreciate your help and support. Make an author smile today. Leave a review! Thank you so much. From Lizzie :)

facebook.com/lizziechantree

x.com/Lizzie_Chantree

instagram.com/lizzie_chantree

Praise for Lizzie Chantree

'Wow what a fantastic book. I didn't want it to end!'

'Sublime! 5 stars!'

'Brilliant book. Couldn't put it down.'

'I would recommend this book to anyone.'

'My recommendation: Get a copy!'

'This book will keep you turning pages until you reach the last one and then leave you looking for another novel by this author.'

'I have read and loved all of Chantree's books, and this is not even my favoured genre. Chantree has a way of creating an intriguing and seemingly innocent plot that slowly draws you in and all of your emotions are set afire.'

'This is the first book of Lizzie's I have read and I loved it. I loved the characters and could visualise them. I will definitely be reading the rest of her books. I look forward to the next one.'

'Lizzie Chantree writes lovely romance novels and her latest is no exception. Her strengths lie in creating wonderful characters, beguiling settings and simple but effective story lines.'

'Couldn't put it down.'

'A great bit of escapism!'

'I would happily devour a second sitting.'

'I was enthralled by this beautiful book.'

The Windsor Love Connection

Arthur and Daisy's story. Forced proximity, ex-door neighbour romance!

Chapter 1

Daisy puffed out her cheeks and then swore as she stepped on a plug lying innocently on the floor. She hopped around holding her foot and gave the plug an evil stare as if it was the cause of her predicament. She was trying to forget about her broken relationship, the distressing way she'd found out that her errant husband had died, and the hushed voices of her neighbours. The tiny apartment she lived in, on a pretty street in the south-western city of Carcassonne in France, seemed oppressive all of a sudden. She'd spent years creating a safe haven there for herself and her four-year-old daughter, Brontë, but looking around now she realised that she'd been kidding herself that she'd made the right choices. She shivered and wished she'd remembered to put on an extra pair of socks.

Daisy felt her bottom lip wobble, but then her doorbell chimed. She angrily brushed any stray tears aside and when she opened the door her lips curled into a genuine smile.

Nico, a dreamboat and part-time model, lived a few doors down. She guessed that he flirted with her because they were the youngest tenants in their block of flats by at least twenty years. There was no way she'd ever take him up on his offers of a sleepover, because love hurt. She'd learned that the hard way – twice! She'd be thirty next year and she knew he didn't want love, just some fun. His friendship meant too much for her to risk it, however tempting his knowing smile and sparkling blue eyes were.

'You're here!' he said happily, leaning forward and kissing her on both cheeks. Daisy closed her eyes for a second and inhaled his spicy aftershave, wondering what it would be like to open the door to a handsome lover like Nico and not worry about the consequences. 'Are you busy?' he asked, his sexy French lilt making Daisy forget her problems for a moment and step back to let him inside. Brontë was playing happily in her room, so Daisy shook her head and led him into the tiny kitchenette, clicking the switch on the wall as there was hardly any natural light in the building, even though the sandy coloured walls were beautiful and made of local stone.

'No. I was just thinking about Harrison and wondering what the hell to do with my life,' she sighed, taking two mugs out of the cupboard, wishing she'd bought some bottles of beer. His forehead creased and he pulled her into a hug, which she sank into. He sat her in one of the few chairs in the apartment while he made them both a cup of tea. She looked around and wondered if it was weird that she had more flowering plants in the house than she had chairs. Most of the other colourful things in her apartment were about Brontë and her happiness. It wasn't exactly as if Daisy had many visitors, so what was the point of spending money on furniture, she reasoned. The plants kept her company.

Nico handed her the steaming mug of tea and perched

his pert bottom on her tiny work desk, placed under the living room window, which was half obscured by condensation. The window faced a wall, so wasn't exactly inspiring to work from, but at least she tried.

'You still thinking about starting a gardening business?' he asked with interest, moving a few of the mood boards and design ideas she'd printed using the old printer that Harrison had left behind when he'd moved out.

'I don't know...' she dithered. 'I've got to do something,' she said, jumping up as she'd also left her paltry bank statement on the desk and Nico could probably read that too from his position. She quickly scooped up the papers and shoved them in a floral storage box on one of the shelves she'd built next to the desk. 'I just don't think I'm ready. I need to sort out a school for Brontë soon and most of this...' she pointed to the mood board, 'is just daydreaming.'

'Your ideas are spot on, though,' Nico insisted. 'What about when you helped the neighbours on this floor grow indoor gardens and herbs and spices? We don't miss not having outdoor spaces so much now. Your designs were genius!' he applauded, making her blush.

'That was just practice,' she brushed off. 'Plus you all paid for your own plants and planters. And I would never have made the designs if you hadn't badgered me for months,' she added.

Nico chuckled. 'We all wanted to live in your apartment,' he waggled his eyebrows suggestively at her and finally she laughed. 'It's a mini oasis in here, even though it's tiny.'

Daisy flushed at the praise. For now, creating more indoor gardens was out of reach – as were her dreams of designing outdoor spaces. She was just about managing to function and keep a roof over her daughter's head, and there was nothing left over for a gardening business. She didn't have anyone to help her with Brontë and she couldn't ask Nico. He was always flying across the globe on modelling assignments and wanted to spend the next year abroad – another reason why romantic entanglements were off the menu.

'Come travelling with me,' he asked, not for the first time.

'Brontë needs stability,' she said, shaking her head at his mad ideas. Had things been so simple when she was his age? She thought back, then winced. She'd been twenty-four when she'd had Brontë. She'd got pregnant, married in haste, and then been persuaded that a new life abroad was the answer to her broken heart. She still found it difficult to think of her best friend Arthur. When their relationship had changed, so had he. Meeting Harrison soon after had been a disaster. Except for her precious daughter, of course. It hadn't taken Harrison long to tire of his little family and move on. She felt bile hit the back of her throat and quickly sipped her tea.

She'd love to go back home to her beloved Windsor and her family in the U.K., but her credit card bill told her that would never happen. Anyway, she'd let her parents down and left her friends, including Arthur, behind. She felt her lip wobble again. She watched Nico pick up a framed photo of her and Brontë and wondered what he thought of the fact that there were no pictures of her with friends. What friends? She barely had time to wash, let alone find friends, and she certainly couldn't afford to splash out on the trendy frothy coffee and cakes that social outings seem to involve these days. Plus, while Brontë spoke French fluently and adored chatting away to Nico and their other neighbours, Daisy's own language skills were embarrassingly lacking, although she could get by when she needed to.

Harrison had only spoken French to Brontë, which meant she'd grown up bilingual. It also meant that Daisy had been shut out of those moments. She'd struggled to grasp the nuances of what they were saying, until Nico had begun to gently help her understand the beauty of the language. Harrison's strict regimes hadn't been fun for anyone, but at least her precious daughter would have a wider world and more opportunities now. It was one thing Harrison had given his daughter before he'd moved out last year, if nothing else.

'Nico,' Daisy said as she reached for her phone. 'I know you hate having your photo taken...' she teased, 'But can I take a picture of us together? I've just realised I don't have many of friends.'

Nico fanned his face with his hand and laughed, giving her one of his standard model pouts. 'Are you going to post it on social media and finally inform the world I'm your lover?' he teased. 'I've been telling you how good we could be together for months!' He took the phone out of her hand and leant in to kiss her on the cheek, whilst expertly snapping a few photos on her phone. She felt her skin grow warm as he brushed her blonde hair out of her face and then pressed his lips to hers softly, making her insides squirm. He stepped back and took her hand.

'I'm really sorry about Harrison,' he said, his tone becoming serious. 'Even though we all hated him,' he added.

She flinched. She knew her neighbours hadn't liked her ex's brusque manner, not that he had been at home much.

'It's ok,' she shrugged, even though her shoulders

suddenly felt heavy. 'We'd been separated for almost a year. It was just a shock to find out how he died.'

Nico's face hardened and he went to look out of the window, despite the uninspiring view, while she thought back to her disaster of a marriage.

Opening the door to a police officer and being informed her husband had died had sucked the breath out of her. She'd had to hold onto the door for support. The fact that he'd been staying with a woman and a child had been a knife to her heart. He barely saw his own daughter. It made Daisy's head pound and her eyes smart with tears. This in turn made her blood boil, as she angrily dashed them away. She'd spent enough negative energy on that man to last a lifetime. Brontë didn't really know her dad, so when Daisy had gently explained that Daddy was now an angel, Brontë had just gone quiet for a few hours and then carried on playing with her toys. She didn't ask questions and after a few days actually appeared happier. Now she shook her head when Daisy asked gently if she'd like to talk about Harrison.

Harrison had told her he was moving out and had left devastation behind. Discovering he had died in a simple accident – slipping on a child's toy and hitting his head on the kitchen counter of all things – had been like a punch to the solar plexus and she'd doubled over, winded. 'He'd been living with one of his indiscretions when the accident happened,' she explained to Nico.

'Though visits to his own child had dwindled to nothing,' he replied angrily, just as Brontë realised he was there and rushed into the room, to be swung up into his arms as they began to chatter excitedly about her day in French. Daisy could literally feel the fires of hell radiating from every pore of her body as she pictured her husband crouching down to offer a kind word to another child, those precious hours and days when Brontë should have been his sole focus. She recalled her husband being charm personified on occasion and she'd been suckered in along with everyone else, so the joke was on her.

'You need to get outside more and stop staring at nothing but these four walls, however beautiful you have made the room,' said Nico as he propped Brontë on his hip. 'Let's go out for hot chocolate!' he said loudly and Brontë whooped with joy, making Daisy wince because a hot chocolate with whipped cream and marshmallows wasn't cheap, from the fancy corner shop Nico liked to frequent. She knew he would offer to pay, but her pride wouldn't allow that. Harrison had kept the purse strings tight. Now she did some online design work for a small gardening company to keep them afloat. She had never told Harrison about that because he would have scorned her for even trying. The company often used her designs, even though she didn't get credit for them and they sometimes forgot to pay her invoice for ages, but the photos they posted on their website of the finished gardens looked beautiful.

One day she might have her own business and customers, but for now her most pressing worry was how to pay for her daughter's *choco chaud*.

Also by Lizzie Chantree

Romantic Fiction

The Windsor Riverside Romance Series

Book 1

The Windsor Love Pact

Book 2

The Windsor Love Connection

Book 3

The Windsor Love Match

The Little Shop By The Sea Series

Book 1

The Little Ice Cream Shop By The Sea

Book 2

The Little Cupcake Shop By The Sea

The Cherry Blossom Lane Series

Book 1

My Perfect Ex

Book 2

The One That He Wants

Book 3

The Eternal Bachelor

If You Love Me, I'm Yours

The Woman Who Felt Invisible

Ninja School Mum

Babe Driven

Love's Child

Finding Gina

Shh... It's Our Secret

Non-Fiction

Networking For Writers